Praise for Mary Daheim and her Emma Lord mysteries

THE ALPINE ADVOCATE

"The lively ferment of a life in a small Pacific Northwest town, with its convoluted genealogies and loyalties [and] its authentically quirky characters, combines with a baffling murder for an intriguing mystery novel."
—M. K. WREN

THE ALPINE BETRAYAL

"Editor-publisher Emma Lord finds out that running a small-town newspaper is worse than nutty—it's downright dangerous. Readers will take great pleasure in Mary Daheim's new mystery."
—Carolyn G. Hart

THE ALPINE CHRISTMAS

"If you like cozy mysteries, you need to try
Daheim's

"[A] fabulou   tradi-
tional, domestic mystery."
—*Mystery Lovers Bookshop News*

By Mary Daheim
Published by Ballantine Books:

THE
ALPINE
ADVOCATE

Mary Daheim

BALLANTINE BOOKS • NEW YORK

A Ballantine Book
Published by The Random House Publishing Group
Copyright © 1992 by Mary Daheim

Published in the United States of America by Ballantine Books, an imprint of The Random House Publishing Group, a division of Random House, Inc., New York, and simultaneously in Canada by Random House of Canada Limited, Toronto.

Ballantine and colophon are registered trademarks of Random House, Inc.

www.ballantinebooks.com

ISBN 0-345-37672-2

Manufactured in the United States of America

First Edition: December 1992

OPM 19

To all those who lived the real Alpine story, and in the process, created a legend. These courageous men and women embodied the spirit of the Pacific Northwest.

Author's Note

THE TOWN OF Alpine no longer exists. But from the early part of the century until the late 1920s, it was a small but thriving mill center off Stevens Pass in western Washington. The mill's owner, Carl Clemans, was a relative of Samuel Clemens (a.k.a. Mark Twain), though a discrepancy in spelling the family name had arisen between the two branches early in the nineteenth century.

Alpine, which saw the doughboys pass through during World War I, was consumed by such patriotic fervor that sales of victory bonds far exceeded the quota for any other community in the state. Old Alpiners still take pride in their contribution to Over There.

My mother grew up in Alpine and returned as a bride when my father took a job with the mill. When the logging operation was shut down, the town was intentionally burned to the ground so that transients off the freight trains wouldn't start forest fires. In over sixty years, the second stand of timber has obliterated all signs of the town.

But since Alpine anecdotes have played a large part in my life, I felt this rustic, picturesque place deserved to be revived. Thus, the background is genuine Pacific Northwest history, and now the town lives again in more than just the memories of those hardy souls who embodied the spirit of Alpine.

Chapter One

IN MY DREAM, Vida Runkel had her clothes on backward. In real life, Vida only wore her hat the wrong way to. Obviously, the poor woman had regressed in my subconscious. Maybe people who spend a lifetime working on small-town newspapers tend to deteriorate in every possible way. Maybe, I thought hazily, as the phone rang, that will happen to me. . . .

"Emma Lord here," I mumbled, trying to make sure I wasn't talking into the earpiece. "Who died?" A call at two A.M. had to be bad news. Unless it was my son.

It was. "Nobody's dead, Mom," replied Adam, his usually strong young voice sounding a bit reedy over the five-thousand-mile cable between the shining sands of Honolulu and the foothills of the Cascade Mountains. "What are you talking about? You working on a story for the paper?"

I sat up, fumbling for the light switch on the lamp next to my bed. "Why else would you be phoning in the middle of the night unless there was a disaster? Are you in jail?"

Adam laughed, and I relaxed a little. "Hey, everything's fresh. It's not the middle of the night. It's only eleven o'clock. How come you're asleep so early?"

Single mothers, married mothers, even stepmothers are basically a patient lot. They have to be or they would devour their offspring early on, like guppies. I repressed a sigh. "Gee, Adam, you've only been going to the University of Hawaii for two years. When are they planning to teach you about time differences? The earth is round, remember? You're three hours behind us, you nitwit. Are you broke again?"

"No." The incredulity in Adam's response struck me as incredible. This was the kid who could lose money as fast as he could spend it. He could lose just about anything, if it came to that, having once misplaced his baby-sitter when he was eight. She thought it was the other way around, but it wasn't. So if Adam wasn't broke, he must have robbed a bank. Ergo, he was probably in jail after all. I finally managed to locate the light switch. "It's Chris Ramirez," Adam was saying, as I blinked against the brightness of my cozy little bedroom. "He's coming home. Can you put him up at our house?"

"Chris?" I sank back against the pillows. A cool breeze blew in through the two-inch span of open window. I could smell the evergreens and the damp earth. As always, they gave me strength, like an elixir. "Why on earth is he coming back to Alpine after all these years?"

"He's quitting school." Adam made it sound simple. He also made me sound as if I were simple, too. "He wanted to quit even before his mom died. He registered, but he didn't go to any of the classes. He can get his money back, but it's a big hassle."

My son's attitude toward extra effort rankled, as usual, but I decided not to run up the phone bill by saying so. Undoubtedly, Adam had charged the call to my credit card. "Okay, when will he be in?"

"Let me see . . ." Obviously, Adam was consulting an airline schedule. I marveled that he'd bothered to pick one up. "It's a six-hour flight. He'll be there in about . . . uh . . . five hours. But you don't have to pick him up at the airport. He'll hitch a ride up to Alpine."

I bolted upright, clutching at the phone. "What? You mean he's on his way? Hell, Adam, it's over a two-hour drive to the airport! I've got a paper to put out! It's Wednesday!"

It was Adam's turn to exhibit patience, a virtue he seemed to reserve only for parts on his '82 Rabbit and his considerably older, if more reliable, mother. "Yeah, I know. That's why I called now, to give you some advance notice. But you don't have to go clear into Sea-Tac. I told him it'd be a cinch to find somebody driving over the Pass."

Visions of various serial murderers danced through my mind. In my opinion, hitchhiking should be outlawed not only on the freeway, but everywhere. "Never mind," I said grimly. "I'll go get him."

"That's up to you," my son said, and I could see him shrug. "Hey, I gotta run. I got some dudes with a half-rack waiting for me, okay? I'll write this weekend and tell you about Deloria."

"Deloria?" But Adam had hung up.

I put the phone back and ran a hand through my short brown hair that somehow had not yet turned gray, despite a conspiracy by the rest of the world. Instead, my teeth kept trying to fall out. Thank God for Dr. Starr and giggle gas, I thought as I reset the alarm for four-thirty. The Seattle-Tacoma Airport was over ninety miles from Alpine, but at least I shouldn't run into much traffic.

Unfortunately, I was now wide awake. Even if Chris's plane was on time, I wouldn't get back to Alpine until ten. As for Chris himself, I had seen him twice, on trips to Honolulu to get Adam settled in at the university. He was dark, spare, handsome, and more moody than most young men his age. A bit of the poet about him, or would have been, if he, like the rest of his generation, didn't seem to be semiliterate. But then I was prejudiced. You get that way when you spend a lifetime in journalism and watch the circulation figures drop. I keep waiting for *The New York Times* to make the endangered species list.

Or at least *The Alpine Advocate*. Granted, except for the fact that both are printed in English and appear on newsprint, there isn't much of a comparison. But then Alpine isn't New York. Originally, the town where I live and work was called Nippon because of the Orientals who helped build the railroad. Later, a sawmill was opened by a relative of Mark Twain's, one Carl Clemans, whose father had changed the spelling of the family name back to its Welsh origins. Carl, in turn, had rechristened the scattering of buildings along the railroad tracks as Alpine. The town thrived, if that's the word, from the pre–World War I era until the Depression when it should have folded and disappeared, like other railroad semaphore spots along the old Great Northern route, such as Tonga and Korea. But a farsighted entrepreneur named Rufus Runkel joined forces with a Norwegian immigrant called Olav the Obese, who decided that putting boards on people's feet and letting them fall down steep hills could be fun—and profitable. They built a lodge in the early 1930s and saved the town from extinction. The mill had closed in 1929. Logging had continued in the vicinity but was jeopardized in the last two years by the controversy over the spotted owl.

Sixty years ago, when both owls and trees had still seemed plentiful, the former mill workers who didn't want to log found other jobs, first in building the ski resort, and then in staffing it. Meanwhile, the silver mines that had originally lured Mark Twain's relative continued to draw visitors who were more curious than greedy. A good thing, since nobody I know has found any silver worth having assayed since 1942.

I turned the alarm off, got up, and got dressed. The *Advocate* office is less than a mile from my house, and I often walk. But, since I'd need the car for the trip to Sea-Tac, I drove. Many of the four-thousand souls who live in Alpine are now commuters to Everett and Seattle. The spectacular beauty of the Cascades, the sharp, fresh mountain air, and the comparatively cheap real estate prices have kept Alpine—well, thriving. During ski season, the town is full of visitors, but in late September, we can still call our souls—and our grocery store—our own. The first snows weren't due for another two weeks, at least.

The *Advocate* office is small but up-to-date. We have three word processors, though Vida Runkel insists on banging out her House & Home section on an old Royal upright. Every Wednesday at nine in the morning, we ship the finished layout off to a printer in Monroe, some forty miles away. It comes back around three, ready for our carriers to deliver and the post office to mail. Then we sit back and wait for the irate phone calls to the publisher and incensed letters to the editor, both of whom happen to be me. I love it. Usually.

My desk is always a mess. At three A.M. it looked even worse, like Adam's room. Fortunately, I had almost everything in hand before I'd gone home last night about seven. I checked over my editorial on the need for a public swimming pool adjacent to the public tennis courts and the public park, and then revised the layout. Twenty-four pages, which was the usual, except during holiday season. For the next hour and a half, I proofed the ads that Ed Bronsky, our one-man business staff, had solicited; tried to make sense out of Vida's column on recycling potato peelings; and corrected the numerous spelling errors on all the copy supplied by my young, eager, and dizzy reporter, Carla Steinmetz. Carla is straight out of the University of Washington, and so zealous that she makes me tired. Maybe I was like that once, too, before the world caught up with me. Maybe that was before I fell in love and got pregnant and had Adam and neglected to acquire a husband in the process. Maybe that was how it was in that brief springtime of my life when I still thought all things were possible, and then discovered that even *probable* usually didn't mean anything good.

Except for Adam and the half-million dollars. They were both better than good. After nine months, Adam didn't exactly come as a surprise, but the five hundred thousand did. I never dreamed that my ex-fiancé, Don Cummings, would forget to remove me as the beneficiary of his life insurance policy with The Boeing Company. But then I didn't expect him to die at forty-five, either. When he did both, I ended up with a windfall—and the cash to buy *The Advocate*.

I left a detailed memo for Carla, a brief note for Vida, and a question for Ed on the Harvey's Hardware and Sporting Goods Store ad. I headed for the car, finding Front Street as deserted and dark as should be expected so early in the day. Alpine is set a mile off Stevens Pass, twenty miles below the summit where the Tye River joins the Skykomish, and smack on the Burlington Northern railroad line. The town founders built compactly on both sides of the train tracks, there being a dearth of level ground and a tendency for residents to walk a bit like mountain goats. Hills surround us, and mountains tower over the hills. In winter, Alpine is cold and dark and often isolated, with the tang of sawdust and woodsmoke carried on the wind. In summer, the town is fragrant with wild flowers, and the sharp, clean air is intoxicating. I love the place, though it's not Eden. Small towns have vices, too. When you run the local newspaper, you know every one of them by name.

I crossed the bridge over the South Fork of the Skykomish River and found first light about ten miles down the highway. I loved this part of the drive, where the road was still narrow and the tall second-stand evergreens framed the asphalt like stalwart sentries. Seventy years ago the original inhabitants of Alpine had hacked down the Douglas fir and the red cedar and the Western hemlock and the white spruce, but their heirs had done more than inherit the earth—they'd reforested it. I blessed them every time I drove this stretch of road.

One of those farsighted Alpiners had been Constantine Doukas, known for reasons I've never heard as *Neeny*. His parents had come from Greece at the turn of the century, and his father had gone to work in the mill. The family was prone to saving and scrimping; by the time the mill was shut down, Grandpa Doukas was able to buy up most of the town. Neeny had been selling it off by bits and pieces ever since. His grandson was Chris Ramirez, and if Neeny was as rich as everybody said, it was no wonder Chris wasn't worried about getting his tuition money back from the state of Hawaii. Neeny could probably afford to buy Waikiki.

But I wasn't sure that Chris would ever see any of that money. His mother, Margaret, had married "beneath her," as Vida Runkel and half the town were fond of saying. A handsome Mexican laborer had passed through Alpine twenty years ago to help put in a new sewer system. He had swept Margaret off her feet—and Neeny Doukas had tried to sweep the romance under the carpet. Failing that, he had threatened to disinherit his daughter if she married Hector. She did—but, as far as I knew, Neeny didn't carry out his threat.

That, however, resulted from Hector's abandonment of Margaret when Chris was about six. Or so the story went. I rely on Vida for Alpine's history, since I arrived in town only a little over a year ago. A small town's past is very important, I've discovered, since its inhabitants seem less concerned about the future than their city counterparts. Maybe that's because they figure their towns don't have a future. Or else their lives have become so intertwined that a local history is more like a family album than a textbook. Whatever the case, Vida Runkel was the current Keeper of the Archives.

According to Vida, Margaret was overcome by grief. Furthermore, she had never liked the rain. Or her father. So she bundled up young Chris, left Alpine, and moved to Hawaii. About a year ago, she died of cancer.

Adam had made friends with Chris Ramirez at school, the two of them having the common bond of an association with Alpine and growing up virtually fatherless. Later they discovered a mutual fondness for basketball, surfing, girls, and half-racks, though not necessarily in that order. Now Chris was coming home after fourteen years. I wondered how much he'd remember. I also wondered what his grandfather would think of him after all this time.

The fragile silver sky of the past few mornings was dimmed, promising rain later in the day. Over the mountains and above the trees, the sun came up behind me, looking wan in the early mist.

It was beginning to drizzle when I reached the freeway. I turned on the windshield wipers and realized I was not the only driver on the road. It was after five A.M., and the commute had begun, a thin trickle of cars headed for Everett to the west and Seattle to the south. I'd avoid city traffic by taking the Eastside route through Bellevue.

Or so I thought, always forgetting that Bellevue was a city. In my youth, it had been a sleepy little suburb. But that was almost forty years ago, and time and invading Californians had changed all that. I kept driving in traffic that grew more dense and aggravating. A year in Alpine had spoiled me; twenty years in Portland had been dismissed as if they had never existed.

The flight from Hawaii was a mere fifteen minutes late. Chris emerged into the terminal wearing a Hard Rock Cafe T-shirt, a Dodgers baseball cap, and a sullen expression. He registered no surprise at seeing me in the role of his personal chauffeur but at least had the grace to mumble something that passed for thanks. His luggage, he told me glumly, consisted of one suitcase and a gym bag.

"How long will you be staying, Chris?" I asked when we finally collected his belongings and had reached the dark green Jaguar that is, next to Adam, the light of my life.

Chris's black eyes roamed somewhere in my direction. "I don't know," Chris said. "A couple of weeks, maybe."

"Oh." Call me crazy, but I can never figure out how the hotel-motel industry keeps going when nobody I know supports it. My house is small, with two bedrooms and a den. When Adam is home, the only place guests can stay is in sleeping bags on the front porch. Or that's the way it should be, but I have been known to put up a family of five in the living room, the dining nook, and even the laundry room. Of course that was my cousin, Trina, and her brood, which hardly counts because I figure they usually sleep in trees and eat out of troughs. "Sure," I conceded, "you can sleep in Adam's room. He might even have made the bed before he left."

"Cool." Chris's voice was remote. His gaze was fixed on the passing traffic, now bumper-to-bumper, mostly headed for Boeing—where Don worked until his fatal heart attack and fortuitous insurance policy. I would have felt guilty about the money had he not also taken out a second personal policy in the same amount which covered his wife and three children. As it was, I counted my blessings. I might not have wanted to be Don's bride, but I never wished him ill. Ironically, the reverse may not have been true. Don was not a happy man when I told him I was carrying Tom's child. Come to think of it, Tom wasn't too thrilled about it either. At least he never told his wife.

"Do you remember much about Alpine?" I asked as we swung onto the Eastside freeway and found ourselves going against traffic for a change.

Chris gave what I assumed was a shake of his head. "Just the trains going through. And the snow."

"It's grown some," I offered. "Your uncle Simon has two new partners in his law firm now."

"I don't remember him." Chris's voice was uninterested.

"Your cousins are both still in town." I was struggling to make conversation, raking up a past that I wasn't sure meant a rat's behind to Chris. Except that it must, somehow, or he wouldn't be coming back. "Jennifer is married to Kent MacDuff. He works at his dad's used car lot. Mark manages property for your grandfather. He had a girlfriend, but they broke up."

"Mark used to lock me in the cellar at Grandpa's." He spoke matter-of-factly, but the fact that he mentioned the incident at all spoke volumes.

The rain was coming down harder; I switched the windshield wipers on to high. "Will you see them while you're in town?" I asked, trying to sound casual.

I sensed rather than saw Chris shrug. "I don't know. They've never come to see me." He was silent the whole time I drove past Bellevue.

Resisting the urge to ask about Deloria, I kept closer to Chris's home turf. "Your grandfather isn't too well," I remarked at last. That was what Vida told me, anyway. She'd run into Neeny Doukas at young Doc Dewey's office about a week ago. He'd definitely looked *poorly* to her, but so did Sheriff Dodge's Siberian husky.

"Neeny's old," Chris replied in a tone that assumed anyone over seventy was expected to be ailing. "He never liked me."

I slowed down as the first of the logging trucks pulled onto the highway. "Chris," I began, a bit surprised at the annoyed note in my voice, "if you don't think much of your relatives, why are you coming back to Alpine?"

Chris glanced at me, then looked down at his battered but expensive gym shoes. "That's my business." He scuffed one foot against the other and relented a bit. "I've got a score to settle with Grandpa. I hate him so much I could kill him."

Chapter Two

Now BOYS WILL be boys, and all that, but I still found Chris Ramirez's response disturbing. I hardly knew the kid, but he struck me as too unmotivated to do much of anything, let alone stage a face-off with Neeny Doukas. I laughed, a bit lamely, and gave him a quick sidelong glance.

"Just wait awhile. Vida Runkel already has him halfway to death's door."

"I don't know her." Chris was staring straight ahead through the rain-streaked windshield. The freeway felt vaguely slick, for it hadn't rained since Labor Day. Indian summer had held sway until this last week of September.

"Chris . . ." I began, then stopped. I sensed his seriousness and recalled my description of him, however inaccurate, as a potential poet. But moodiness can beget other things than verse. "Did he and your mother ever write or talk?" I posed the question with less than my usual professional aplomb.

"Sometimes." He resettled the baseball cap on his head. "Afterward, my mother would be mad for a week."

"Is that why you're so angry with him?"

Chris shifted in the leather-covered seat, his feet now pigeon-toed. "He wrecked my mom's life. She died sad. She lived sad. He sent my dad away. He owes me. And them."

This was serious stuff indeed. I recalled the time I'd been sent by *The Oregonian* to cover a story about a woman who was going to jump off the roof of a down-

11

town Portland hotel. The policemen and firemen weren't having any luck talking her out of it, so they dispatched me, as the only woman on the scene, to give it a try. I hadn't had the wildest notion what to say to her. I vividly remembered walking out onto the rooftop and wracking my brain for words of wisdom. The first thing that popped out of my mouth was "Where'd you get those green shoes?" She had gone right over the ledge. A decade later, I didn't have a lot more confidence in my abilities at persuasion.

I hedged a bit. "You never saw your father again?"

"Nope. Neither did Mom. Never heard from him either. He just . . . disappeared." Chris paused, fidgeting with the baseball cap. "Whatever my grandfather did to him must have been pretty freaking grim."

Whatever, according to Vida Runkel, had involved a large amount of money. At least that was what she and her fellow town gossips had figured. But nobody knew for certain.

"Maybe he went back to his own people," I suggested, veering further away from the topic of Neeny Doukas.

"Maybe." Chris fell silent. We turned off the main freeway, heading toward Monroe, where I hoped this week's *Advocate* had arrived an hour ago. If only Carla Steinmetz could screw her head on the right way long enough to get the paper properly routed, I'd have my faith restored in her and, to some extent, in the younger generation in general.

"Say, Chris," I said, reverting to more practical—and comfortable—matters. "Have you got enough warm clothes?"

He shrugged. "I can buy some."

"Okay." I suddenly felt weary. I'd been up for eight hours, and it was only ten A.M. I cursed Adam for sending Chris to me; I cursed myself for being sappy enough to drive all the way to the airport. I wondered why Chris had confided in me. Maybe it was because I, like his mother, had raised an only son on my own. I experienced a familiar pang of regret, not for my sake, but for Adam's. Chris had had a father for the first six years; Tom had never seen Adam. I wouldn't let him, and sometimes I was sorry.

"Hey, this is fresh!" The young man beside me had suddenly metamorphosed into an enthusiastic passenger. He was straining at his seat belt, staring out the window at the dark green hills and the occasional fertile field. "This is like forest! Are there any deer?"

"Sure. We just went by a deer crossing sign a couple of miles back. Your uncle Simon used to hunt before he got some environmentalists as clients."

Chris didn't react to his uncle's change of heart. He was still gazing out the window, the faintest hint of a smile touching his wide mouth. In profile under the bill of his Dodgers cap he looked very young. I hoped it was only bravado that was setting him up for a confrontation with his grandfather. Maybe, once we were settled in and I'd fried up some chicken and made milk gravy and mashed potatoes, I could talk some sense into him.

I shot another swift look at his face. It was set in stone. I'd be better off talking shoes to would-be suicides.

To look at Ed Bronsky, you wouldn't figure he could sell mittens to the three little kittens. Almost as wide as he was tall, Ed had the gloomiest face this side of a basset hound, and his ears were nearly as long. He was the most negative man I ever met, except for my seventh grade math teacher. I'd actually heard Ed try to talk advertisers out of buying space in *The Advocate*.

"The town's too small. There's no competition. You've been around forever. Everybody knows you already." I still shudder every time I hear Ed chatting with one of the local merchants. After ten years in the job, it's a wonder the paper isn't in worse financial trouble than it already is.

Which, I must confess, is bad enough. Marius Vandeventer, who started out as a raving Socialist in the 1930s, had evolved into a patriarchal capitalist by the time I met him in 1990. At eighty-five, he was still sharp, but he had lost his crusading zeal along with his hair. He was also ready to retire. I thought the asking price of $200,000 cash was a steal. As it turned out, I was the one who got robbed. A kindly newspaper broker told me later I could have acquired *The Advocate* for $150,000, with one-third down and ten years to pay. I guess it was the Jaguar that gave me away.

My debut was not auspicious. I was an outsider; worse yet, a City Person. At first, the locals assumed I was divorced or widowed. While I didn't flaunt my status as an unmarried mother, I didn't hide it either. There are, as my mother used to tell me when she was especially mad at my father, Worse Things Than Being Married. Some of the Alpiners didn't agree, and the usual spate of outraged letters ensued. I printed every letter in full. Without rebuttal. The letters stopped. But of course I was still an Outsider.

So, in fact, were two members of my staff. Carla had been on the job for only three months, but Ed had worked on *The Advocate* for almost a decade. He was gradually assimilated, but acceptance took time in a small town.

So we muddled along under my untested managerial skills. We weren't losing money—yet. But we were teetering, just making ends and the payroll meet, but I was determined to make a go of *The Advocate* and had actually upped the circulation by almost fifty subscribers, most of them in outlying areas. The same, alas, could not be said for the advertising income.

"The Grocery Basket wants to cut its ad to a half page," Ed reported in his rumbling, mournful voice. "No more coupons. They're losing money on the fifty-cent eggs."

"Promotion," chimed in Carla, whirling around the office like a wind-up doll. "The Grocery Basket needs to promote its specials more. Take squash. It's the season. Do you know there are twenty-eight varieties of squash available this time of year?" Her long black mane sailed around her slim shoulders.

Ed looked affronted. "I hate squash."

"Pumpkins are a squash," Carla went on blithely.

"They'll be in next week. The Grocery Basket could sponsor a jack-o'-lantern carving contest."

Ed was shaking his head, his heavy jowls undulating. "Halloween is getting dangerous, even in a town like Alpine."

"Ed, you're a ninny," asserted Vida Runkel, who had just stumbled across the threshold carrying a megaphone. "You think Arbor Day is dangerous."

Ed gave a mighty heave of his body and got up from his desk. "It can be, around here. All that controversy with the environmentalists and the loggers. A bunch of nuts want to picket Old Mill Park."

I sighed. The park was the site of the original sawmill, complete with a small museum and a half-dozen picnic tables next to the railroad tracks. "How can you picket a memory?"

"Symbolism." Carla nodded sagely. She turned to Ed. "Besides, that's only a rumor, probably started by the loggers. There are too many rumors in this town. It's impossible to verify everything if you have to make a deadline. Like finding that gold this morning."

I frowned at Carla. Ed swiveled slightly, his hand on the coffeepot. "Gold?" I echoed. "What gold?"

Carla was taking off her suede flats and examining the heels. "These are really worn down. Maybe I should put on my running shoes and go to the shoemaker's."

"Carla . . ." My voice held a weary warning note. Carla's attention span was as fragile as her five-foot frame.

"What?" The big black eyes were wide. "Oh! The gold mine!" She giggled. Carla was a world-class giggler. "I got a call when I came in first thing saying that Mark Doukas had found gold in . . . some place."

"Bunk," Ed said, sloshing coffee into a Styrofoam cup.

"Rubbish," Vida said, tapping the megaphone with her stubby fingers.

"Who called?" I inquired, feeling that familiar unease I often experience when Carla goes off chasing wild geese.

"Mmmmmm." She danced a bit in her stockinged feet.

"Kevin MacDuff, I think. He said Mark Doukas was trip-
ping out. Isn't Kevin the kid with the pet snake?"

Kevin was. In addition, his eldest brother was Kent,
who happened to be married to Mark Doukas's sister,
Jennifer. Despite the snake, Kevin was as easygoing as
Kent was touchy. Kevin was also one of our carriers.

"That snake eats mice," Vida declared, putting down the
megaphone and taking off her ancient velvet cloche which,
as usual, she'd been wearing backward. "I don't care for
mice, but I think that's disgusting."

I was bearing down on Carla, which only took about
four paces, since our front office is quite small and very
crowded. "The gold, Carla. What exactly did Kevin say?"

Carla turned vague. "Oh—that Mark had been panning
or digging or delving and he'd hit pay dirt, or whatever
you call it, and he came racing out of the woods looking
half nuts. Kevin said Mark must have found gold. You
know how he likes to play prospector."

Mark did indeed, though *playing* was the word for it, as
he expended no more energy on prospecting than he did
on any other endeavor that might qualify as work. Neeny
Doukas's oldest grandchild had never held a steady job in
his twenty-six years, despite the family's efforts to make
him a responsible citizen. As far as I could tell, his alleged
duties as property manager for his grandfather consisted of
harassing tenants he happened to run into in various bars
around the county. It was no wonder that Heather Bardeen
had dumped him the previous weekend.

"I doubt it was gold," I said. "Nobody's ever found any
around here, and not much silver, either, in the last forty
years." I glanced at Vida for confirmation, but she was
wiping off the mouthpiece of the megaphone with a tissue
soaked in rubbing alcohol. A sudden horrible thought as-
sailed me as I turned my gaze back to Carla. "You didn't
write this up, did you?"

Carla's long lashes flapped up and down like spider
legs. "Well, of course I did! I made room for it by pulling
that two-inch story on the zoning commission meeting.

They meet every two weeks and never do anything. Who cares?"

"Oh, Carla!" I didn't try to hide my exasperation. It wouldn't faze Carla anyway. Nothing ever did. "Where is it? Let me see your hard copy."

Undismayed, Carla obliged. The short article was fairly innocuous—for Carla:

Bonanza days may be in store again for Alpine. Mark Doukas hit the jackpot yesterday when he struck gold outside of town near Icicle Creek.

According to a colleague of Doukas, the local resident was prospecting close to the old silver mine shafts and found a large deposit of gold. An excited Doukas returned to Alpine to report his findings to Sheriff Milo Dodge, but the local law enforcement agency was out to coffee. As of this morning, Doukas was unavailable for comment.

I handed the story back to Carla. At least Carla hadn't misspelled Dodge's first name this time. In her first article involving the sheriff, she'd made a typo, calling him *Mildo*. Fortunately, I caught it in time, telling myself that it could have been worse. "Okay," I said to Carla, "this probably isn't libelous, unlike your piece on Grace Grundle's bottle cap collection—where you insinuated she stole it from Arthur Trews. You're very lucky that Arthur died the week after that story came out."

"Not so lucky for Arthur," remarked Vida.

I ignored my House & Home editor. "However, you shouldn't have pulled the zoning commission story. We'll catch hell from Simon Doukas for that, since he's the chairman. As for the gold: you have only the word of a fifteen-year-old boy. And you didn't contact Mark Doukas. Where was he when you called?"

"I didn't call." Carla's eyes were so wide and innocent that I thought her face might split. At least I hoped it would. "I didn't have time. I had to get the paper off to Monroe."

"Monroe's getting too big," said Ed, sitting back down. "You see that new development going up? Thirty houses, at least. They'll ask an arm and a leg. I couldn't afford one of those three-car garages."

I also ignored my advertising manager. I hadn't yet finished with Carla. "Look, I appreciate your initiative. But this isn't the kind of story we need to get in at the last minute, if at all. Next time, wait until Mark runs in here with a ten-pound nugget, shouting—"

"Eureka!" Vida blasted the word through the megaphone, and both Carla and I jumped.

"What on earth are you doing with that thing?" I demanded, sounding more cross than I really was.

Vida shrugged, her rumpled blouse quivering over her big bosom. "I interviewed the high school cheerleaders this morning. They gave it to me as a souvenir. Actually, I stole it. I've always wanted one." She started to give me her smug little smile, but stopped when a car door banged outside her window. Vida glanced through the rain-spattered pane. "Oh, swell, now I'm under arrest. It's Sheriff Moroni. The old fool."

Enrico Moroni was actually the former sheriff, having given up his office on account of his diminishing eyesight, and, according to Vida, his diminishing hold on the electorate. Moroni's impaired vision didn't keep him from driving a battered old Cadillac de Ville, but his status as an ex-sheriff kept him out of jail. Nothing else could, since he averaged about one accident per month. No doubt he was now parked on the sidewalk. Moroni and Neeny Doukas had been chums since boyhood, and Enrico was known as *Eeeny*. Some day I intended to ask Vida what had happened to Miny and Moe.

"Che bella!" Moroni burst into the office, making straight for Carla. His parents had been immigrants from Palermo, and while Eeeny had been born in Seattle, he retained a few fragments of their native tongue, especially

when he wanted to impress pretty women. "Hey, Carla, you want to make pesto with me?"

Carla giggled. "I can't. I have to interview Henry Bardeen about the improvements at the ski lodge."

Moroni, who was spare and sinewy, looked over the top of Carla's head to Vida. "Vida, *cara mia*, let's go in the broom closet and make beautiful music, eh?"

Vida gave him her gimlet eye. "I'll play the dust mop on your head, Eeeny. Why don't you marry one of those silly widows who are always having you to dinner?"

Moroni pulled a long face. "You're a widow, Vida, but you never feed me. How come?"

Vida's expression was sour. "Because you're an idiot, that's why. Isn't Moroni the Italian plural for moron?"

The former sheriff laughed and made a slashing gesture with his hand. "Ahhh! You never forgave me for arresting your husband as a Peeping Tom, right, Vida? Give up the grudges. Think of the good times we could have."

Vida shot back in her chair. "Ernest never peeped! That was his brother, Elmo! And that halfwit cousin of theirs, from Skykomish!"

Eeeny leaned on Vida's desk and wagged a finger at her. "Now, Vida, you know what I always say—'The Family That Peeps Together, Keeps Together,' eh?"

Vida was about to boil over with outrage, but Moroni had already swung around to face me. "Say, what's this I hear about young Chris? Harvey Adcock just told me he showed up at the hardware store not half an hour ago. Where'd he come from?"

"Hawaii," I replied as the phone rang and Ed answered it in his lugubrious voice. I'd dropped Chris off at the house about an hour earlier. He hadn't mentioned any plans to go out, but there was no reason why he shouldn't. Yet I somehow felt uneasy. "I brought him in from the airport this morning."

Moroni was studying me closely through his thick glasses, his usual leer displaced by a scrutiny that I felt he'd probably reserved for hardened criminals in bygone days. "Does Neeny know?"

"I don't think so." I glanced at Ed, who seemed to be trying to talk Driggers Funeral Home out of its standing four-inch ad. "Chris came over here all of a sudden. He quit school."

"Aaargh!" Moroni made another slashing motion with his hand, this time more emphatic. "These kids! No staying power!" His dark, lined face displayed a grimace. "So why come to Alpine? Does he expect a big welcome-back party?"

I shrugged, trying to ignore Ed's doleful arguments and Vida's aggressive typing. Carla had slipped out the door, presumably to interview Henry Bardeen up at the lodge. "Alpine is home, after all. Where else would he go?"

Eeeny Moroni seemed to take the question seriously. He rocked back on his heels, rubbing his hands together. "Damned if I know. But why is he trying to buy a gun?"

I blinked. Unfortunately, I thought I knew. But I was not going to say so to the ex-sheriff.

Chapter Three

WEDNESDAYS ARE USUALLY set aside for catching up. The paper is finished for the week; the reactions haven't yet started to come in; and the next edition is just beginning to take form in my mind. After Eeny Moroni left, I went into my cubbyhole of an inner office and sat down to look at the books. It was the end of the third quarter, and I needed to assess *The Advocate*'s current financial position. A cursory scanning of the columns told me we weren't in any worse shape than I feared. But we weren't any better, either.

Ginny Burmeister had come to *The Advocate* directly from high school three years ago. She ran the tiny front office, which had its own entrance and led to the former back shop, which was now mainly used for storage in this age of high tech. Ginny answered the phone, took classified ads, sold stationery supplies, filled out small printing orders, and handled the books. A tall, thin girl with auburn hair, she was far more reliable than Carla but had no literary gifts whatsoever. Money was her metier, and I was glad of it.

I opened the drawer of my old oak desk and took out some gum. No wonder my teeth kept trying to fall out, but at least I wasn't smoking a pack and a half a day anymore.

It was almost noon, and I suddenly realized I was starving. I also knew I should go out looking for Chris. Handguns—if that's what he was trying to get—were sold in the sporting goods section of the hardware store, but I convinced myself that he wanted a rifle. For deer, or maybe birds. The season was upon us, after all. I didn't care to dwell on its being open season on Neeny Doukas.

Not that I was an avid fan of Neeny's. Like a lot of big frogs in small puddles, Neeny was borderline obnoxious. He was accustomed to getting his own way, whether buying people or things. Since his wife's death in 1986, he had lived alone in a big old stone and stucco house on what was known as First Hill, beyond the high school. Frieda Wunderlich, maybe the homeliest woman I ever saw, came on a daily basis to cook and clean. It was said—by Vida—that employer and employee rarely spoke. Frieda, in fact, might have been the only person who ever got the better of Neeny Doukas.

Before heading for the Venison Eat Inn and Take Out next door, I called my house to see if Chris was there. I didn't get an answer, except for my own voice, babbling on the recorder. Buzzing Ginny on the intercom, I discovered that she'd already left for lunch. Still stalling, I checked the little mirror above the filing cabinet. I looked awful, with circles under my eyes and the faint mark of a cold sore lingering on my lower lip. Not that I could ever put in a claim to beauty—but there were days when I was quite presentable. This just didn't happen to be one of them.

The rain had stopped, but the clouds hung low over the town, gray and heavy. The trees that marched up the hills into the mountains looked black and somehow sad. Above the dense forest, Mount Baldy brooded, its long ridge not yet wearing its first cap of snow. In late summer and early fall, Baldy's crest boasted wild flowers and heather. The colors had faded now, leaving the mountain dark and seemingly bare. I tied the belt to my black trench coat and wondered if autumn had really arrived. Judging by the gold and red and russet of the maples and birch, it had. I didn't mind; fall is my favorite season.

Front Street was busy, at least by Alpine standards, with a half-dozen cars and twice as many pedestrians. A couple of scaffoldings and several ladders were lined up along the sidewalk, evidence of the third annual Clean-Up, Paint-Up, Fix-Up project. Obviously, the merchants who had postponed their refurbishing would have to hurry before the bad weather set in. Not for the first time, it occurred to me that we should have made some improvements to *The Advocate*—other than getting a new doorstop for the front entrance.

The noon train, a freight bound for Chicago, slowed, whistled, and kept going. So did I, but not to the inn. Instead, I tramped across the street in the direction of Harvey's Hardware and Sporting Goods, two blocks away. On the near corner, I glanced up at the marquee of the Whistling Marmot Movie Theatre. Oscar Nyquist, the bombastic owner, was contenting himself with having the glass on the outside poster displays washed. Originally, the Marmot had been housed in the social room above the old pool hall on Railroad Avenue; but during the 1920s, Oscar's father, Lars, had built a real theatre on Front Street at Fifth. A miniature, if less lavish version of its art deco city cousins, the Marmot had also undergone a name change early on. Carl Clemans had mused in his droll manner that Lars Nyquist ought to choose something more imaginative than the Alpine Bijou, perhaps a name that would evoke the majesty of the surrounding mountains and forests.

"Goddamn, Carl," replied Lars, whose origins on the edge of a spectacular Norwegian fjord had hardened him against any less dramatic beauty, "look out the vindow and vat do you see? Nothing but trees and more trees and those goddamn pesky warmints that pop out of the ground and act sassy. Yah, sure, you got it—Vistling Marmot it is, and vill serve you right, py golly!"

Clemans, finding himself hoist on his petard (or perhaps secretly amused), didn't argue. The grand opening had taken place in 1924, with Greta Garbo's first film, *Gösta Berling's Sagg*. The show was a big hit with Alpine's Scandanavian population, but residents of different nationalities demanded Hollywood movies. Lars Nygnist never booked another foreign film. Over seventy years later, Oscar Nyquist was offering *Dances with Wolves*. It, too, was popular, though some of the old-timers ventured that Kevin Costner couldn't hold a candle to William S. Hart.

The hardware and sporting goods store, which was divided into two separate sections, smelled of sawdust and paint thinner. Harvey Adcock was a pixie of a man, no taller than I am, with pointed ears and a balding head and quicksilver movements. He was behind the counter of flooring samples, waiting on, of all people, Mark Doukas. I considered beating a hasty retreat, but figured Mark couldn't stick around forever. Besides, I really should talk to him, too.

Harvey looked past Mark and smiled with lots of small, perfect teeth and twinkling green eyes. "Mrs. Lord! Don't tell me your hallway panels have come unglued!"

I smiled back. "I'm the only one who has come unglued, Harvey. No, I wanted to get . . ." I paused, and nodded at Mark, realizing that there was a considerable resemblance between him and his cousin, Chris. Mark was older, taller, and heavier, but the long mouths were the same and so were the jawlines. Both had dark eyes, but where Chris's were vaguely hooded, Mark's were faintly shifty. Still, Mark was the better-looking of the two, possibly owing to style, rather than substance. In fact, Mark Doukas was incredibly handsome. That, coupled with the inheritance he would no doubt one day receive, should have made him the catch of Alpine. Yet he remained single, reputedly antagonizing young women such as Heather Bardeen at regular six-month intervals.

"Hi," he said in a laconic voice, leaning against the counter. His brown bomber jacket looked new; his faded blue jeans looked old.

I was still pausing, now waiting for Mark to mention his cousin's arrival. But he said nothing about Chris. Harvey was looking at me expectantly.

"Oh—I wanted to get some attachments for my cordless screwdriver," I said, latching on to the only excuse I could think of, despite the fact that I already had two extra sets, one courtesy of Adam, the other, a birthday gift from my brother, Ben.

Mark kept lolling against the counter. "Go ahead. Harvey and I were just shooting the breeze."

"Okay. Thanks." I smiled at Mark. "By the way, we've got a small story in the paper today about your prospecting. Frankly, I'm not sure if we got all the facts." Never admit you're wrong when it comes to reporting—that's one of my basic rules of journalism. Allow a margin for error or a lack of detail, but don't suggest you might be mistaken. I tried to look ingenuous, but at forty, I don't do it very well.

To my surprise, Mark drew back. "What about it?" he asked.

Since the paper would hit the streets in less than three hours, I opted for candor. "Carla Steinmetz got a call this morning from Kevin MacDuff. He said you'd found gold near Icicle Creek."

Mark's face darkened, and he banged his fist down on the glass counter. "Hell! That kid's as big a jerk as his brother! Wait till I get hold of him. . . ." The rest of the threat faded as Mark rushed out of the hardware store.

Harvey Adcock's eyebrows, which were only a sketch of red-gold hairs, lifted quizzically. "Gold? Mark never said anything about gold. He wanted to buy a crowbar."

I considered buying one myself and using it on Carla. "Did he mention his cousin, Chris?"

Harvey leaned both elbows on the counter and looked unusually solemn. "Oh, Mrs. Lord, I just about fell over when that young man came in here and told me who he was. He didn't want to, you know, but I had to ask when he inquired about handguns."

I tried to keep my voice casual. "Did you sell him one?"

Harvey shook his head with vigor. "Of course not. I had to ask to see his driver's license. He isn't twenty-one. Even if he were, there would be a sixty-day waiting period since he's just come in from another state." He looked up at a newcomer I recognized only vaguely from the Grocery Basket and called out a greeting. "Hello, Virgil. I've got your lumber out back. Do you want to bring the truck around?"

Virgil did, and Harvey called to his nephew through the door behind the counter. "Jason will help Virgil load up. I didn't say anything to Mark about his cousin. Do you think I should?"

I shrugged. "I'm sure his arrival is all over town, or will be, before the day is out."

"Neeny will have a stroke." Harvey came out from behind the counter and headed in his sprightly manner for the tool section. "Unless he's already had one. Mrs. Runkel tells me he's in very poor shape." He hesitated, his hand on a large cellophane-sealed package of more screwdriver attachments than I could ever find uses for in fifty years. "Gibb Frazier told me Mrs. Pratt left town last week. Do you suppose she and Neeny had a spat?" Harvey spoke in a near whisper, though there was no one to hear us.

"I doubt it," I said, automatically lowering my voice, too. "I saw her Monday driving on the ski lodge road." There was no mistaking the upswept hairdo of Phoebe Pratt or the bright red Lincoln Town Car she'd recently acquired. The car, along with most of Phoebe's other expensive possessions, was rumored to have come from the indulgent hand of Neeny Doukas, her longtime lover.

"People are odd," remarked Harvey, fondly looking at the screwdriver attachments as if he found tools more reliable than humans. "This set has everything," he asserted.

I was dazzled. "Gee, it sure does. Can it decorate cakes, too?"

Harvey laughed, much harder than the comment warranted. He looked more like a pixie than ever. A loud crash out back wiped the mirth from his face. "Oh, that Jason! He's so clumsy! Let me ring this up, and I'll go see what I can to do to help."

"Never mind, Harvey," I said. "Just hold it for me. I'll get it later." Maybe I'd forget. With luck, so would Harvey. "Say—do you know where Chris went after he left here?"

Harvey was already at the back door. "No, I can't say that I do. He should be easy for you to find, though."

"Oh?" My curiosity was piqued. "How come?"

From the doorway, Harvey gave me his impish smile. "Because he's driving your car. That big green Jaguar is hard to miss."

Sure enough, I sighted Chris, pulling in down the street at the Burger Barn. I ran along the uneven sidewalk, calling his name against the wind that had blown off the mountains.

He stopped in the parking lot and waited for me. When I got closer, I noted that his expression was more sullen than ever, and that he didn't seem very glad to see me.

"Chris!" I started to shout, but thought better of it. Two members of the local Chamber of Commerce were just emerging from the Burger Barn. "Chris," I said, mustering calm and waving at the merchants, "why the hell didn't you ask if you could use my car? Where did you get the keys?"

Chris looked almost as vague as Carla. "I thought I did ask," he mumbled. "Do you mind? The keys were underneath, by the left rear door."

They were, of course, since I always kept an extra set with the car in case I locked myself out. Or more likely, if Adam lost the keys, which he had already done four times in two years, despite the fact that he had spent twenty of those months in Hawaii.

I sighed. "Okay. But be careful. I love that car, even though most of the people here think I'm a snot for owning it."

"Most of the people here *are* snots," Chris said. He scowled at the length and breadth of Front Street. "They're worse than that. They're pricks."

"Some are, that's true. One thing about a small town: at least you know who's a prick and who isn't." I tried to keep my voice light as I put a hand on Chris's arm. "Have you eaten lunch? I'm famished."

With only a minor display of reluctance, Chris let me lead him into the Burger Barn. It was busy as usual, with two women clerks from the drug store; the local insurance agent; Dr. Starr's dental hygienist and her new beau; the Episcopal rector and his wife; a quartet of loggers who were passing through—and Heather Bardeen with a girlfriend I knew only as Chaz.

Now and again I have been accused of having a perverse nature, but I prefer to call it puckish. Thus, I steered Chris over to Heather and Chaz, which wasn't difficult since they were seated in the booth next to the door. They were also about to leave.

I introduced them and watched Heather's cornflower blue eyes narrow. "So you're the long-lost cousin from Honolulu," she said, sounding pleasant, if not actually friendly. "You must have heard that Neeny is about to croak."

Chris regarded her coolly. "You said it first."

Heather's pouty mouth opened slightly. "Huh?" She gave me a questioning, sidelong glance.

"Chris just got in this morning," I explained a bit too hastily. "He hasn't seen any of his family yet. He's staying with me."

Heather picked up her purse and the bill. "Well, if you run into Mark the Shark, tell him to go screw himself. For a change," she added with bite. "Come on, Chaz, we're going to be late getting back to work. Dad will flip his toupee."

Heather and Chaz flounced off. I decided not to make an awkward moment any more so by standing around waiting for a booth, so I sat down in the seat Heather had just vacated. The waitress, whose name was Kimberly and who was some relation to Vida, came over to clear the table.

"Heather's the girlfriend?" Chris inquired after Kimberly had departed in a clatter of dishes and rattle of silver-ware.

"Ex-girlfriend." I picked up the menu, though I knew exactly what I was going to order. "She works for her dad at the ski lodge. He runs it for the Norwegians. They all live some place else now—Seattle or Palm Springs."

Chris seemed even less interested in the Norwegians than in Heather. Still, I thought he'd shown a spark of life when Heather had put on her pout. I congratulated myself on my puckishness. What irony, I told myself, if Chris and Heather should fall into each other's arms. What goofy ideas I could get, I reminded myself as Kimberly resurfaced with an order pad.

Making small talk over burgers, fries, and shakes wasn't easy with Chris Ramirez. He evaded any queries about calling on his relatives. He never mentioned trying to buy a handgun. He didn't say where he'd been in the past two hours, except cruising around town. And, like ninety-nine percent of the people I meet, he never asked me anything at all.

"My treat," I said when the bill arrived. Chris didn't argue. I calculated the tip for Kimberly and said hello to the rector and his wife as they went out. "What are your plans for this afternoon?" I asked without much hope of getting a direct answer.

Chris put his baseball cap and his denim jacket back on. "I'm going to see Neeny."

My heart gave a little lurch. "Chris—why don't you wait? He's sick, really he is." Vida might be right. Certainly the rest of the town seemed to agree with her. "Why don't you talk to your uncle Simon first? His office is just down the street, in the Clemans Building."

"I didn't come here to see my uncle." His jaw was set, his eyes staring straight past my shoulder.

I leaned across the table. I wondered if I should ask him why he wanted to buy a handgun, but since he hadn't been able to get one, I decided to let that question slide. Instead, I urged caution. "Damn it, Chris, you're staying with me.

You're my son's friend. Don't you dare do something fool-
ish! At least take time to think things through."

"I've been thinking for fourteen years." He barely
moved his lips when he spoke.

"Then keep thinking for another fourteen hours. Please
talk to your uncle. If you don't go see him, you can bet
he'll come see you." I sat back, my own lower lip thrust
out.

Chris seemed to waver ever so slightly. "Maybe not."

"No maybes about it." I was gaining confidence. "You
don't know small towns. You don't know your family. I'm
surprised Simon Doukas isn't combing the streets for you
right now."

Except that was precisely what Simon Doukas was
doing. He stood in the door of the Burger Barn, and there
were tears in his eyes.

The tactful maneuver was to leave uncle and nephew
alone. For once, I gave in to my better nature as a human
being, rather than my professional voyeurism as a journalist. I made my exit as discreetly as possible.

The office was in its usual midweek hiatus. Ginny
hailed me on the way in, repeating her frequent argument
that we ought to insist on prepayment for household items
in the classifieds. "If they don't sell the stuff, they think
they don't have to pay for the ad," she asserted, pulling
back her curly auburn hair with an elastic band. "I've already talked to four deadbeats this morning." It was an old
argument in the newspaper business, but I was sticking to
Marius Vandeventer's policy of publish first, collect later.
Unfortunately, it didn't seem to be working. I tried consol-
ing Ginny, but she remained adamant. Not for the first
time, I considered her as Ed's replacement.

Carla was fretting over her story on the ski lodge renovations. Ed was complaining that the Hutchins Interiors
and Decor ad was too big. Vida was singing the Alpine
High School fight song as she pounded out her cheerlead-
ing article.

"Fight on, ye Buckers;
    Chop down their trees!
Turn them into suckers;
    Bring them to their knees!
Saw off their . . ."

Miraculously, she stopped. "My grandfather wrote that," Vida announced, using the keys of her typewriter to tap out the rest of the melody. "Back in 1916. There were six pupils in the school, four of them were Blatts."

Vida had been a Blatt before she became a Runkel. It was her father-in-law who was responsible for the original brainstorm about building the ski lodge, but he'd sold out to the Norwegians just before World War II. Ernest, Vida's husband, and the fourth of the Runkels' six children, had been in real estate, working first for his father, and later for Neeny Doukas. Ernie, as he was known, might never have been a Peeping Tom, but he'd had some other curious hobbies, including going over waterfalls in a barrel. It was on one such excursion ten years ago that Ernie had met his demise on Deception Creek. The falls weren't that treacherous, but the truck that had driven off the road and run over his barrel was.

Vida had been left a widow at forty-four, with three children to raise. A natural font of information about everybody and everything in town, she asked Marius Vandeventer for a job. Marius had complied, and Vida had been a fixture at *The Advocate* ever since. She wasn't much of a writer, but she worked hard and had a genuine nose for news. Her only vices, as far as I could tell, were chocolate truffles, her sharp tongue, and the propensity for wearing her endless variety of outdated hats backward.

In the beginning, Vida and I had only one problem: she despised Democrats more than anything else in the world—except Catholics. I was both. Having been forewarned by Marius Vandeventer, I predicted that when Vida learned I'd borne a child out of wedlock, she would be the first to pin a scarlet letter on my raincoat. But Vida had surprised me. On a snowy afternoon last January when the subject came up and I'd casually remarked that Adam's father and I had never been married, Vida had taken off her glasses, rubbed her eyes like mad, and said, "Good for you. You've got spunk." We had been forging a tentative friendship ever since.

"Hey," I asked, as Ed hung up on his latest advertising victim, "what's with Phoebe Pratt? Harvey Adcock said she left town—but I saw her Monday."

"Phoebe!" Vida gave one of her magnificently eloquent shudders, her bosom heaving. "She probably went to Seattle on a shopping spree. With Neeny's credit cards. I still can't believe she convinced him to take her to Las Vegas last month. Neeny hasn't left Alpine in four years. The old fool. He dotes on that brainless hussy. I always said I should have married Clinton Pratt. He asked me first, you know. Even then, Phoebe was fast. She got caught with boys in the boiler room at the high school at least four times before we graduated. Poor Clint, it's no wonder he died young. He'd have been better off with me."

Ed looked up from the classified section he was working on. "And you'd have been Vida Blatt Pratt. You wouldn't have liked that, Vida. *I* sure wouldn't."

Easily diverted as usual, Carla turned away from her ski lodge article. "I thought your own husband died young, Mrs. Runkel."

Vida lifted her sharp chin. "He didn't die," she said with dignity. "He was killed. It's not the same."

Ginny Burmeister had noiselessly entered the editorial office, bringing with her a couple of legal notices for the next edition. "My father worked for Mr. Pratt's plumbing company," Ginny said in her nasal voice. "Dad thought Clint Pratt was really nice, but a wimp."

Vida harrumphed. "He certainly couldn't stand up to Phoebe. She wouldn't give the poor man children, either. I hoped that when she went away after he died, she'd keep out of Alpine for good. But oh, no, back she came not even a year later, looking like the Queen of Sheba, and ready to sink her claws into Neeny Doukas. In fact," Vida added darkly, slamming the carriage of her typewriter for emphasis, "I wouldn't be surprised if she'd been carrying on with Neeny even before Clint died."

"I don't know why our generation is always being criticized," Ginny said, exchanging glances with her peer, Carla. "Think of people acting like that back then. That was twenty years or so ago, when I was a baby. Dad had to get another job after Mr. Pratt died and my folks were really broke. Mrs. Doukas was still alive. Wasn't she heartbroken?"

"About forty times," retorted Vida. "Poor Hazel didn't have the gumption to make a fuss about how Neeny couldn't behave himself. She just sat at home and baked apple pan dowdy."

Gibb Frazier stood in the doorway, thumbs hooked in his suspenders, plaid flannel shirt not quite meeting over his paunch. "Damned post office," he muttered, letting the wind rattle the door. "They're talking about raising the rates again. They'll put you out of business, Emma."

I gave Gibb a wry smile. "Me and *The Christian Science Monitor*."

Gibb banged the door shut and stumped over to Vida. He had lost a leg ten years ago in a logging accident. At not yet fifty, he'd been too young to retire, so after acquiring an artificial limb, he'd traded in his logging rig for a pickup truck and hired himself out as a Jack-of-All-Hauling-Trades. One of his jobs was to take *The Advocate* to and from Monroe every week.

"What's this I hear over at the post office about the Doukas kid coming back to Alpine?" He addressed his question to Vida, who was commonly known as the source of all vital information.

"Ramirez kid," I corrected, but neither Vida nor Gibb paid me any heed.

Vida took off her glasses with the tortoise-shell rims and rubbed her eyes with both fists in a typically vigorous manner. "How should I know?" she replied crossly. Above all else, Vida hated not knowing. "Ask Emma. He's staying with her."

I gave a little shrug. "He quit school. You know how kids are these days. I suppose he figured it was time to get reacquainted with his family, now that Margaret's dead." The fib slipped easily off my tongue; sometimes you have to be glib to protect your sources.

Gibb's wide faced creased into a frown. "If I were Chris Doukas or Ramirez or whatever his name is, I wouldn't bother myself. That arrogant sonovabitch Neeny will give him a bad time. And Simon's a stuffed shirt. As for your Mark—" Gibb stopped and spat into his hand. "That's for Mark, the dirty little creep. He may be rich, but he's still a bum."

It wasn't the first time I'd heard Gibb Frazier cast aspersions on the Doukas clan in general, and Mark in particular. Before Gibb could further revile Mark Doukas, the phone rang in my inner office. I left my staff and hurried to take the call. It was Chris. He wanted to know if he could leave my car at the Burger Barn. He was going to have dinner with Uncle Simon and Aunt Cece and his cousin, Mark, at their house on Stump Hill.

"Sure," I replied, a sense of relief flooding over me. "That's great, Chris. Do you remember Cece? She's very sweet." She was, too, so much so that she frequently made me gag.

"Kind of. Doesn't she have moles?"

"One mole, on her cheek. People find it charming." That was true, too. People found everything about Cecelia Caldwell Doukas charming, especially her enthusiasm for Good Works. "Will you be back later tonight?" I hoped not—I didn't mind having Chris stay with me, but I'd much prefer that he made peace with his family. Spending the night on Stump Hill might very well lay the foundation for a new relationship.

"I guess," said Chris. "Uncle Simon or Mark will probably bring me to your place."

"Okay." My euphoria over the happy Doukas family reunion slipped a notch. "Have a good time. I'll wait up to let you in."

"You don't have to," said Chris in his taciturn manner. "I've got a key."

"Oh." I didn't bother to ask how.

For the next hour, the phone never stopped ringing, which isn't unusual at *The Advocate*. I fended off the president of the Burl Creek Thimble Club, who was threatening to disband the organization; listened patiently to a long-winded diatribe from the Chamber of Commerce's executive secretary; took complaints from two members of the zoning commission abut the deletion of their story; explained why Vida's account of a recent wedding had not included the fact that the bride had set her wedding vows to rap music (Vida had been adamant about leaving it out); and jumped in my chair when I heard Neeny Doukas's deep, gravelly voice at the other end of the line.

"What kind of an outfit are you running there, Emma? What's this bullcrap about my grandson?"

I wasn't sure which of his grandsons he meant, so I hedged. "You know me, Neeny. I just try to do my best."

Neeny snorted into the receiver. "There's no gold around here. That's the trouble with you newcomers. You don't know siccum about Alpine. Mark wasn't prospecting. He was digging up maidenhair ferns for Cece's rock garden."

The resonant growl of Neeny's voice suggested he wasn't as feeble as Vida had reported. I could picture him at the phone, broad-shouldered, barrel-chested, a shock of white-streaked hair with a big mustache, full beard, and black eyes that could bore holes in tree trunks.

I don't like admitting I'm wrong, especially in print. But Carla's flighty reporting had put me in a tight corner. "Look, Neeny, we went off the deep end, I'm afraid. The story should have been verified. It wasn't, because we were right against deadline. I've already spoken to Mark about it. He blames Kevin MacDuff for calling it in, but we take responsibility for running it. We'll do a retraction next week, okay?" A faint smile twitched on my lips. On metropolitan dailies, editors and reporters worried about war and rumors of war, with statements checked out through the White House, the Kremlin, and Vatican City. In small towns, we sink into turmoil over maidenhair ferns and teenaged paper boys.

Neeny was grumbling over the line. "Oh . . . hell, I suppose. What else can you do, unless you rerun the whole damned thing. Could you do that?"

"No." I was emphatic. It wasn't just the expense of printing another three thousand copies of *The Advocate*. It was the principle. Neeny's request was tantamount to asking God to start the day all over again. It occurred to me that he'd probably done just that somewhere along the line.

"You gotta understand," he was saying, apparently for once taking no for an answer, "that it isn't just because of Mark that I'm upset. Do you wanna bunch of half-assed gold seekers tramping all over the woods and tearing the place up? It'd be worse than all them damned hikers and bikers."

I hadn't considered the wider implications, but Neeny was right. Every week, at least three hundred copies of *The Advocate* were mailed to former residents who liked to keep up with the doings in their old hometown. We had subscribers in twenty-seven states of the Union, as well as in Canada, Mexico, Japan, England, Belgium, and Sri Lanka. I had a sudden vision of all of them descending on Alpine with pickaxes and gold pans.

"You're right, Neeny," I said, resorting to a phrase that he'd no doubt heard ten thousand times in his seventy-two years. I felt obsequious and vaguely ashamed of myself. "I apologize." Hearing a rumble of assent, I broached an even more delicate subject. "Are you going to have dinner at Simon's tonight?"

"Paaah!" Neeny seemed to be fumbling for words. "How the hell did you get mixed up with that kid? As far as I'm concerned, he don't exist. Let Simon and that lamebrained wife of his feed the little punk. I'll bet he looks like Hector."

"He looks like Mark."

"Bullcrap. He looked just like his old man when he was a kid. God help him if he acts like him, too. I don't want any part of that Ramirez tribe."

Obviously, the antipathy was mutual. I marveled that Margaret Doukas Ramirez had maintained any contact at all with her father. No wonder she got a case of the glums whenever she heard from him. Still, my conscience was needling me. I decided to put Neeny on the alert. It was the least I could do.

"Chris has a chip on his shoulder, I'll say that. He was very fond of his mother." I spoke carefully, hoping Neeny wasn't in one of his purposely obtuse moods.

"Kids should like their mothers," he said with a grunt. "How old is he? Twenty? They all got chips on their shoulders at that age. Don't worry. He'll get it knocked off soon enough." He paused, and I heard a sound in the background. "Listen, Emma, I got company. Let me see what you're gonna do to fix up your dumb-assed story."

Ordinarily, I never clear copy with anyone, but I decided it wouldn't hurt to make an exception. "I'll do it right now and read it to you over the phone later, okay?"

"Huh?" Neeny was obviously distracted. "Yeah, sure, fine. Goodbye."

Before he hung up, I heard a female voice in the distance. I was almost sure it belonged to Phoebe Pratt.

Ed Bronsky was about to go home to his long-suffering wife and hyperactive children. "Another day, another half-dollar," he said, putting on his wrinkled raincoat. "I haven't had a raise on this job in three years."

I gave him my brightest smile. "If we took in more money, we could pay more. It's that simple, Ed. Why not bring in some new accounts?" Instead of losing our old ones, you dumbbell, I thought in secret annoyance.

Ed was searching in his pockets for his driving gloves. He didn't find them. He never did. Frankly I didn't think he owned a pair. "Now who would I get? A lot of the stores at the mall would rather advertise in the shopper that comes out of Monroe. Those other new places are too far out of town. Some of these merchants want to do inserts, and stuff *The Advocate* full of four-color tripe that just falls out on the sidewalk." He gave a forsaken shake of his head. "You wouldn't believe what advertisers can come up with."

I could, and wished I had the nerve to get rid of Ed and hire an ad manager who shared my imagination. Like Ginny Burmeister. But I was too good-hearted—and weak-willed—to fire Ed Bronsky. "What about Driggers Funeral Home?" I asked, hoping for the best but fearing the worst.

Ed was shuffling toward the door. "I talked them out of running that weekly ad. Once a month—that'll hold them." He tugged at the doorknob, which needed fixing. "Heck, it's the only funeral home in thirty miles. Besides, nobody has died here since July."

It was funny that Ed should mention that. No, it wasn't funny at all. Within twenty-four hours, it would be quite sad.

Chapter Four

WITHOUT CHRIS COMING to dinner, I wasn't inclined to fry up a batch of chicken. I hate cooking for myself, though I'm fairly competent around a stove. I left the office at six, heading for the Venison Eat Inn and Take Out. Except for a new French restaurant ten miles down the highway, the inn had the best kitchen in the vicinity. I often ate alone, which I usually preferred. I brought the printout of *The Advocate*'s financial statement. The conversation with Ed had goaded me into a serious analysis.

Unfortunately, I'm not very good at managing money. In the eighteen years I worked for *The Oregonian*, I succeeded in saving a grand total of $2,146.85. It was just enough to send Adam off to his first semester at the University of Hawaii.

I ordered the broiled halibut cheeks and rechecked the columns of figures. The good news was that the holiday season was upon us; the bad news was that Ed would probably try to cancel Christmas.

Over my green salad, I considered my personal finances. Out of Don's $500,000, less taxes, I'd spent $200,000 on *The Advocate* and $30,000 for the used Jaguar. I'd sold my two-bedroom house in Portland for $145,000 and paid just under $100,000 for the stone and log cabin in Alpine. I'd paid off all my debts and still had a small nest egg. I certainly didn't want to use it to keep *The Advocate* alive. Capitalism wasn't supposed to work that way. But if Marius Vandeventer had updated his technology, he'd let the building run down. In heavy rain, the roof leaked. When the snow piled up, ice covered the inside of the windows. The floorboards in my office creaked ominously. The exterior and interior were badly in need of paint. I figured I was looking at an outlay of at least $25,000. Given our current hand-to-mouth existence, renovation wasn't feasible.

The halibut arrived, snow-white and tender, with just a dusting of charcoal on top. Should I pony up that twenty-five grand? Once I got Adam through school, he'd be on his own. Maybe. I knew a lot of parents who'd congratulated themselves at commencement and four years later were still providing free room and board. Or worse yet, had found their children on the doorstep with *their* children.

I layered my baked potato with butter, sour cream, chives, and bacon bits. Luckily, gaining weight isn't a problem for me. I have too much nervous energy, and I tend to burn off calories. It's a good thing, because I consider physical exercise a deplorable waste of time. I could be eating instead.

The *Advocate*'s spread sheets depressed me. Chris Ramirez's hostility depressed me. Gibb Frazier's comment about the increase in postal rates depressed me. Ed Bronksy's negativism depressed me. Carla Steinmetz's careless journalism depressed me. I should have ordered a drink. Instead, I ate like a pig and watched my fellow diners, which depressed me even more.

There was Dr. Starr's dental hygienist again, holding hands with her boyfriend. There was Harvey and Darlene Adcock, looking devoted after thirty years of marriage. There were the newlyweds whose wedding Vida had just written up. Two other couples I didn't know sat at tables across the room.

Couples. The world was geared to pairs, not singles. I cup up my potato skin and ate that, too. I'd never really been part of a couple. I'd been engaged. I'd borne a child. In the past twenty years, I'd had two more lovers and another fiancé. I wasn't given to casual romance. I never loved anybody but Tom Cavanaugh.

I met Tom when I was an intern on *The Seattle Times* and he was working the copy desk. I was twenty, he was twenty-seven, and we fell for each other like a ton of bricks. My plans to marry Don Cummings after we graduated from college evaporated. Tom talked about leaving his wife of five years. We were wildly, briefly happy. Then I got pregnant. So did Tom's wife. He made a heart-wrenching choice and stayed with Sandra.

I went to Mississippi to have my baby. My brother, Ben, had received his first assignment as a priest in the home missions along the delta. A capable black midwife with a seamless contralto voice delivered Adam, and the two of us struck out on our own.

My parents had been killed in a car accident coming from Ben's ordination the previous summer. I finished my degree at the University of Oregon, instead of at Washington, and took a job on *The Oregonian*. I'd stayed there until a year and a half ago when I inherited Don's insurance money and realized I could fulfill my seemingly impossible dream of owning a weekly newspaper.

I'd stopped dreaming about being half of a couple a long time ago. My last romance was with a twice-divorced professor of philosophy from Reed College who was brilliant, charming, and so claustrophobic that he wouldn't even go to the movies. We went on so many picnics that I developed a phobia of my own—to potato salad. We split up in January of 1987 after I caught pneumonia from eating lunch in a hailstorm.

My depression lifted with the presentation of the dessert menu. Either I am very shallow or I have great resilience. Whichever it may be, cheesecake restores me. I was polishing off the last bite when Eeeny Moroni came into the restaurant.

"Emma, *mio cor*!" Not wanting to show favoritism, he gave the hostess a slap on the backside before gliding up to my table. Eeeny Moroni was light on his feet for an older man and reputed to be the best dancer in Alpine, though Vida insisted it was only because he'd taken professional lessons in his youth. "I thought you had a date with a younger man," said Eeeny, sitting down in the vacant chair opposite me. "Was that Chris Ramirez I saw outside of the Burger Barn with Simon?"

"Probably. Dark, not quite six feet, denim jacket, and baseball cap?" Given Eeeny's lousy eyesight, I marveled that he could tell Chris from Vida. Except, of course, that Vida would have worn the baseball cap backward.

"That was him." Eeeny nodded. "I kept my distance. They seemed deep in conversation. So where's the kid now?"

"He's safe in the bosom of his family," I said as Eeeny stared unabashedly at my bosom. "Simon and Cece asked him to dinner."

Eeeny scowled. "Simon's going to make Neeny mad." He paused, accepting a menu from the waitress and offering her his body. She laughed mechanically and recommended the Idaho trout. Eeeny adjusted his thick glasses and squinted at the entrées. "That Chris is just going to cause trouble, Emma," he continued, back to serious matters. "It was bad with Hector, for the whole Doukas tribe. It almost broke Hazel's heart. I can't tell you how many times she tried to go to Hawaii to see Margaret and that kid."

"Why didn't she do it?"

Eeeny looked at me as if I were dense. "Neeny wouldn't let her. That's why."

"Hazel Doukas must have been a wimp," I declared, trying in vain to imagine my own independent-minded mother knuckling under to my father in similar circumstances. Then I remembered the concessions I'd made to Neeny that very afternoon and gave Hazel a little mental slack.

Eeeny Moroni ordered cracked crab and a half bottle of Chardonnay. I excused myself, recalling that after a few drinks Eeeny's amorous words could turn into lecherous deeds. I'm not much of a flirt.

I got home just after seven, still stewing over *The Advocate*'s finances. The wind was up, making the stately evergreens sway and rattling the lid on my garbage can. I changed clothes, looked through *The Seattle Times*, heard somebody's dog howl at the brewing storm, and winced as the electricity flickered several times. I needed some business advice, so I called Dave Grogan, the newspaper broker who had handled the deal between Marius and me. He lived about a hundred miles away, in a small town not far from the ocean. After listening patiently to my tale of woe, he advised caution.

"You aren't going broke yet, Emma," he noted in his kindly voice. "Your repairs can wait. Take a look at those ledgers in January. Even Ed can't wipe out the Christmas spirit single-handedly."

"He'll probably try, though," I said, sounding almost as gloomy as Ed.

Dave Grogan, who knew virtually every small daily and weekly newspaper in western Washington inside and out, chuckled. "Have you ever considered that Ed may be using reverse psychology?"

"No," I said bluntly. "And if he is, I don't think it's working." I sighed. "I'm probably overreacting. But I want to make a go of this so much."

Dave paused, and I could hear the shuffling of papers over the miles. "You've got several options, Emma. One thing you might mull over is a partnership."

"No." I was emphatic. "The big attraction for me—or at least part of it—is being my own boss. I'm awfully independent, Dave."

"I don't mean an editor-publisher relationship per se," Dave said in his mild manner. "I'm talking about the kind of setup where a—I guess you could say silent partner—has a financial interest in the paper but no hands-on control. I've got a couple of people looking for that sort of a deal right now. They want an investment, but they don't want to get actively involved in the operation or else they don't want to live in a small town."

I frowned into the receiver. "What's the payoff?"

"For them? Money. That type of person is usually willing to sink a pretty good-sized amount of cash into expansion. Generally, they're interested in suburban weeklies, where the growth potential is obvious. But once in awhile you find someone who's a bit more adventuresome. Or farsighted."

I hesitated. "It's a thought." My ears caught the sound of a car outside. "I'll take your advice and hang tight until after the first of the year. If conditions look grim, maybe you can find me a pigeon." The car drove off; no one came to my door. A false alarm, I decided, figuring it was too early for Chris to come back anyway.

"I've got one right now," Dave said, accompanied by the sound of more paper shifting. "He's an old newspaper hand whose wife came into a lot of money a few years ago. He's bought into three weeklies in eastern Washington, four in Montana, one in Idaho, and has a deal in the making up in British Columbia."

I was impressed. "Who is this moneybags?"

At the other end, Dave's wife was calling to him. "What?" he said, momentarily distracted. "Oh, he used to work for *The Times*, 'way back. His name's Tom Cavanaugh."

By midnight, I was ready to give up waiting for Chris. Maybe he'd changed his mind and decided to stay with his relatives after all. It wouldn't be unusual for a kid that age not to call. Adam had always thought my rules about checking in with old Mom were arcane—and weird.

Besides, I was beat. It had been a busy, exceptionally long day. I marveled that I'd kept awake all evening, and figured I probably would have nodded off hours ago if it hadn't been for the jolt from Dave Grogan.

All I knew about Tom Cavanaugh was that he'd stayed on at *The Times* for another five years, had a second child with Sandra, and then moved to Los Angeles. After that, his history was a blank—except for a chance remark three years ago at a Sigma Delta Chi Journalism Awards banquet when a retired city editor had mentioned Tom's name, and added, "Poor guy." I pretended I didn't care and failed to ask for amplification. Of course I'd kicked myself ever since.

But *poor* apparently didn't describe Tom's financial state. I recalled that Sandra Cavanaugh came from a wealthy Bay Area family, and it would follow that she would end up rich in the wake of her parents' demise. So would Tom, since it appeared the couple had remained together. Good for them, I reflected grimly. I hoped Sandra had turned out to be every bit of the ditz she seemed to be. My better nature doesn't always win.

My back and my head both ached as I pushed the last of the logs into the cavernous stone fireplace. It dominated the room and provided enough space to roast a small ox. The wind was blowing down the chimney, sending the sparks flying against the smoke-blackened stones. I still had the poker in my hand when Chris came through the door. I must have looked menacing, because he actually jumped.

"I thought you'd be in bed," he said, his face not so much sullen as it was wary. His dark hair was windblown, and I suspected he hadn't shaved since yesterday morning in Honolulu.

"Almost," I admitted, setting the poker back in place. "How was dinner?"

Chris shrugged out of his jacket, which I noticed had suddenly turned from denim into leather. "Fine. They had steak."

"Were all your relatives there?" I had moved to the door to put the chain on for the night, a habit of my city days in Portland.

Chris was ambling around the living room, hands shoved in the pockets of his jeans. "Some of them."

I could see this was going to be the usual tooth-extraction sort of conversation I had grown accustomed to with most of Adam's friends and occasionally with Adam himself. "Not Neeny?"

"No." He had his back to me, apparently admiring a Monet print hanging above my recently reupholstered sofa.

I picked the leather jacket off the back of the rocker where he'd thrown it. "Where'd you get this?" I asked, trying not to sound like an inquisitor.

"Huh?" He shifted his weight, turning slightly to glance at me. His wiry frame seemed tense. "Oh, it's Mark's. He couldn't find it when he went out so he borrowed mine. Then I had to borrow his because it was so windy and stuff. I'll take his back tomorrow."

The explanation made as much sense as anything else at the end of a long, tiring day. I surrendered on eliciting further information from Chris. Maybe he'd talk more over ham and eggs at breakfast.

"I'm going to bed. Is there anything you need?" I inquired.

"No. Thanks," he added as an afterthought. His back was still turned. Maybe he was crazy about Monet. Certainly he was absorbed in something I couldn't fathom. His relatives, probably—seeing them again after all these years must have been a traumatic experience.

"Okay," I said, taking him at his word.

It wasn't the first mistake I ever made, but it was one of the worst.

I wasn't entirely surprised that Chris wasn't around when I got up at seven the next morning. I still felt a bit groggy, and it was raining like mad, a dark, wet September morning that could drain all but the hardiest native of enthusiasm for a new day.

Chris had slept in his bed—or maybe Adam really hadn't made it before he'd gone to Hawaii at the end of August. I didn't snoop in my son's room while he was away. I couldn't bear to; the disarray gave me the twitch. As long as there were no overpowering aromas and nothing slithered out from under the door, I figured everything else could wait until the Thanksgiving break.

Instead of ham and eggs, I ate two shredded wheat biscuits and drank a cup of coffee. By ten to eight, there was no sign of Chris, and I had to be on my way to the office. To my surprise, the Jag was parked in the carport. Deferring to the downpour and my new green suede shoes, I drove to *The Advocate*.

Ginny was in the front office, efficiently typing up the end-of-month statements. No one else had arrived yet. Carla was chronically late, Ed breakfasted with the Chamber on Thursdays, and Vida usually didn't come in until eight-thirty. I put the coffee on, checked the answering machine, and went over some notes I'd made on next week's editorial calling for the resurfacing of County Road 187 between Icicle Creek and the ranger station.

By the time Vida got in, I'd taken four phone calls, including two subscribers who were dead set against the public swimming pool, one who was for it, and a woman named Hilda Schmidt who wanted to take out a classified ad to sell her exercise bicycle. Instead of referring her to Ginny, I took the ad myself and felt like cheering her on.

I went out into the editorial office to greet Vida. She was shining her glasses and looking sly. I recognized that expression. "What's new?"

Vida stuck her glasses back on her nose but retained the smug look. "Phoebe Pratt did leave town—but only for a couple of days. Darlene Adcock says she went to Seattle to see an eye specialist. If she ever gets her vision fixed, she'll see how homely Neeny is and dump him."

"Not with all his money." I parked myself on Carla's desk.

"True," Vida conceded. "Phoebe always was one for the main chance." She rummaged around in her enormous purse and pulled out a tarnished gold compact. Flipping it open, she applied powder on a hit-and-miss basis. "According to Bill the Butcher, Cece Doukas bought enough New York steaks—not on sale—for six." She cocked her head to one side, the overhead light bouncing off her glasses. "Who do you think? Cece, Simon, Mark, Jennifer, Kent—and your Chris? No Neeny, right?"

"Right so far," I agreed. "Except I didn't know Jennifer and Kent MacDuff were there."

Vida sniffed at my ignorance. "Of course they were. Dot Parker saw them from her driveway. She was on her way to pick up Durwood. He fell off the barstool at Mugs Ahoy again." She paused to smear on bright pink lipstick. "Last but not least, Heather Bardeen has an appointment with Doc Dewey this afternoon. The *senior* Dewey," she added with a knowing look.

Since Dewey the son had been the recipient of Dewey the father's practice, with the exception of maternity cases and a few stubborn patients who refused to be tended by a young whippersnapper, Vida's meaning was clear: Heather must be pregnant. Or thought she was.

"Where did you hear that?" I asked, fascinated as always by Vida's sources.

She gave a careless shrug, powder flying from the ruffled, wrinkled collar of her blue blouse. "Marje Blatt. My niece. She works for old Doc Dewey." Vida obviously thought I had a faulty memory.

She was right. "I forgot." The phone rang, and I grinned at Vida as I reached to answer it. I stopped grinning immediately. It was Sheriff Milo Dodge. Mark Doukas had been murdered—and Christopher Albert Ramirez was wanted for questioning.

Chapter Five

ED AND CARLA entered the office just as I hung up the phone. I was in virtual shock. I stared at them open-mouthed, while they stared back. I'd had to ask Milo four times if he meant Mark Doukas rather than Neeny. He insisted he did. There was no mistaking the grandson for the grandfather.

"I've got to go down to the sheriff's office," I announced, pulling myself together and grabbing my handbag and raincoat.

Carla's cheeks had turned pink with excitement. "Should we put out a special edition?"

The idea hadn't crossed my mind. Although this was my first Alpine murder—if in fact that was what had happened—I knew the town didn't have a blameless track record. A drunken, jealous husband had strangled his wife two years ago. A pair of loggers had gotten into a brawl only months before that, and one had beaten the other to death. And going back almost a decade, there had been the Claymore family, some four miles out of town, with a brooding, schizophrenic father who had shot his wife and six kids before turning the .22-caliber rifle on himself. Murder was no stranger to Alpine. I decided this event didn't merit an extra.

The phone rang before I could get out the door. To my surprise—and relief—it was Chris. I started to tell him about his cousin, but for once he launched into a monologue.

"Hi, Mrs. Lord. This is Chris. Hey, thanks for picking

me up and stuff." His voice was perfectly natural. "I decided to split. Alpine isn't my kind of place. I hitched a ride into Seattle. I'd like to see the city and maybe go on a ferryboat. Then I think I'll head for L.A."

"Chris!" I couldn't keep the panic out of my voice. "Wait—don't go anywhere! Your cousin's been killed!"

"Huh?" He sounded understandably dumbfounded. "What did you say?"

"It was Mark," I said, clarifying my report. "Sheriff Dodge just called and said he'd been murdered."

Chris gave a short laugh. "That's lame. I just saw Mark last night."

Fragments of song and verse about Yesterday and Tomorrow skipped through my agitated brain. "I guess it must have happened after you saw him," I said somewhat stupidly. I took a deep breath; I had to convince him to stay put. "Chris, this probably sounds idiotic, but Sheriff Dodge would like to talk to you about Mark."

He hesitated. When he spoke again, a wary note had surfaced in his voice. "Why me? The whole family was there. Except Grandpa. They all know Mark a lot better than I do." He made a strange, muffled noise. "Hey, this is weird! All things considered, I don't ever want to see Alpine again."

"It's not that simple," I began, but an operator came on the line and told Chris his three minutes were up.

"Got to go," he said, and rang off.

I stood by Ed's desk, with the receiver in my hand. The city of Seattle was home to half a million people. I had no idea where Chris's ride had dropped him off. I dialed the operator and asked if the last call made to *The Advocate* could be traced. She said no. So much, I thought, for modern communications technology.

"Chris has gone to Seattle," I told my staff. "If he calls again, find out where he is."

Ed looked mildly puzzled. "I thought you said he was in Seattle."

I clamped my mouth shut and left the office. We have

no police chief in Alpine, since it's an unincorporated town, despite the best efforts of civic-minded citizens to change the status. The mayor and the city council have been empowered through a charter allegedly drawn up during World War II in an air raid shelter under Mugs Ahoy. But when it comes to law enforcement, we rely upon the state police and the sheriff, which works out well enough since Alpine is the county seat. The Skykomish County Sheriff's office is two blocks away, so despite the rain and my green suede shoes, I walked. I needed time to collect my thoughts. I couldn't imagine why Mark had been murdered. A drug-crazed vagrant passing through, maybe. Or someone who had taken the discovery of gold seriously. Mark was no gem, but he didn't seem like the type to inspire homicide. Of course there was always Heather Bardeen and her appointment with Doc Dewey Senior. Maybe her father had decided to take the notion of a shotgun wedding seriously.

But why, I wondered, nodding vaguely at the handful of passersby I knew only by sight, did the sheriff want to question Chris Ramirez? Just because he happened to come to town the same day—or night—that Mark had gotten himself killed? I heard the morning freight whistling in the distance. Traffic was heavy on Alpine's main street—by Alpine standards. There must have been at least a dozen cars. Life was going on, with or without Mark Doukas.

Sheriff Milo Dodge was a big, shambling man, well over six feet, with broad shoulders and pale graying blond hair. He had a long face, sharp hazel eyes, and a square chin. In appearance, he was totally unlike his predecessor, Eeeny Moroni. But in terms of efficiency, he more than matched his mentor and was considered one of the best law enforcement officials in the state.

Which, I must admit, was the main reason I was disturbed over his desire to question Chris. Milo Dodge didn't act precipitously. His intentions sounded serious.

Dodge looked up from the paperwork strewn all over the desk. His office was finished in knotty pine and a thirty-pound steelhead was mounted over his filing cabinet. He stood up and proffered his hand, which was long and strong. I winced a little as he ground my bones together.

"Where's the kid, Emma?" he asked without preamble.

"Seattle," I replied, knowing it was useless to try to hide the fact since Vida Runkel had probably spread the word in the five minutes since I'd left the office. I saw the speculative look in Dodge's hazel eyes and lifted my sore hand. "I don't know where. He had to hang up before he could tell me."

"Damn." Dodge sat down, making his faux leather chair creak. "Emma—this is urgent. A dead Doukas isn't just another stiff. You know that. Now I suppose I have to call the SPD and King County and the State Patrol. Couldn't you have kept an eye on the kid?"

"I can't keep an eye on my own," I confessed, sitting in the chair across the desk from Dodge. "Chris Ramirez was a guest. He's twenty years old. And how the hell was I to know he'd get involved in a murder case?"

Dodge picked up a roll of mints, offered me one, which I declined, and turned the package around in his fingers. "I've known you for a little over a year," he said thoughtfully. The hazel eyes fixed on my face. "How well do you know this boy?"

I lifted my shoulders. "I've met him a couple of times when I was in Honolulu with Adam."

He popped a mint in his mouth. "Are Chris and Adam pretty tight?"

"Yes." As far as I could tell, they were best friends. Adam is more gregarious than I am. He knows a lot of other students. But like me, he doesn't form close attachments easily. "He and Chris were roommates last year."

The door opened and Jack Mullins, one of Dodge's deputies, poked his shaggy red head inside. "You want to see Doc Dewey now, Sheriff?"

Dodge waved a hand. "In a minute." Mullins left. Milo turned back to me. "Old Doc Dewey's still the coroner, you know."

I did, of course. He was waiting until the next election to turn over the duties to his son. I was beginning to get my thoughts back in order. My presence in the sheriff's office wasn't confined to my roles as Chris's hostess and the mother of Chris's friend. But before I could start playing journalist, Dodge asked me a question:

"What do you make of Chris, Emma?"

"I told you, I don't know him very well." I searched my brain for any help from Adam. But twenty-year-old men aren't into character analysis, at least not into articulating the subject. "He seemed nice enough. Quiet, polite. He hadn't declared a major, so I don't know what kind of ambitions or interests he has. Adam mentioned that he had a bike." I gave another little shrug. "A motorcycle, I mean. His mother bought it for him." I paused, watching Dodge's mobile face take in my scant information. Clearly, he wasn't satisfied. "Look, Milo," I said, going on the offensive, "I need the facts. All I know is that Mark is dead and you want to question Chris. What actually happened?"

Milo leaned back in the chair and put his feet on the desk. His cowboy boots, which had recently been resoled, reached almost halfway across the littered surface. "You don't publish again until next Wednesday. What's the rush?"

"The outside media, for one thing," I replied. "The Seattle and Everett papers will be interested. So will the TV and radio stations. You said it—the Doukas family is rich enough and venerable enough to make news outside of Alpine."

Dodge looked pained. "I don't want a bunch of reporters nosing around town."

I gave him a flinty smile. "Then give me the story. I can be the media contact and save them all a trip."

Dodge cracked the mint with his teeth and swung his feet back onto the floor. He picked up a sheaf of papers and scanned them rapidly. "I got a call last night from Mark Doukas asking me to meet him up at Mineshaft Number Three at nine o'clock. I didn't take the call personally, because I was at an all-day meeting and a dinner in Monroe. I got to the mine right on the dot, and Eeeny Moroni was already there. It seems that Mark had called him, too." He leaned forward, resting his elbows on the desk and adjusting the expansion band of his watch. The hazel eyes were shadowy, and it dawned on me that unlike his counterparts in Portland's Multnomah County, dead bodies weren't a common occurrence for Milo. Especially bodies he was used to seeing on Front Street or in the bar at the Venison Inn.

"Eeeny was having a fit," Dodge continued in a quiet voice. "He'd found Mark with his head bashed in. He was lying near the old mineshaft. He was still warm. I doubt if he'd been dead for more than a few minutes."

I cringed a bit and allowed for an appropriate moment of silence. Dodge was now fidgeting with a small figure of a spotted owl around whose neck hung a sign: EAT ME—I'M YOURS. Logging humor often eludes me; any kind of humor was hard to come by at the moment. The significance of Dodge's words struck me: "His head was bashed in? How?"

Milo's gaze shifted to the opposite wall that was covered with maps of the county. "We aren't sure yet."

"But he was . . . uh, clobbered, right?"

"Right." Dodge stood up; he seemed to loom over me. "Emma, I've got to see Doc Dewey. I'll give you more later, okay? Meanwhile, you help us locate Chris. Deal?" He extended his hand.

I kept mine in my lap. I also remained seated. "Not until I know why you want to speak to him."

The pained expression returned. Milo Dodge knew I could be stubborn. On at least two occasions, he had compared me to his ex-wife, Tricia, whose nickname was Old Mulehide. In a perverse way, I was flattered. Generally, however, we got along, engaging in the symbiotic relationship that is inherent between the press and law enforcement. "You can keep your mouth shut," Milo conceded, more to himself than to me.

"It's part of the job description."

He nodded. "Right." He sighed, leaning one hand against the wall next to the steelhead's snout. "Chris Ramirez was going around town yesterday trying to buy a gun. He couldn't, of course, having just arrived in this state. But he didn't ask about a hunting license. So what should we make of that, Emma?"

"Not much," I answered. "Mark wasn't shot, was he?"

He eyed me with a smirk. "And if Chris wanted to whack somebody, he didn't have a gun. Mark and Chris had a big argument at dinner last night, according to Kent MacDuff." Suddenly, Dodge swung around the desk and stood next to my chair. He was definitely looming now. "Why did you keep asking me if I meant it was Neeny who'd gotten killed?"

The sheriff had caught me off-guard. Fleetingly, I wondered if this was a ploy he reserved for interrogation. "Because he's old," I said, hoping I hadn't missed more than one beat. I stared up at him with my best brown-eyed look of innocence. "I thought there might have been a mistake. Maybe Neeny had simply had a heart attack and somebody had jumped to conclusions."

Dodge cocked his head to one side. "Not bad," he remarked with a wry smile.

"Well?" I stood up rather awkwardly. "Are you absolutely certain Mark didn't fall?"

The wry expression intensified. "Oh, yes, we're sure of that."

"I still think you're nuts trying to direct suspicion at Chris. He didn't even know Mark."

Dodge ignored the comment. "What time did Chris get home last night?"

Damn, I thought. I was in the dark about so much when it came to Chris Ramirez. To make matters worse, I wasn't entirely certain why I was so eager to defend him. Except that he was Adam's friend, and a mother hates to admit her kid has lousy judgment when it comes to people. "Midnight," I answered weakly.

Dodge nodded. "He left Simon and Cece's a little before eight-thirty. I don't suppose he told you where he was for the rest of the evening?"

"I didn't ask."

For a long moment, Dodge was silent. At last, he loped toward the door and opened it. "Get him back here, Emma. Otherwise, I'll have to send out an APB."

I hoisted my handbag over my shoulder. "Then do it PDQ. I don't expect to see him again. He's going to California."

The hazel eyes bore down on me. "Like hell he is," Dodge said.

I brushed past him. "Don't call me. I'll call you."

"That's fine," the sheriff said to my back. "But don't call me dumb. I'm not."

I didn't reply. I already knew that.

I took Vida with me to the murder site. Carla had begged to come along, but this was a tricky story, dealing with the most powerful family in the county. Vida might have the tact of a bull elephant, but she knew the cast of characters, and they knew her. In a small town, that was crucial.

It was a mile from *The Advocate* to Mineshaft Number Three, just off the county road that wound up through the foothills to the ranger station and Icicle Creek Camp Ground. The wind had blown itself out against the mountains, and the rain was coming down in a straight, steady drizzle. In the older residential section of frame houses on the edge of downtown, smoke spiraled out of chimneys and many of the lights were on. Russet leaves drifted into gardens that still sported dahlias, roses, chrysanthemums, and marigolds. Yet the splashes of color in the gray morning seemed more brave than bright.

I followed the curve of the road past a tract of newer homes, mostly split level, almost all with some sort of recreational vehicle parked in the driveway or the two-car garage. These Apliners were outdoor people who spent their leisure time fishing and hunting, hiking and camping. I, too, have been known to do a little stream fishing. Unfortunately, since arriving in Alpine, all I've had to show for it are two small rainbow trout and an extremely ugly bullhead. Even this far from the urban center, I'm told the halcyon days of trout fishing are over.

At the edge of town, on the sidehill, the cemetery crept up into the evergreens. I glanced that way, thinking of the new grave that soon would be dug, no doubt near the final resting place of Hazel Doukas, Neeny's wife.

"Did Mark have any enemies?" I asked Vida, who would know if anyone did.

She was sewing a button on the cuff of her blouse, no easy task considering the ruts and curves in the road. "Dozens. He was a twerp."

Up ahead on the jutting bluff known as First Hill, I saw Neeny Doukas's big house, all gray stone and dark stucco, with a massive front porch. It stood on a full acre and was reached by a switchback driveway that wound above Icicle Creek and the woods around Mineshaft Number Three.

"I mean, *real* enemies," I said, slowing for the left-hand turn to the mine.

"Oh." Vida bit the thread. "Well, no. He's gotten into oodles of fights, usually when he's been drinking. But they don't count. He's never worked much, so he hasn't put a crimp in anybody's career. There have been a slew of girls, but most of them have dumped him, instead of the other way around. He had a bona-fide feud going with Josh Adcock, Harvey and Darlene's oldest boy, but Josh has a Fulbright to Cal Tech, so he's not around. Their quarrel had something to do with a high school football game. Mark fumbled one of Josh's handoffs in the league championship."

Alpine's grudges still amazed me. Mark Doukas and Josh Adcock had graduated from high school at least eight years earlier. Forgiving and forgetting weren't small-town virtues.

The mine was only about twenty feet from the main road, just off the turn into Neeny's long driveway. I pulled over when I saw two sheriff's cars and a van barring the way. A half-dozen men were scrutinizing an area roped off by yellow and black crime scene tape.

"In other words," I said to Vida as I turned off the engine, "you don't have a favorite suspect."

Vida shrugged. "Not off the top of my head."

"Gibb didn't like him," I noted, recalling the venom our driver had exhibited the previous day. "How come?"

For once, Vida didn't have a ready answer. "Oh—lack of respect, maybe. Gibb needs respect, especially since he lost that leg." She took off her glasses and rubbed at her eyes, always a sure sign that she was either agitated or lost in rumination. "There was something about a hermit's cache years ago. You know the sort of thing around this part of the country—abandoned shacks or cabins in the woods where recluses hole up."

I did. Often, they would bury their belongings, especially money. In the modern era, Sunday prospectors would trot out their Geiger counters and go in search of buried treasure. Once in a great while, somebody got lucky and actually found some.

"Anyway, there was a story around town about—oh, ten years ago, I guess—that Mark and Gibb got into a fight over some valuable coins one of them had dug up. Mark was just a teenager then, but he was always pigheaded. Then again, so is Gibb. I think they split the loot down the middle." She replaced her eyeglasses and stared out the car window. "I suppose Gibb has never forgiven Mark. But he wouldn't have waited this long to kill him."

I had to agree. "So who do you think murdered Mark?"

"Well." Vida buttoned up her serviceable brown wool tweed coat. "I'd say Chris Ramirez is as good a pick as anyone."

There was no arguing with Vida. There never was. "Are you getting out?" I asked.

Always game, Vida unwound herself from the front seat. We tromped across the muddy, leaf-strewn ground, careful to avoid branches that had blown down in last night's wind. My green shoes were a mess.

Bill Blatt, who had recently graduated from a two-year college in criminal justice and wasn't much older than Adam, broke away from the others to meet us.

"Hi, Aunt Vida, Mrs. Lord!" His round, freckled face beamed out from under his regulation cap. Bill was one of Vida's numerous nieces and nephews, an engaging young man with ash blond hair and deep-set blue eyes. "Isn't this something?" He stopped grinning, but the excitement remained in his voice. This was his first murder investigation, and he was clearly thrilled.

"It's wicked," Vida declared. "What are you boys doing, Billy?"

Bill Blatt glanced at the others who were crawling around on the sloping wet earth. We were surrounded by trees, with Icicle Creek tumbling downhill amid thick ferns and cattails. The road into the mine was no more than a dirt track that ended in a turnaround by a post marking the trailhead into Surprise Lake. "We're systematically going over the scene," Bill said, now very serious. "You'd be amazed at the stuff we're finding."

"No, I wouldn't," Vida replied. "Human beings are pigs." Her sensible shoes squelched in the mud as she pulled her hat down to her eyebrows. This morning she wore a black derby with a swatch of net. It was impossible to tell if she had it on frontward, backward, or sideways. "The point is, what have you found that's pertinent to Mark's murder?"

"Now, Aunt Vida," Bill began, looking nervous. "You know I can't divulge—"

"Rubbish!" Vida snapped her fingers. "I'm your own flesh and blood. Who used to take care of you when your crazy parents were gallivanting off to Reno every three months?"

Bill's heavy lids blinked over his blue eyes. "Well, it's not much anyway. Just a bunch of junk, like paper and gum wrappers and cigarette butts and a plastic fork." He gazed off in the direction of the creek, avoiding his aunt's keen stare.

"That's it?" Vida was incredulous.

Her nephew shuffled a bit. "Yes, ma'am. Except for the flashlight and the crowbar." Bill Blatt swallowed hard.

"Ah." Vida turned smug. "The crowbar was the weapon? Or was it the flashlight?"

"We aren't sure yet." Bill Blatt was virtually mumbling, his fresh, fair face downcast.

Discreetly, I had taken out my notebook but refrained from transcribing Bill's comments. I didn't want to intimidate him, though it was clear that he found his aunt more daunting than a sea of Camcorders. As for Vida, she never took notes. Her memory was extraordinary.

"Where did Eeeny Moroni find Mark?" I asked in my gentlest manner.

Bill perked up. "Over there." He pointed toward the mineshaft that had been sealed off very recently, no doubt to prevent curiosity seekers from getting inside and causing a cave-in. As far as I knew, the mine had been closed for decades, but apparently Milo Dodge was taking no chances. "We took a ton of pictures," Bill said, following my eye. "It's hard to draw an outline in the rain."

I nodded. "Hard to get footprints, too, I suppose."

"We got some," Bill said dubiously. "But you're right. Even though we made it here pretty fast, between the rain and Eeeny stomping around and carrying on, the ground's pretty chewed up. Same for tire tracks." He gestured back to the road, visible between the trees. "If the killer drove, he—or she—could have parked like you did, on the verge. That's all gravel."

Casually, I jotted down a few key words. "Where did Mark leave his car?"

"It was his Jeep," Bill replied. "He'd parked it in Neeny's drive halfway up. Mrs. Wunderlich found it when she came to work this morning."

I wondered how Neeny was taking his grandson's death. But that wasn't a question for Bill Blatt. I stuck to the basics. "What about dogs? Any scents?"

Bill swallowed hard, his Adam's apple bobbing above his crisply pressed tan shirt. "We did that already."

"And?" I kept my expression bland. The rain was pattering on the leaves, and my hair had gotten quite wet: I hate umbrellas, and I seldom wear a scarf. The air smelled of damp and decay. Only a foot away, a rotting log sprouted colorful clusters of red and brown toadstools.

Bill coughed into his fist. "I don't know exactly what conclusions Sheriff Dodge has come to." He sounded very formal.

"You'll find out, though." Vida thrust both chin and bust at her nephew.

With an anxious glance at his colleagues, Bill mumbled something in the way of reluctant assent.

I tried to bolster him with a smile. "Does anybody know why Mark wanted Dodge and Moroni to meet him up here?"

Bill considered the query. "He'd called the sheriff once or twice before, but Milo was out. I suppose it had to do with his prospecting. Maybe he really did strike gold."

"Was he working in the mineshaft?" I inquired.

Bill looked over toward the entrance, now covered with old moss and new two-by-fours. "He may have. But usually he panned in the streams."

Vida, who had meandered over to the quintet of deputies and specialists, turned back to us and sniffed. "That lazy lout didn't find gold." She swept a hand in a windmill gesture, encompassing the small clearing, the encroaching woods, and the steep hillside. "We're twenty feet from the road. This whole area has been gone over by every professional and amateur prospector in the Pacific Northwest, not to mention numerous unsavory Californians. Mark Doukas might have discovered a lost diamond ring or a stash of cash, but he didn't strike gold. Or silver, either. That mine is empty as the tomb."

Vida was right. Up to a point. But we didn't find out where she'd gone wrong until later.

Chapter Six

Simon and Cecelia Doukas's pseudo-Colonial house was situated west of town in a small but expensive development. Called The Pines by residents and real estate personnel, to everybody else the subdivision was known as Stump Hill—having been clear-cut during World War I, reforested in the 1920s, and partially hacked down again about ten years ago.

Neeny Doukas's father had bought Stump Hill early on and let some shirttail relation named Bump farm the land for about five years until he drank himself into a fit. The original house on what was known as Bump's Stump Ranch had burned down shortly thereafter. A couple of hobos who were passing through on the old Great Northern line stopped to spend the night and set the place—as well as themselves—on fire with the aid of old stogies and white lightning.

The neighborhood had definitely moved up in class since then, unless you prefer virgin forest to civilization. I suppose I do, except that trees don't buy newspapers. They just make them. I love trees for a lot of reasons.

There were several cars parked in the driveway of the Doukas house, including Simon's ecru Cadillac, Cece's silver Mercedes, Mark's Trans Am, and Kent MacDuff's blue Buick. I hesitated, but Vida gave me a whack on the arm.

"What's the matter? Are you going to let this bunch of goons scare you away? If nothing else, you can offer your condolences. I intend to, even if it chokes me."

In the newspaper business, being part voyeur, part ghoul, and all-around snoop is essential. But even after twenty years, once in awhile I get a twinge of guilt. Or an attack of good taste. This was one of those times. The white house with its pillars and green lawn and well-tended garden spoke not so much of Doukas wealth and power as it did of Cece's sweet nature. The woman could be cloying, but she was also decent. I didn't give much of a damn for the rest of the family, but I felt a genuine pang of sympathy for the mother of the murdered young man.

"Let's hit it," I said, getting out of the car.

Vida was already in the driveway, trudging toward the house with her peculiar flatfooted gait. I glanced at my watch; it was just after eleven-thirty. I hoped Cece wouldn't feel obligated to ask us to stay on for lunch. Just as we rang the doorbell, another car, bearing the Driggers Funeral Home logo, pulled into the drive. Our timing was awful. On the other hand, maybe I could talk Al Driggers into reverting to the weekly ad schedule.

Al, a suitably grave man of about fifty with gray hair, gray eyes, and gray skin, joined us on the long veranda just as Jennifer Doukas MacDuff opened the door. She was a pretty young woman, in her middle twenties, with her mother's honey-blond hair worn shoulder-length. Her pale blue eyes showed signs of fresh tears. Al put out a hand, but it was Vida who took over:

"Jenny, you look puny. It won't do for you to get sick right now. Your mother needs you to buck her up. Where is everybody?" Vida was already in the entry hall, darting glances into the study on the left, the living room on the right, and the kitchen down the hall. "Ah! There they are!" She wheeled into the living room, long coat flapping and hat askew.

The grouping included a very white Cece, a taut Simon, and a frowning Kent MacDuff. Cece, wearing black slacks and an off-white cashmere twin set, started to get up, but her husband laid a hand on her shoulder.

"Vida. Emma. Al," intoned Simon Doukas, as if he

were taking roll. He was of average height but seemed taller. His black hair, now graying at the temples, and his sharp beak of a nose gave him a melancholy mien. Had Simon Doukas smiled more often in less tragic circumstances, he would have been attractive. As it was, he verged on the alarming. His courtroom demeanor, which I had observed on various occasions, was dry, concise, and often sarcastic. He was, however, successful, for he came prepared. On this gray September morning, he was tight-lipped and high-strung. He was out of his element; life had not prepared him to face the loss of his son.

"Please sit," he said, after shaking hands with all of us and gesturing at the harmonious melding of comfortable beige and brown and sea-green furniture. "There's coffee. And tea. Unless," he added on a too-eager note, "anyone would like something stronger."

"Tea for me," said Vida, plopping down next to Kent MacDuff on a long brown sofa. "Cream, no sugar. Where's Neeny?"

Simon actually jumped. Kent scowled even more. Cece dabbed at her eyes with a flowered handkerchief. "Dad's taken to his bed. Doc Dewey Senior has gone up to see him." She placed a hand over her cashmere-layered breast. "It's his heart," she added in a faint voice.

"No wonder," remarked Vida, wrestling out of her coat. She glanced around the room, no doubt taking in every detail of decor and nuance of emotion. "You got new drapes. I think I like them."

Cece looked at the nearest panel as if she'd never seen them before. "What? Oh, yes, we had them made in Seattle."

Simon, aided by Jennifer, was pouring coffee and tea from a sterling silver tray on the glass-topped table. Kent MacDuff held his cup and saucer in his lap and put up a hand. "I'm over-coffeed," he said in the rather high voice that didn't fit his square shoulders and bulging biceps. Even in a subdued navy blazer the muscles seemed to ripple through the wool. Kent was close to thirty, with curly sandy hair and a florid complexion. He and Jennifer had been married for almost five years. So far, there were no children, and Jennifer had continued her job as a receptionist in her father's law office.

I had sat down in a striped armchair next to Al Driggers and across from Kent. "We owe you an apology," I said to Kent as Simon handed me a cup of coffee. "I think we misquoted your brother."

Kent MacDuff looked momentarily blank, then gave a little snort. "Oh, *Kevin*. He shot his face off about Mark and the gold, right? Dumb kid." He set the Royal Worcester cup and saucer down with a clatter and straightened his dark blue socks. "Does it matter now? I mean, with Mark gone and all. Or do you think somebody zapped him to get at the gold?"

Cece shuddered and Simon turned away. Kent seemed oblivious. He was lighting a cigarette with a sleek gold lighter that hadn't come off the rack at the local 7-Eleven.

"What did Mark really find?" I asked to break the awkward silence as much as to get the story straight.

Jennifer and Kent looked at each other, and both came up empty. "He never told us," Jennifer said at last in a listless manner.

I steeled myself and turned to Cece. "Neeny told me Mark was digging up maidenhair ferns for you."

Cece burst into tears. Simon leaped across the room and sank down beside her chair. "Dearest! Please! You're going to collapse!"

"But it's so like him!" Cece wailed. "Mark was so *thoughtful*!" She peered at me over the wrinkled handkerchief. "Especially of his mother. He always said I was his best girl." The sobs started up again, and this time, Simon pulled her to her feet.

"Come along, dearest. I'm putting you to bed. I'll talk to Al about the arrangements. Don't fret. We know what you would . . ." His voice trailed away as he led her out of the room and toward the spiral staircase.

"Well," said Vida, snatching a sugar cookie off a Wedgwood plate, "I don't suppose Mark would have called the sheriff to tell him he couldn't find any maidenhair ferns, would he?" She fixed her hawklike gaze on Kent and Jennifer.

"What's that?" asked Kent. Even Al Driggers's carefully composed face showed puzzlement.

Vida shrugged and munched. "Mark called the sheriff two, three times to tell him something. He asked Milo—and Eeeny Moroni, the old fool—to meet him up at Mineshaft Number Three. Now if that was all about a bunch of ferns, I'll eat my hat." She touched the brim as if to verify it was still there should the bet be called in. "Well?"

"Well what?" Kent was getting annoyed. "Damn it, Vida, what are you yakking about?"

Vida glared at Kent. "I'm yakking about the fact that Mark must have found something pretty significant to send for the sheriff. Maybe you'd better ask your little brother, unless you want to go on being as dimwitted as you act, Kent MacDuff. I remember when you had to repeat fourth grade. Twice."

Kent turned crimson. He fairly bounced on the sofa. I was reminded of a bantam rooster. "It was only *once*! And that was because old Miss Grundle was too drunk to add up the grades right!"

"Rubbish." Vida took a big swallow of tea, presumably to wash down her cookie. "Grace Grundle doesn't drink. She has an inner ear problem. That's why she staggers so much."

I decided it was time to intervene before we got off onto a tangent about public education in Alpine, chronic alcoholism of various inhabitants, insidious diseases, or any combination thereof. "Jennifer, is it true that Mark and Chris quarreled last night?"

Jennifer, who had been pleating the folds of her baggy dress in her thin fingers, looked up with a mystified expression. "I don't think so." She turned to her husband. "Did they, Kent? I forget."

"Hell, yes." Kent thrust out his chin in a pugnacious manner. "They had a hell of a row outside, just before Mark left."

"What about?" I asked.

Kent shrugged. "I don't know. I didn't stick around. None of my business." He started to drink from his cup, realized it was empty, and put it back down again. "Who knows? That Chris struck me as big trouble."

"I kind of liked him," Jennifer murmured.

"Where is he?" Al Driggers asked, and I was surprised to hear him speak. Somehow I was getting the impression that he'd filled himself with embalming fluid and was sitting there corpselike, waiting for his own eulogy.

I gazed unflinchingly into Al's somber gray eyes. "He left town."

"Oh, my." Al shook his head sadly.

"Skipped town, you mean," said Kent.

"Is he coming back?" asked Jennifer.

I opted for candor. "I doubt it."

Kent stood up, smoothing the creases in his rumpled slacks. "Don't worry. They'll haul his ass back. Old Neeny has sworn revenge."

"Phooey." Vida sniffed. "Old Neeny is full of it. What he needs is a good purge."

Jennifer looked shocked, Al Driggers winced, and Kent scowled even more ferociously than before. "That's none of your damned business, Vida. Neeny's a sick man."

"Maybe, maybe not." Vida was unruffled. "I think I'll go cheer him up."

"Please don't." It was Simon's ice-cold voice, emanating from the doorway. "Mrs. Pratt is looking in on him."

"Ha!" Vida sprang to her feet. "That old tart! Some nursemaid. She's got a terrific bedside manner, I'll give her that."

"Please!" Simon was holding up both hands. "Cece's trying to sleep." He motioned to Jennifer. "That casserole Mrs. Adcock sent over—why don't you put it in the oven for our lunch?"

The words seemed to be our exit cue, but Simon had come over to my chair. "Before you go, could we speak alone for a moment?" Not waiting for my assent, he glanced at Al Driggers. "We'll get down to business in about five minutes," Simon said. "It shouldn't take long." Apparently Al wasn't going to partake of the casserole either.

I followed Simon across the hall into his study. Like the rest of the house, the small room was tastefully appointed, with an unlighted fireplace, an antique oak desk, two chairs, and tall bookshelves boasting an eclectic collection. Unlike the comfortable living room, the study wore a stilted air. Perhaps it was the difference between Simon's occupancy and Cece's touch.

Simon Doukas sat behind the desk, looking like a coiled spring. "I have to ask about Chris," he said dryly.

I could hardly believe I'd seen this man less than twenty-four hours ago with tears in his eyes. If he had wept for Mark, he gave no sign.

"I have some questions of my own," I responded, sitting in the chair across from him.

He stiffened even more, if that were possible, and looked down his long nose at me. "I'll go first. What did he tell you about his relatives in Alpine?"

I felt as if I were in the witness box. "He didn't remember any of you very well. Except for Neeny."

Simon inclined his head. I guessed that he'd spent a lifetime being overlooked in favor of his father. "Didn't he speak of Mark?"

"No. Well, yes, once. Some prank when they were kids, I think."

"Oh." Simon seemed bored by pranks. "What else?"

"Nothing." I raised my palms. "Really, Simon, you were strangers to Chris as far as I could tell."

Simon put his hand to his head. "I don't understand any of this. Emma," he said in a plaintive voice, "do you think Chris killed my son?"

"No." It was the truth. I scarcely knew Chris Ramirez,

but despite the acrimony for his grandfather, I genuinely didn't believe he could commit murder.

Simon drummed his fingers on the desk. It was almost bare, except for a fresh blotter, a calendar, and a matching pen and pencil set. "If not Chris, then who?"

I shook my head. Outside, the rain continued to fall, spilling from the downspouts by the room's single window. "Who stands to gain from Mark's death?" I inquired.

"Gain?" Simon's heavy dark eyebrows lifted. "No one."

"He had no will?"

"No." He gave me what might have passed as a smile before warmth was invented. "Typical, eh? The lawyer's son without a will, the cobbler's children with no shoes. Oh, I tried talking to him about drawing one up, but it upset him. You know how young people are. They think they're immortal. They don't want to discuss death." Simon grimaced, his sad and empty gaze somewhere beyond my right shoulder.

"He had money, I take it?" It seemed the logical conclusion to draw. If he hadn't, then there would be no need for a will.

"Some." He clamped his mouth shut as if he'd been wildly indiscreet. But Simon Doukas must have had the need to talk. There was so much repressed within the man, and his wife wasn't very helpful at the moment. As for his daughter and her husband, I couldn't imagine Simon engaging either of them in meaningful conversation. "Fifteen years or so ago," Simon went on, "my father set up trusts for each of our children—two-hundred fifty thousand dollars apiece, to be turned over to them absolutely on their twenty-fifth birthdays. Naturally, the sums have grown considerably. Mark came into his money almost two years ago. Jenny will get hers next month." He fingered his sharp chin and waited for my response.

"So Mark's money will revert to you—or to Neeny?" I asked.

"To Cece and me, as his next of kin." He gave a pathetic little laugh. "You aren't thinking we killed our son to inherit his trust fund, are you?" His voice showed a trace of his well-known sarcasm.

Stranger things had happened, of course, but I knew Mark Doukas's nestegg couldn't compare to Simon's. I also assumed Mark had probably already blown a portion of the money. I ought to know; I'd done it myself.

I passed over Simon's comment. "What about this quarrel between Mark and Chris? What started it?"

Martin frowned. "I don't know. I didn't hear any of that."

"But they *did* quarrel?"

"Kent says so." His tone suggested that Kent wasn't the most reliable source in town. I tended to agree, but my own suspicions were based on something more concrete. The problem was, I couldn't remember exactly what.

"Simon," I began, taking another tack, "do you remember much about Chris as a little kid?"

A spark of life flickered in his black eyes. "He was a good-natured little fellow. Cute as a button. I used to try to make up to him, but he . . ." Simon paused, a catch in his voice. "He was a bit shy. And of course Margaret and Hector kept to themselves."

I tried to imagine Simon Doukas fifteen or twenty years ago, coaxing a small boy into a romp. The picture was out of focus. Even as a young attorney, Simon must have been stiff and intimidating, especially to a child. "Where did they live?" I asked, wondering how long it would take to wear out my welcome at this interview.

"East of town, by the golf course. It was one of my father's rentals." He gazed at the desk calendar; it hadn't been changed in a week. Simon carefully turned the pages. "Who would have thought . . ." he murmured, then placed his hand on today's date: Thursday, September 26. "Emma." Pushing back from the desk, he again looked down that long nose at me. "You don't intend to publish any of this, do you?"

"What?" I bolted forward in the chair.

Simon straightened his tie. "Over the years, we've been

very loyal to *The Advocate*. I presume you're willing to show your gratitude for our family's support. We certainly don't want the Doukas name smeared all over the newspaper."

I was aghast. Neeny's demand for a reprint was bad enough, but Simon's request was outrageous. And impossible. I leaned on the desk, suppressing an urge to pound my fist on the smooth oak surface. "Simon, you can't keep a story like this quiet. I'm surprised the met dailies haven't been up here. It might not make page one outside of Alpine, but it'll certainly find its way into the regional sections."

Simon's face had grown very tight, his shoulders rigid. "I think you're wrong. We haven't heard from anyone. And if we do, I know the phone numbers of some very important people in the media." He raised his head slightly, as if he were looking over a courtroom full of rabble, and I was the lowliest of the bunch.

I stood up. "Sorry, Simon. It won't work. You haven't got that big a Rolodex." I spoke with more confidence than I actually felt. There had been, alas, a couple of recent occasions when the local media had indeed suppressed stories. "You've got almost a week of peace as far as *The Advocate* is concerned. We'll be as careful and as tasteful as possible."

Simon had also risen to his feet. He was so angry he was shaking. "If you print this, I'll run you out of town! Do you hear me? You ... *whore!*"

My own temper was about to explode. But miraculously, I kept my wrath under control. "I was wondering who'd be the first one to call me that to my face," I said in a musing manner. "Funny," I went on, turning toward the study door, "I honestly didn't think I'd run into anyone that small, even in a small town. Until now."

I slammed the door behind me.

Chapter Seven

EXCEPT WHEN SHE was eating sugar cookies and chocolate truffles, Vida was always dieting. It wasn't easy coaxing her into driving down to Index for lunch. I didn't want to eat in Alpine, because I knew we'd be overheard. Index was just far enough away that we were guaranteed a certain amount of anonymity.

Naturally, Vida was wild-eyed when I told her about Simon's insistence that we not run the murder story. It took me most of the drive to calm her down. By the time we reached the little café just off the highway, she had stopped shrieking and rubbing her eyes long enough to look at the menu.

"I'm not hungry," she announced, and promptly ordered the hot turkey sandwich with gravy and cranberry jelly.

After raking Simon over the coals one more time, we finally moved on to Mark's murder. "Did you find out what happened at dinner last night?" I asked as an elderly waitress brought us each a small green salad.

Vida pitched into her lettuce. "Not much, from what I could tell. Of course I only had that idiot, Kent, and that ninny of a Jennifer to go by." She huffed a bit between mouthfuls of salad. "Simon and Cece and Chris sat around and visited before dinner. Since Kent and Jennifer weren't there yet, I haven't a clue as to what they talked about, but everybody seemed to be on good terms when the MacDuffs got there around six-thirty. Mark showed up a few minutes later, drank a beer, and then they all sat down to dinner. They finished up around seven forty-five. Chris talked quite a bit about Hawaii." Vida paused, noting my look of incredulity.

"Chris opened up?" I asked.

Vida shrugged and brushed a crouton off the front of her blouse. "He drank beer, too. Maybe it loosened his tongue. Anyway, about eight-fifteen, Mark said he had to go out. Which he did. Chris left about ten minutes later." She pursed her lips and gave me a shrewd look. "Simon dropped him off at your house. It was eight-thirty."

"At *my* house?" I almost dropped my fork. Then I remembered the car I'd heard while I was talking to Dave Grogan on the phone. "But Chris never came in. Where did he go?"

"You should have asked him," Vida said matter-of-factly. "As for Kent and Jennifer, they went home right after Chris and Simon left. Cece cleaned up from dinner, read the paper—both papers, ours and *The Times*—and went to bed." She gave me a significant look.

"So when did Simon get home after allegedly dropping Chris off?"

Vida paused as the waitress delivered her turkey and my BLT. "I'm not sure," she admitted. "I got most of this from Jennifer, so the part about Cece is second-hand. She never came back down, as you may have noticed when you flew out of Simon's study." She sprinkled her plate with lavish doses of salt and pepper. Across the aisle, three middle-aged fishermen eased into a booth, ragging each other about their abysmal luck. An elderly couple moved past us, the woman wheezing, the man shuffling. A Persian cat swished by, its plumelike tail exuding disdain.

"Cats!" Vida exclaimed, making a horrible face. "Dreadful animals. Have you ever dissected one of those things?"

I considered reminding Vida that we were eating, thought better of it, and replied that I had not. Luckily.

"It had to be the crowbar," she remarked, apparently apropos of nothing, except that I knew Vida well enough by now to follow her train of thought—which had led from dissecting cats to the autopsy on Mark Doukas. "Emma," she said in a more serious tone, "are you trying to cover this story—or solve the murder?"

Despite having raised three children, Vida wasn't particularly maternal. But she was old enough to be my mother, and once in awhile, she acted like it. I appreciated that. After all, I'd been an orphan for almost twenty years.

I mulled over the question. "Maybe I have to do one to do the other," I said.

But Vida shook her head, the derby slipping further down over her forehead. "No, no. That takes away your objectivity. Stick to the facts, Emma. That's your job. Don't try to play detective."

She was right, of course. Over the years, I'd covered a variety of murder investigations in Portland. Except for some random piecing together of information, I'd never concerned myself much with solving the cases themselves. But then I'd never had a personal stake in any of those homicides. The victims were all strangers; the killers, if indeed they were discovered, were just names.

"I feel responsible for Chris," I asserted. "He's my son's best friend. I may not need to find out who killed Mark, but I have an obligation to prove who didn't."

Vida chewed on her white meat and looked thoughtful. "Are you sure you just don't want to get back at Simon Doukas for being such a jackass?"

I hadn't told Vida exactly what Simon had said in dismissal, but she was shrewd enough to guess that it had something to do with my status as an unmarried mother. "The only way," I said slowly, "I could get back at him is if he did it. That may not be the case."

"It might be one of the other Doukases." Vida lifted her graying eyebrows, which met the brim of her derby. "Simon wouldn't like that."

I suppressed a smile. "But you would, Vida?"

She cut up her gravy-slathered bread with vigor. "You bet I would. If any family ever needed a comeuppance, it's that bunch."

The cat sidled past again, looking even snootier than before. Vida made another face, then she leaned closer, almost dipping her bust in her lunch. "All right, Emma, you've made up your mind. I'll do what I can to help, but you have to be candid with me. Why was Chris trying to buy a handgun from Harvey Adcock?"

I was wondering when Vida would get around to asking me that. I debated, but not for long. I not only like Vida, I trust her. She could tell the world about every scrap of gossip, but she could also keep a secret. It was one of the reasons she knew so much; I wasn't the only one in Alpine who trusted Vida Runkel. So I told her about Chris's animosity toward Neeny and the frightening conclusions I'd drawn.

Vida's reaction was typical. "Well, good for Chris. He's got some spunk. But that doesn't mean he intended to shoot his grandfather, tempting as the prospect may be. In fact, it doesn't mean much, since it was Mark and not Neeny Doukas who got killed."

I agreed. "The only reason I can think of for Chris trying to buy a gun is for self-defense. His mother may have told him some pretty hair-raising stories about her family."

Vida rolled her eyes. "As Margaret well might." Polishing off the cranberry jelly, she dabbed at her mouth with the paper napkin, then pitched it at the cat, which had parked its carcass next to our booth. The cat flinched but stayed put. "I wonder," she mused, rummaging in her purse for compact and lipstick, "whatever happened to Hector Ramirez?"

So did I, but at the time, it didn't seem pertinent.

This time Vida was right and I was wrong.

Vida took her own car up to see Neeny Doukas. I suggested joining her, but Vida was adamant. "Let me handle the old sap this time. If he's really sick, I may have to use tact. It's not a pretty sight."

Back at the office, Carla was agog about the murder, but Ed, who always expected the worst anyway, took it in stride. I fended off their questions as best I could before barricading myself in my office.

Predictably, a stack of phone messages had piled up. Ginny, Ed, and Carla had tried to intercept the ordinary snoops, but at least twenty callers had insisted on speaking personally to the editor and publisher. Before I could start dialing, Ginny Burmeister slipped into my office to complain that Gibb Frazier hadn't brought back the overage on the print run. She needed at least two dozen extra copies to mail for special requests, and we needed the rest for our files. I told her to give Gibb a call; it wasn't like him to be so absentminded.

For almost an hour, I wielded the phone, talking to the Methodist minister, the owner of the Venison Inn, two of the three county commissioners, the city's head librarian, and Cal of Cal's Texaco and Body Shop. All of them prefaced their inquiries with other, unrelated business, but the bottom line was Who Killed Mark Doukas? I kept repeating that Sheriff Dodge was working hard to solve the case. I certainly wished him luck, since I was baffled. None of the callers was satisfied, but at least they didn't cancel their subscriptions.

I had just hung up on Cal Vickers when Fuzzy Baugh, our current mayor, lumbered into my office. Fuzzy was the retired owner of Baugh's Fine Home Furnishings and Carpet, which had recently moved from Front Street to the new mall, causing a ruckus over whether or not downtown Alpine was dying. Since the entire commercial district was only eight blocks long and two blocks wide, the controversy struck my city-bred mentality as odd. But all things are relative, and when, two months later, Barton's Bootery also vacated Front Street, I actually asked Carla to poll the remaining downtown merchants and find out if they planned to stay put. As far as she could tell, they did. But with Carla, you could never be quite sure of her data.

Fuzzy was a tall, heavy-set man with curly blond hair, which I presumed was dyed. His face was nicely crinkled and his eyes were green and small. He had been mayor for the past six years, though his first election back in '84 was also steeped in controversy. It seemed that Fuzzy and Irene, his wife of thirty years, had decided to split up. Irene stayed at their house in town, and Fuzzy moved out to a cabin he'd built on the Skykomish River, about ten miles downstream. When Fuzzy announced he was running for office, the opposition declared he wasn't a resident and therefore was ineligible to stand for election. Fuzzy moved back in with Irene, a gesture that was dismissed by his detractors as merely expedient, but the couple actually reconciled and went on a second honeymoon to Mexico. Politics might make strange bedfellows, but in this case, they had reunited a pair who probably should never have stopped sleeping together in the first place.

"This is bad, Emma," Fuzzy announced, dropping into the vacant chair on the other side of my desk. "Drugs, of course."

"Drugs?" Though that was often a factor in homicides I'd covered on *The Oregonian*, I hadn't seriously considered the issue. Not that we didn't have our share of substance abuse—but for all of Mark Doukas's failings, I'd never heard him accused of taking or dealing drugs. "What makes you say that, Fuzzy?"

Fuzzy leaned forward in the chair, trying to find a bare spot to place his elbows. As usual, he was dressed impeccably in suit and tie, never having overcome his salesman's need to look his best. Perhaps he felt such formal attire was worthy of his mayor's role, though his predecessor, Elbert Armbruster, had never been seen in anything but overalls. "You haven't been here long, Emma," Fuzzy said in a kindly tone that suggested it wasn't entirely my fault. "This town was originally filled with Orientals. That's why it was called Nippon. What do you suppose those people brought with them?"

I resisted the urge to answer *tempura* and merely looked curious. Fuzzy gave me his sage half smile. "Opium. I'll bet dollars to doughnuts Mark found a stash of it at the old mine. Other stuff, too, probably brought up there by modern-day drug traffickers. The question is, who's the kingpin?"

Every first and third Tuesday, I sit in on the city council meetings, so I was used to Fuzzy Baugh's strange—and imaginative—hypotheses. Last spring, damage to one of the Burlington Northern spurs had, he insisted, been caused by neo-Nazis. The Fourth of July fireworks hadn't all gone off due to the devious machinations of the Monroe Elks Club, who were jealous of Alpine's display. The theft of a birdbath from young Doc Dewey's front yard was the plot of irate loggers who wanted to avenge their endangered livelihoods by getting back at all avian species, spotted owls or not.

Thus, I regarded Fuzzy's latest flight of fancy in context. "Mark might have found something up at the mine, Fuzzy," I allowed, "but I doubt it was drugs."

Fuzzy's small green eyes opened wide. "See here, Emma, you haven't thought this through like I have. I know human nature. I had to as a salesman. I still do, as mayor of this fine town. Mark was real anxious to get hold of Sheriff Dodge and get him up there to Icicle Creek. Now what could Mark have wanted to show Milo unless it was drugs?"

Fuzzy's conclusion might be off base, but his reasoning wasn't. Despite his lamebrained ideas, he was no dope. "Well, everybody agrees it wasn't gold or silver," I conceded. "As far as the mine goes, I understood it had been closed for years. Isn't it a safety hazard?"

"Definitely," Fuzzy agreed, sagely nodding his head. "There's a real danger of cave-ins. Plus, the springs can rise up and flood those shafts. That's one of the reasons they quit working the mines in the first place."

"You mean there was still ore?"

"Oh, maybe some. Not enough to risk lives over, though." Fuzzy made the statement with some authority, as if he had personally been in charge of the closure some seventy-five years ago. He sat up straight, turning so that I could catch his profile, which was still a fine one. "Mark my words. It's drugs. I intend to ask for a resolution at the city council meeting next Tuesday to open Mineshaft Number Three."

I tipped my head to one side. It didn't seem like a very helpful idea, but on the other hand, it couldn't do any harm. As long as nobody wandered inside and got hurt. "Who owns those old mines, Fuzzy?"

"Nobody. That is," he went on in his low, soft voice that still held just a hint of his native New Orleans even after twenty years, "the rights to the mines expired years ago. The Forest Service owns the land that Mineshafts One and Two are on, Number Four belongs to the railroad, Five is gone, and Three is on Neeny Doukas's property."

I lifted my eyebrows. "Do you have to get Neeny to approve of opening the shaft?"

A flicker of uncertainty passed over Fuzzy's crinkly face. "I hope not. But he'd do it, especially if it'll help find out who killed his grandson." Standing up, Fuzzy put out his hand. "I'm off, Emma. Nice as always visiting with you." He gave me his best marketing-mayoral smile. "You'll handle this with care, I'm sure."

"From now on," I replied with a smile of my own, "my middle name is *Alleged*."

Briefly, Fuzzy looked puzzled; then he nodded and let go of my hand. "Yes, that's right. Circumspection. That's the ticket." He started for the door, then turned back to face me. "In fact, it might be better to let matters sit for a time. There's no point in riling everybody up, is there?"

I feigned innocence. "How do you mean?"

Taking a step back toward my desk, Fuzzy assumed his best good-ole-boy air. "Well, the way I see it, if you run just an obituary on Mark this coming week, that pretty well covers it. The funeral will be over by then, I imagine. If Milo's arrested somebody, fine. If not, why upset folks?"

Neeny Doukas had Fuzzy Baugh, along with almost everybody else in town, tucked in his pocket. I wondered if Neeny, supposedly sick, had delegated his influence to Simon. I said as much to Fuzzy: "Have you been talking to Simon Doukas?"

Mild surprise registered on Fuzzy's face. "I offered him my condolences, of course. And to that fine wife of his, Cecelia." He gave a sad shake of his curly locks, reminding me of an aging cherub. "You realize how hard it is on the family, Emma." His voice had grown rather faint. "I know you'll want to spare them any further grief."

I decided to play the game. "Certainly. I have no intention of rubbing salt in their wounds, Fuzzy. You know better than that. Good journalism isn't cruel."

The green eyes turned cold, like agates. Fuzzy filled the doorway, and for the first time since I'd met him, I was aware of the menace of the man, seventy years and all.

When he spoke again, his voice was still very soft. "You behave now. There's no need to embarrass fine folks like the Doukases." He gave another shake of his head. "We sure don't want any more tragedies around Alpine, do we, Emma? I mean, you never know who could be next."

Giving me the most empathetic of looks, Fuzzy Baugh made his exit.

I tried not to let Fuzzy's thinly veiled threat bother me. Neither he nor Simon Doukas was the first in Alpine to attempt to scare me out of a story. There had been trouble with some of the loggers the previous winter. At least one irate taxpayer had promised to send me a bomb after I'd backed a school levy. And somebody had actually thrown a rock through the window of my office after I'd made the editorial comment that Alpine remained basically an unintegrated community because most of the residents weren't hospitable to people of other races. Threats were also part of the job description.

But the intimidation I'd faced twice in one day over Mark Doukas's murder unsettled me more than I liked to admit. It was no longer just a matter of Chris Ramirez's involvement, but of preserving my right to publish. I did not, however, intend to perish in the process. The more I thought about it, the more I became convinced that the only way to secure the story was to find the killer.

I put in a call to Adam. Nobody answered, but I wasn't surprised, since it was only one-thirty in Honolulu. I'd try again, after five, our time.

Meanwhile, Vida returned and reported on her visit to Neeny Doukas. She'd been gone for over two hours, and, given the sudden threatening atmosphere hanging over *The Advocate*, I'd begun to worry.

"Oooh—" she exclaimed impatiently, rubbing at her eyes, "you might know I was fine. I just nosed around a bit here and there after I left Neeny's. Not that it did me much good. People ought to pay more attention to what other people are doing."

"What about Neeny?" I asked, pulling a chair up to Vida's desk. Ed had left for the day, and Carla had gone to a hospital board meeting.

Vida breathed on her glasses, wiped the lenses on her slip, and settled the tortoise-shell stems over her ears. "I got lucky. Phoebe was just leaving to get her hair dyed."

"Neeny isn't at death's door, I gather."

Vida snorted. "Of course not! Oh, he's upset, I suppose he would be, he regarded Mark highly, which proves what an old fool he really is; but, except for gastritis, I don't think there's much wrong with him." She wagged a finger at me. "*He* says otherwise, but I don't believe him. He just wants to be babied."

Given the fact that Neeny had just lost his favorite grandchild, I felt Vida was being a bit harsh, but I didn't say so. "Had he seen Mark last night?" I inquired.

Vida took a sip from the hot water she always drank in the late afternoons. "No. He didn't realize Mark had parked that Jeep or whatever it is in the drive. Neeny said he heard sirens by the mine some time between nine and nine-thirty. He thought it was a wreck on the highway. Sheriff Dodge didn't tell him about Mark until this morning."

I gave Vida a quizzical look. "How come?"

The wry expression on her face told me she also thought the delay was strange. "Milo called around ten-thirty and talked to that idiot, Phoebe. She said Neeny was resting—I'll bet!—and shouldn't be disturbed. The sheriff should wait and give Neeny the bad news in the morning, after he'd had a good night's sleep. Ha!"

I reflected briefly on Vida's words. "So Phoebe knew?"

Vida rolled her eyes. "Taking a lot on herself, isn't she? Imagine Hazel Doukas making decisions like that for Neeny! Why, Hazel couldn't even decide for herself whether to broil or bake her pork chops!"

Not having known the late Hazel, I couldn't imagine much. But Vida's remark gave me an idea. "Phoebe doesn't live up there, does she?"

"She might as well," Vida huffed. "You should see her house over on Pine Street—I'll bet she hasn't washed her curtains in four years. And the yard—it's a mess. Nothing but a few ratty rose bushes and some poor bedraggled perennials. She spends most of her time up there at Neeny's, holding his—whatever." Vida's expression showed rampant distaste.

Out on Front Street, a car horn honked and somebody yelled a greeting to a passerby. Darkness was settling in over Alpine, but the rain had stopped shortly after my return to the office. I examined my sad suede shoes and considered heading home. I was anxious to get hold of Adam.

"Did Neeny say anything about Chris?" I asked.

Vida cocked her head at me. "Now that's odd. He didn't! At first, I expected him to launch into one of his diatribes about how Chris must have killed that nitwit, Mark, but he never let out a peep. I have to admit, Neeny was a little subdued. He figures Mark was murdered by bikers."

The theory was more plausible than Fuzzy Baugh's. About every four years, sort of like the Olympics, a horde of rough-and-tumble bikers descended on Alpine. They raised hell up and down Front Street and usually tried to smash up the bar at Mugs Ahoy. But on their last foray, the previous spring, they had taken on a bunch of disgruntled loggers at the Icicle Creek Tavern at the edge of town. The leader of the bikers had made the mistake of imitating a spotted owl. The final score had ended up something like Loggers 48, Bikers 3. Still, it wasn't impossible that they might have returned for revenge. But it was unlikely that they'd pick on Mark Doukas.

"I think it's odd that Neeny didn't mention Chris," I said.

"So do I." Vida raised her eyebrows above the rims of her glasses. "But what does it mean?"

I shook my head. "I don't know. Did he say anything about our running the story?"

Vida batted a hand at the air. "Oh, of course! I told him to go soak his head. I won't stand for that nonsense from Neeny Doukas or anybody else." She gave me a quick, shrewd look. "Who else has been trying to scare you?"

I told her about Fuzzy Baugh. Vida hooted in derision. "That nincompoop! He should have stuck to selling rugs! In fact, I'll bet he's wearing one. That mop can't be his real hair, and if it is, he ought to be ashamed of himself!"

In spite of my more serious concerns, I was amused. "What was his hair like when he was younger?"

Vida shrugged. "Fuzzy was never younger. Not by much. He came here only about twenty years ago and bought out my brother-in-law, Elmo, who owned the furniture store first. Elmo had to go away for a while, and the business had gone downhill. Fuzzy's wife was a Pratt whose first husband lived in Baton Rouge."

As ever, the intricate, inbred background of Alpine's citizenry never ceased to amaze me. But Vida, who apparently felt she'd finished dispensing all usable information, had begun pounding away at her old upright. I stood up and went back into my office to collect my gear and call it a day.

I was driving down Front Street when I realized that for the first time in years, I didn't much like heading home alone.

Chapter Eight

ADAM TOLD ME I was weird. "Chris wouldn't hurt a bug," he insisted after I'd explained the events of the last two days in Alpine. "Sure, he talked about having it out with old Neeny. It was his favorite subject after he'd had a couple of beers. But get violent? No way, Mom. You're too weird to even think it."

I assured Adam that I wasn't the one who thought Chris might be implicated in Mark's murder. Then, aware that I'd already used up over five minutes of long distance clock, I asked my son if he knew of any relatives or friends Chris had in Seattle. Adam didn't. The only family Chris had ever mentioned was the Alpine contingent. Margaret hadn't kept up with Hector's relations. She'd started a new life in Hawaii, and all her real friends were still there.

I was coming to a dead end, but I had a sudden inspiration. "Adam, did Margaret have a boyfriend?"

"Huh?" He sounded shocked. Obviously, women in my peer group should not be allowed to date due to encroaching senility. "Gee, I don't think so. She was like you—sort of, like, well, you know, antisocial."

"I am not antisocial!" I bristled. "I'm choosy, damn it. Do you want a mother who's a tramp?"

My son gave out with a little laugh that was part sneer, part embarrassment. "You could go out with some guy once in awhile, Mom. You haven't done that since the Nutty Professor in Portland."

"Never mind my love life," I snapped. "How much money has Chris got with him?"

There was a pause. "I don't know," Adam finally answered. "He does okay. He got his mom's insurance and some attorney dude over here has rented out the house for him. He worked, too, at the Hilton."

No trust fund, I thought. Simon hadn't mentioned one for Chris, but there was always a chance that Neeny had kept his own counsel. Apparently Margaret had been completely cut out of the family money.

"Oh," Adam added as I mulled, "he has some plastic."

It sounded as if Chris could get by for a while without having to send back to Honolulu for more money. For the dozenth time that day, I wondered if Chris had stayed in Seattle or headed south. "Okay, Adam, I can't think of anything else to ask you. Is everything all right over there?"

"Sure," Adam replied. "Deloria and I are going to a movie tonight." I was about to pry when Adam continued: "Hey, what should I do with Chris's mail?"

"Hang on to it, I guess. Unless he settles some place." Like jail, I thought grimly.

"There isn't much," Adam noted, "except his *Sports Illustrated*, a couple of ads, and a letter."

In the past few years, I'd come to regard the writing of personal letters as dead as the dodo. My curiosity was piqued. "Who from?" Maybe it had something to do with the rental house; if so, Adam should attend to it in Chris's absence. It would help teach him responsibility, or so my unrealistic maternal mind-set ran.

"Let me see." Adam rummaged in the background. I reached over to click on the TV. I usually watch the early evening news, not just to keep informed, but to check out any possible local tie-ins. "It's postmarked Seattle," Adam was saying as the image of a sinking ship appeared on the screen. "That's weird," he remarked. "There's a printed return address from Alpine. Phoebe Pratt. Oh, I remember

her. Isn't she the old bat with all the clown makeup and
the hairdo that looks like a pineapple?"

I took in a sharp breath. "Open it," I commanded in my
best breach-of-ethics tone.

"I can't do that," Adam protested. "It's addressed to
Chris. That's *snooping*."

"That's my job. Come on, Adam," I coaxed, "just this
once. It could be important. To Chris."

It was his turn to sigh. "Okay, hang on . . . It's dated
September twenty-third. Jeez, I don't like this. . . . Why
don't I just stick it in another envelope and send it to you
so you can give it to Chris?"

"Why don't you just stick that idea in your ear? Phoebe
is Neeny Doukas's girlfriend, get it?" I stopped just long
enough to let that fact sink in on Adam. "It's very strange
that she would write to Chris. Read me the blasted thing.
Then you can mail it to me, okay?"

The stationery fluttered in my ear. I had visions of it being pale lavender and scented. I was probably wrong. No
doubt it was typed on a word processor—but sometimes I
cling to illusions.

" 'Dear Chris,' " Adam began. " 'This letter may come
as a surprise to you. You probably don't remember me, but
I certainly remember you as a little boy. You were such a
handsome lad and so well-behaved.' " Adam paused.
"This is a bunch of bilge, Mom. It'll make Chris puke."

"Go on." I gritted my teeth and gave only fleeting attention to the TV image of a North Seattle bank, the site, presumably, of an afternoon holdup.

"Where was I? Oh—'I'm sorry your poor mother
passed away last year. You must feel her loss sorely. I
should have written sooner to offer my sympathy, but time
goes by so fast, even in Alpine.' What a crock!" exclaimed Adam. I could picture him shaking his head. Nev-
ertheless, he went on reading: " 'I've been looking after
your grandfather, and I hate to tell you this, but he's failing. I know he would love to see you, so if you could
come over to the Mainland on your next college vacation,

do consider it. Meanwhile, I stand ready to help you any way I can. Though bridges may be burned—' Get this, Mom. You're gonna blow chunks. '—the way home remains. Be assured, you still have one friend in Alpine. Sincerely yours, Phoebe Pratt.' Retch-making, huh?"

"Puzzle-making," I murmured. On Channel 4, a disabled Metro bus was blocking traffic on the freeway. I wished all the Doukases, plus Fuzzy Baugh, were trapped inside. "I think you had better send that to me. Overnight. I'll pay for it."

"It's just a bunch of birdcrap. What's it got to do with Mark Doukas getting whacked?"

"I don't know," I admitted. But deep down I had a feeling there might be a connection.

For the next minute or so, I listened to Adam try to weasel out of a trip to the post office. He was short of ready cash—of course. He had to study for a test—maybe. He didn't want to be late picking up Deloria—naturally. But eventually he gave in; the post office was only two blocks away. I figured he could throw the letter that far, which is how I assume the mail is often delivered anyway.

Still resisting the urge to ask more about Deloria, I poured myself a glass of English ale and sat back to catch the last fifteen minutes of news. Except for a feature on a couple in Kirkland who'd adopted a pair of aardvarks, the rest was weather and sports. Mark Doukas's murder hadn't made the Seattle television scene, and I didn't know whether to be glad or sad.

I turned off the set and realized I hadn't listened to my answering machine. I'd been too anxious to call Adam to notice the flashing red light. Luckily, there were only three calls: an old friend from Portland, Darlene Adcock asking if I could fill in for a sick bridge player Saturday night, and Sheriff Dodge. I dialed Milo first, hoping to catch him still at work.

He was. "The crowbar did it," he declared. "I tried to call you at the office, but Vida said you'd just left."

"Prints?" I asked, taking notes.

"Wiped clean except for some smudges we can't use. The weapon belongs to Simon Doukas—he thinks." Dodge sounded annoyed. "The flashlight was Mark's."

"What do you mean, Simon *thinks* it was his? Mark was trying to buy one from Harvey Adcock that afternoon."

"Seen one crowbar, seen 'em all. Simon said he had at least one, maybe two, but he couldn't find either of them," Dodge explained. "It sounds as if Mark had been trying to pry open the mine."

"Mayor Baugh wants to open it," I said in a casual voice.

"Jeez! That's great, we'll end up with fifty men trying to rescue some poor little kid who wandered in by mistake." Dodge's annoyance was turning into anger. "Why can't people leave well enough alone?" His tone changed quickly. "Have you heard from Chris again?"

"No. Are you looking for him?" I didn't sound quite so casual this time.

Dodge sighed. "I was hoping we wouldn't have to. By the way, did you know the story made the five o'clock news on the Everett radio stations?"

I gave a little gasp. Apparently, the Seattle media hadn't had the time—or the inclination—to pick up on the item yet. "No. Well, it's out in the open anyway."

"Simon's pitching a fit," Dodge said, not without a hint of pleasure. "Hey, you want to go get some dinner? How about that French place down the highway?"

In the past few months, Milo Dodge and I had shared a half-dozen meals, usually accidental luncheon encounters. This was the first time he'd issued a formal invitation. Rankled by my son's gibes, I accepted. Besides, what better way to ferret out more information than over boeuf Bourguignon and a glass of Beaujolais?

I was changing into a white crepe blouse and a black pleated skirt when Vida called.

"Can you swing a crowbar?" she demanded.

I allowed that I thought I could.

"So can anybody who's not feeble," she retorted. "So

where does that leave us? Did you hear about the Everett stations?" She was gleeful. "Let that moron Simon put that up his nose. As for Fuzzy, it'll make his hair fall off."

While trying to button my blouse and juggle the receiver, I told Vida about Phoebe's letter to Chris. She was flabbergasted.

"Well, if that doesn't beat all!" A teakettle whistled in the background and Vida's canary, Cupcake, competed with the sound. "Why would she do such a thing?"

"Sucking up, my son would say," I suggested, marveling that he hadn't. "How does Phoebe get along with the rest of the Doukases?"

"Like cat and dog," said Vida. "Except for Cece. Cece Doukas gets along with everybody, which is a sure sign that there's something wrong with her. Simon's never approved of his father carrying on with Phoebe, but he doesn't dare speak up, the little weasel, and Kent's been downright insulting. Jennifer sticks up her nose, and Mark—well, Mark considered Phoebe a world-class leech. Which she is, but I hate to admit to agreeing with Mark, even if he is dead."

I slipped into my sling-back black pumps. "You don't suppose Phoebe is angling to marry Neeny, do you?"

Vida scoffed. "After all these years? You know the old saying about the cow and the free milk—Phoebe's been a regular dairy farm for Neeny Doukas." She huffed a bit, then suddenly changed her tune. "Emma, people are *very* strange. Do you suppose that's why Phoebe dragged Neeny to Las Vegas?"

I'd forgotten about the trip the previous month. "Gee, it could be. At least it's something we could check out. Or Milo could. I'm going to dinner with him. I'll mention it."

"You're *what*?" Vida's voice exploded into my ear.

I cringed. I hadn't wanted to confess my date with the sheriff, but I knew that by tomorrow morning, it would be all over town. "We're going to discuss the case." It wasn't a lie: Given the circumstances, of course we'd talk about Mark's murder.

Vida huffed and puffed some more. "Ooooh—just be careful, Emma."

"Hey, I'm safe. I'll be with a law enforcement person."

Vida's tone turned dour. "Don't let him finagle any more out of you than you get from him. In *any* way," she added darkly.

"Don't worry, I'm a big girl," I insisted. But I sounded more confident than I felt. I had the feeling that Vida knew it.

The Café de Flore was run by a Frenchman who had married a Californian. Together, they had fled north with dreams of opening a restaurant that featured prime examples of cuisine from Paris, Brittany, and Normandy, with a dash of Beverly Hills.

The decor was as simple as it was predictable: one wall covered with wine racks, gleaming copper pots suspended from the ceiling, and bunches of dried wildflowers. The tables and chairs were an odd-lot collection that looked as if the owners had bought up kitchen donations to St. Vincent de Paul. But the food was excellent, and though the menu was small, the wine list was long. I chose the beef I'd envisioned, while Milo let me recommend the pork chops baked with apples. We didn't mention Mark until our entrées arrived.

"How did the radio people in Everett get the story?" I inquired after he'd raised the subject by remarking that murder investigations were exhausting.

"The usual way," he answered. Milo's shambling frame was decked out in what I guessed he considered semiformal attire—a brown corduroy sports coat, tan shirt, dark brown slacks. No tie. "They check our blotter over the phone every morning," Milo explained. "Then we got a couple of calls, so one of the deputies doled out the bare facts. We didn't know about the crowbar for sure at that time." He gave me a wry grin. "You'll be glad to hear they didn't mention Mark finding gold."

I was relieved. It's embarrassing to find yourself a

laughingstock among your peer group. "Are you still after Chris?" I asked bluntly.

Milo, who was trying to figure out the identity of his vegetable, gave a shrug. "We certainly need to question him, yes. I'm putting out an APB tomorrow if he hasn't shown up by tonight. I would have done it earlier, but Eeeny talked me out of it."

Inwardly, I thanked the former sheriff. "He doesn't think Chris is . . . involved?"

"He doesn't think we have any evidence." Milo surrendered and ate the unknown vegetable. My guess was that it was turnip; I had tiny brussels sprouts. "I think Eeny's overly cautious."

Judging from that remark, I gathered that Milo Dodge did indeed have some sort of evidence. My appetite flagged. I approached the matter obliquely. "Have you figured out where Chris went last night?"

Milo nodded once. "Oh, yeah. We know quite a bit about that." He pushed aside the single candle that flickered between us. "Don't you?" His gaze was very level.

"I sure don't." I bristled a bit. "He was like a clam when he got back to my house. Where was he?"

Chewing on his pork chop, Milo shot me a disapproving glance. "I can't tell you that, Emma. Hell," he chuckled, "you won't even tell me what I'm eating. What's a *pomme*?"

"It's a walrus tusk," I snapped. "Okay, then I won't tell you about Phoebe Pratt eloping with Neeny Doukas."

Milo's sandy brows arched. "Where'd you hear that?"

"Never mind." I would have hummed a bit if we hadn't been sitting down to dinner. My mother had never allowed singing at the table. "If you don't believe me, check it out. Clark County, Nevada. August of this year."

To my satisfaction, Milo was hooked. "We will. Hell, Emma, this is a community property state. Neeny must have rewritten his will. If he hasn't, everything will go to Phoebe, should she outlive him."

"Simon would make sure it didn't," I pointed out. "Assuming he knows they got married."

Milo waved to a couple coming across the room. I didn't know them. In fact, I only recognized four of our fellow diners, both younger couples who lived on the fringes of Alpine. The rest of the two dozen customers had probably come up from Monroe, or even Seattle and Everett. The Café de Flore's reputation was growing beyond the boundary of Skykomish County.

"Whether or not Phoebe and Neeny eloped doesn't help us with Mark's murder," Milo noted. "It'd be more likely that somebody would have knocked off Phoebe. Or even Neeny."

I sipped my Beaujolais and tried to figure out the flaw in Milo's argument. I couldn't find one. I sighed. "What about Heather Bardeen?"

"Heather?" Milo looked puzzled. "She'd already broken up with Mark. Why would she want to bash his head in?"

"Maybe he done her wrong," I said lightly.

"I'm sure he did. More than once. But so what? When did you last meet a twenty-year-old girl who went gaga over her lost honor?"

Milo had a point. Even if Heather was pregnant, she wasn't likely to rush off to Icicle Creek and bust Mark's head with a crowbar. I savored my last mouthful of beef and wondered if the bikers had really returned.

Milo's plate was clean as a whistle, turnips and all. He took out a small spiral note pad with a ballpoint pen. "By the way, I'll need a description of Chris for that APB."

I grimaced, feeling like a traitor. But dissembling wouldn't serve any purpose. The Doukases, Harvey Adcock, and a dozen other people could provide the information Milo needed.

"Twenty years old, five-eleven, about a hundred and fifty pounds, straight black hair worn just a little too long, black eyes, straight nose, slight dimple in chin, no distinguishing marks." I hesitated, giving Milo time to finish writing. He was quick and looked up with approval. I went on: "Faded blue jeans, maybe Levi's, faded denim jacket, maybe ditto, Hard Rock Cafe—Honolulu T-shirt, Dodgers baseball cap, Reebok tennis shoes in white with black and green stripes. No, hold it."

Milo looked up again, pen poised over the pad. "What?"

"He'd changed his T-shirt." I shut my eyes, trying to picture Chris as I'd seen him last. "It was something about Hawaii—a cocktail, with SUCK 'EM UP! on it, I think. And . . . let me see . . . I can't . . . Oh!" I put a hand to my mouth. "He wasn't wearing that denim jacket. He'd loaned it to Mark. Chris had on Mark's leather bomber jacket."

Frowning, Milo flipped back through the pages of his note pad. "You're right. Mark had on a denim jacket, J. C. Penney issue." He regarded me very seriously. "Tell me more about the baseball cap."

"More? What can I say? That it was autographed by Tommy Lasorda?" I gave Milo a perplexed look. He didn't so much as flicker an eyelid. Then I saw Chris in my mind's eye again, standing in front of the Monet. "Chris wasn't wearing the cap when he came home. Is that what you mean?"

Milo nodded once and tapped the note pad with his pen. "Mark wore the cap. They found it next to his body. It's got his blood and his hair on it."

"Of course," I said slowly. "It was raining. Mark borrowed both the cap and the denim jacket. Chris's hair was wet when he came home. I remember that now." Struck by a sudden thought, I leaned eagerly across the table. "Now reconsider your suspicions regarding Chris—if he'd killed Mark, wouldn't he have taken back his own jacket?"

Milo looked at me as if I'd been sniffing Elmer's Glue. "I've never said Chris murdered Mark," he replied carefully. "What are you implying? First they swap clothes, then they try to kill each other? My sisters used to do that, but fortunately, nobody ever ended up dead."

The waitress came for our dessert order, but for once I abstained and ordered a King Alfonse. Milo settled for the café's version of burnt cream and a snifter of brandy.

There was something else about Chris and Mark and their jackets that bothered me, but my brain was numbed by the excellent meal. The fragmentary idea slipped away, and I changed the subject from violence to domesticity. "Where are your kids?" I asked Milo when the waitress had left.

"The youngest—Michelle—is living with Old Mulehide and her second husband, Peter the Snake, in Bellevue. Tanya is shacked up with some would-be sculptor in Seattle." He shook his head. "She supports him, and he makes erasers out of Play-Doh. I don't get it. My son, Brandon, is going to school in Oregon. Corvallis. He wants to be a vet."

"At least he has a goal."

Milo shrugged. "Of sorts. He wants to move to Kentucky and take care of million-dollar thoroughbreds. He'll be lucky to come back to Alpine and unruffle the feathers of Vida's canary."

I sympathized, briefly. Furtively, I glanced over at Milo, who was immersed in his burnt cream. He was attractive in his way, with regular, if unremarkable features, tall, solid, smart enough. He even had a sense of humor. So why did I feel about as thrilled by his presence as if I'd been dining with Vida? The truth was, I'd hoped the evening might provide a springboard for future intimacies. Maybe it was Adam's needling, or the thought of spending the night alone in the wake of a murder. Perhaps I was lonely and didn't know it. But whatever had spurred me into wishing for some sparks to fly with Milo Dodge, the truth was that nothing was happening. I fervently hoped it was the same with Milo.

I didn't get to find out. When we pulled up in front of my house half an hour later, Bill Blatt was waiting for the sheriff. Fuzzy Baugh had been rushed to Alpine Community Hospital with an apparent heart attack; he was listed in critical condition. Milo Dodge put the siren on and raced off toward Front Street, leaving me alone.

* * *

The last person I expected to see on my doorstep that night was Jennifer Doukas MacDuff. She knocked just before ten, about a half hour after I got home. Wearing another sack of a dress and with her long hair straggling over her shoulders, Jennifer was definitely waiflike. I took in a deep breath of fresh, pine-scented air and ushered her into the living room.

"Kent and I had a fight," she said, collapsing onto the sofa. "Over you."

"Me?" I had just changed into my bathrobe and was drinking a Pepsi. "Why?"

Jennifer slumped against the cushions, looking even more drab than usual by contrast with my emerald-green upholstery. "Kent thinks your story about the gold got Mark killed. He said you all but admitted it at my folks' house. And he also thinks you're hiding Chris Ramirez." She gave me a plaintive look. "Are you?"

"No. Want some pop?"

Jennifer did and opted for 7-Up. I returned from the kitchen to find her in tears.

"What's wrong? Are you crying for Mark?" I inquired gently, sitting next to her and putting the glass of soda on the coffee table.

Jennifer sobbed on but shook her head. "Mark was a jerk in a lot of ways," she said between sniffs. "I'll miss him, sure. But it's Chris I feel most sorry for."

"How come?" I shifted on the sofa while Jennifer tried to compose herself and sit up.

"I was the only one he'd make up to when he was little," Jennifer said. "Aunt Margaret had me baby-sit a couple of times. That was just before Hector disappeared. I never understood that. I was only a kid, about ten, but I liked Uncle Hector. He wasn't educated, but he was nice. He seemed to really like Aunt Margaret—and Chris, too. His running off has never made any sense to me. Maybe I was too young to take it all in."

"Tell me about Hector." It had occurred to me that in more ways than one, Hector Ramirez was the missing link in the Doukas family history. "What did he do for a living?"

Jennifer reached for her pop and looked vague, which I realized was typical. "Labor stuff. Not logging, but construction, maybe. My father said he was lazy. Hector didn't work all the time, but sort of off and on."

"Construction's like that," I remarked. Vida had said Hector had come to Alpine to help put in a sewer line. It would follow that he'd try to get work as a manual laborer; it would also follow that Neeny Doukas would try to prevent his despised son-in-law from getting employment. "Maybe Hector left town to find another job and something happened to him."

Lapping at her soda like a cat, Jennifer shook her head, the honey-blond hair swinging across her face. "If he had, wouldn't somebody have notified Aunt Margaret? He must have had an I.D. Besides, he and Margaret did go away for a while, when they were first married. In fact, Chris was born in Seattle. But I guess she got homesick. Or else she thought the rest of the family would change their minds. They didn't."

"Was Hector an American or a Mexican National?" I asked.

Jennifer considered. "I think he was from Los Angeles. He had kind of an accent but not much." She sat back, her shoulders hunched. The Doukas arrogance seemed to have been obliterated in Jennifer by Cecelia's self-effacing nature. In some ways, it was a pity. I wondered how Jennifer faced up to Kent MacDuff.

I finished my Pepsi and realized that the rich food and red wine had given me heartburn. A bit guiltily, I thought of Fuzzy Baugh, lying in the intensive care unit at Alpine Community Hospital. If his heart attack had been severe, he would be moved to Everett or Seattle. Alpine's medical facilities were limited.

I came back to the subject at hand. "Do you remember much about Hector's disappearance?"

Jennifer fiddled with her hair and squirmed a bit. "Not

really. Margaret didn't tell anybody at first. At least not the family. Then I guess she called the sheriff, but they didn't start looking for him right away. Grandpa interfered, I think, and told Eeeny Moroni not to bother."

Recalling that Vida had said there were rumors about Neeny paying Hector to hit the road, I decided to broach the topic. "Do you think your grandfather might have bribed Hector to leave town?"

Jennifer turned her pale blue eyes on me in astonishment. "Oh! I don't . . ." She swallowed hard, blinked and put her chin on her fist. "Gosh, I don't know. I never thought about it." For a few moments, she apparently did just that. Then she gave a tentative shake of her head. "I can imagine Grandpa trying it, but honestly, I don't see Hector going along with him. Like I said, Hector really loved Aunt Margaret and Chris."

The living room was silent while we each reflected on the life and times of Hector Ramirez. I hadn't built a fire, and there was a definite chill in the air. The wind was gentle tonight, a soft sigh in the trees that surrounded all but the front of my house. I heard a logging truck rumble down the street as someone came home, no doubt after a long stop at Mugs Ahoy or the Icicle Creek Tavern.

I was the first to break the silence. "I'm puzzled about Chris and Mark. Your brother borrowed Chris's cap and jacket, yet Kent says they had a fight. That doesn't make sense."

Suddenly edgy, Jennifer avoided my gaze, hiding behind her veil of fair hair. "There was no fight," she said in a mumble.

"I'm glad to hear it," I said, trying to sound cheerful. "Is Kent trying to cause trouble or is he always so full of bunk?" My guess was both, but I waited with a smile for Jennifer's reply.

She prefaced it with a deep sigh. "Oh, Kent can be such a pill! He doesn't mean to be, but I think he feels he has to act like a big shot because he married into the Doukas family. It's really very immature."

"It sure is. It's also harmful to people like Chris. It gave Sheriff Dodge the wrong impression. I'm very relieved to hear there was no quarrel."

Jennifer seemed to be brooding over her husband's faults. She looked up suddenly, pushing the long hair off her face. "I didn't say there was no quarrel. I just said there wasn't one between Chris and Mark." She thrust out her small chin in a surprisingly pugnacious manner. "Kent and Mark got into it, just before Mark left. Having him go off and get killed is enough to make me cry for him, too."

"Oh." I took note of the uncharacteristic spark in her eyes. "Yes, I can understand that. What did they fight about?"

Her shoulders slumped again. "Kevin. Mark was mad because Kent's brother had told your reporter about the gold. Except there wasn't any, of course. Mark blamed Kent for having such a dopey brother."

I'd meant to talk to Kevin but hadn't gotten a chance. By the time he was out of school, I was knee-deep in phone calls and Fuzzy Baugh's visit. Now it was too late to call a teenager who had to get up at seven in the morning. At least that's the way it had worked at our house.

I wondered how far I could push Jennifer. I sensed that her anger—or in her case, anguish was a better word—with Kent might temporarily overcome her protective instincts. "Was it a serious quarrel?"

"Well, they didn't hit each other this time. I heard some of it. They just yelled a lot, mostly about who had the stupidest relatives." A flash of alarm crossed her face. "Don't take this wrong, Ms. Lord—Mark and Kent were always on each other's case. It was some kind of macho deal. But they weren't enemies. They even partied together."

The kind of partying Mark and Kent had done depressed me. I could envision raucous nights with a half-dozen kegs, stale nachos, and bad jokes, culminating in ghastly trips to the bathroom. By comparison, my bathrobe and a can of Pepsi didn't look half so bad.

"But on that note, Mark left?" I asked innocently.

"I guess." Jennifer looked glum.

"Then I gather your dad gave Chris a ride home?"

She drank more soda. "Yes. A few minutes later, we went home, too."

"You didn't see Chris again?"

"No."

"You stayed home the rest of the evening?"

Jennifer looked faintly belligerent. "Sure. It was a work night."

"When did you hear about Mark?"

"We'd gone to bed. Around eleven, I guess." She glanced at her wrist, which was bare. Maybe she was confirming the fact that she didn't wear a watch. "Dad called. I got dressed and went over to be with him and Mom."

"Kent didn't go?" I was mildly surprised.

Jennifer shook her head. "No. He'd gone to see young Doc Dewey about a muscle pull. Kent was Dewey's last patient for the day, and he had to wait forever. That's why we were late getting to my folks' house for dinner. Kent had taken one of those muscle relaxant things before he went to bed, and he was out of it."

I couldn't think of anything else to ask Jennifer except how her grandfather was doing. Okay, she answered vaguely, all things considered.

"Look," I said, "tell Kent I'm sorry we ever ran that story in the first place. I'll tell him so myself if it'll help. But even if we hadn't printed it, rumors about Mark and the so-called gold find would have spread all over town." Jennifer didn't look convinced, but neither was I. While I didn't believe Mark had discovered gold, our black-and-white reporting job automatically gave authenticity. That's just the way it works with the media. We're supposed to be trusted to tell the truth. Fighting down regrets, I changed the subject. "Jennifer, are you going home?"

Her hair and shoulders drooped in unison. "I don't know. Maybe I'll go stay with Mom and Dad. They could use my help, I suppose."

Fleetingly, I considered asking her to stay with me. But my earlier fears of being alone had been tempered by good food and red wine. Besides, I wasn't having much luck with houseguests this week. I didn't want Kent MacDuff breaking down my knotty pine front door at three A.M. Then again, maybe he'd taken another muscle relaxant and was out for the count.

Jennifer got to her feet, the sacklike dress hanging unevenly. "I'm sorry I bothered you, but I was upset and I didn't want to go crying to my folks. Mom's pretty racked up. Mark was her favorite. She spoiled him something awful. It wasn't fair." The belligerence was back in her eyes.

"Lots of things aren't fair," I remarked, making one of those useless, if true, comments that serve no other purpose than to fill a void. "Feel free to drop in again."

Jennifer looked faintly surprised at the invitation. "Okay. Thanks for the pop."

I watched her go out into the overcast night, a bulky all-weather jacket thrown over her shoulders. Her white Japanese compact was parked at the edge of the short driveway.

Poor little rich girl, I thought—she was as unlikely an heiress as any I'd ever met. I'd known wealthy girls at Blanchet High School in Seattle; I'd rubbed elbows with their big sisters in Portland. They not only reeked of privilege, but they were often supremely self-confident. Jennifer, by contrast, could have been a gyppo logger's daughter. She'd married at twenty, stayed in Alpine, and seemed to have neither ambition nor curiosity. The Jennifer Doukas MacDuffs of this world bothered me.

Even after she'd driven away, I lingered on my small front porch, inhaling the fresh, cool mountain air. Tonight it was tinged with wood smoke, a sure sign that autumn had settled in. I peered around my front yard, still amazed that the dahlia tubers I'd planted last March had actually come up. There wasn't much lawn—just enough to separate the walk from the drive on one side and the narrow flower bed and the split-rail fence on the other. A big maple stood in one corner, by the street. In the back, where the grass sloped gently upward, a half-dozen evergreens protected me from the rest of the world.

The phone broke my reverie. To my surprise, it was Chris, calling from Seattle. He sounded troubled.

"Hey, Mrs. Lord, I can't find your address. Maybe it was in my denim jacket. I need to send back Mark's leather jacket. I mean, I know he won't need it, but I don't feel right keeping it, you know?"

Carefully, I gave him my address. "Chris, the sheriff really has to talk to you. I'll drive down and pick you up first thing in the morning."

His reply was sharp: "No. I'm going to L.A." He sounded not only incisive, but older.

"Why? What's wrong?" There was no mistaking the sound of panic.

"I just want to get away from here," he said, trying to keep his voice calm. "It . . . it rains too much. I miss the sun."

"Okay," I said reasonably. "I'll buy that. Can I ask you a question, just to set the record straight?"

"Sure." Despite the response, Chris didn't sound so positive.

"Where did you take my car last night after your uncle dropped you off?"

"I just sort of drove around. I tried to find the house where we lived when I was a kid." He hesitated, and I heard a tapping sound, as if he were drumming his fingernails on the phone. Impatience or anxiety, I wondered. Both, maybe. "Just for kicks, I went up to the ski lodge to see Heather Bardeen. But she wasn't there. Not then. I ran into her later, at the Burger Barn."

I kept my voice casual. "So you just cruised for over three hours?"

"I guess." Apparently, it didn't strike Chris as strange. For the moment, I gave up pressing him. "Where are you right now?"

There was a faint pause. "In a motel, near downtown."

"Which one?"

"I don't know."

He could have been hedging. On the other hand, his lack of awareness was typical of his generation. "Have you got a view?" I asked.

Another pause. "Yeah. Of a parking lot. And the Space Needle. I went up there today." He definitely sounded more like himself, though I had the feeling it wasn't without effort.

"Forget about mailing the jacket," I counseled him. "I have to come into town tomorrow for a meeting." It was a lie, but made in a good cause. "I'll meet you for breakfast. Adam is sending your mail over. I talked to him today."

"Oh? Cool. Maybe I got my check."

I didn't disillusion him. "It should be here in a couple of days. Why don't you wait?"

"No way." The incisiveness returned. "I'll send you an address from California. Oh, hey, when you talk to Adam again, ask him to send my other denim jacket, okay? It's at the house. The people who rented it let me store a bunch of stuff in the garage."

I agreed to convey the message. In some ways, I was ambivalent about keeping Chris around, so I didn't try arguing with him further. But I was determined to see him before he left. "Is there a restaurant in the motel?"

"Yeah, I saw it when I checked in. But I want to catch the nine-thirty bus."

"No problem," I said easily, but inwardly groaning at the prospect of another early-morning run into the city. "I'll meet you in the restaurant at eight. Look on the table by the phone, Chris. There must be some advertising to give you the motel's name."

"There's some postcards and a sort of phone book thing—oh, yeah, here. It's a Ramada Inn. But I don't see an address."

"No problem," I repeated. "I know where it is. I'll see you in the restaurant at eight."

"Okay," he said a bit dubiously. "Mrs. Lord?"

"Yes?"

"You're not bringing anybody with you, are you?" The suspicion in his voice bounced off my ear.

I laughed. "Hardly. Do you think I'm a police dupe?"

"Well, it's all pretty strange, isn't it?" He sounded very young again.

"Yes, it is," I agreed. "Are you sure you're okay?"

"Huh? Yeah, I'm fine." He hesitated, then spoke with less certainty. "It's just that, well, like, this is really scary, you know?"

"Yes," I replied, grateful that Chris couldn't see my grim expression. "It's scary, all right. I've never been this close to a murder before."

"Me neither," said Chris. He sounded frightened. I wished I knew why.

Chapter Nine

THE SUN WAS trying to break through during the last half hour of my drive into Seattle. I'd given myself plenty of time and arrived at the Ramada Inn at seven forty-five. Fueled only by coffee, I was starving by the time I reached the restaurant. It was half full, a mixture of off-season tourists and business types. I drank more coffee but held off ordering breakfast until Chris came down. The pancakes tempted me, but so did the crab and cheese omelette. On the other hand, the ham and eggs special was appealing, too. I amused myself by playing my finely honed game of juggling the menu around in my head. It was a practice borne of countless hours of eating alone.

I'd picked up a morning paper in the lobby and scanned it for news of Mark Doukas's murder. Sure enough, the story was tucked away on an inside page. The brief, two-inch item stated that the body of Mark Doukas, twenty-six, had been found in Alpine, just off Stevens Pass. Sheriff Milo Dodge was investigating what was a probable homicide, since Doukas had apparently died from a blow to the head. There was no mention of gold. There was no allusion to the Doukas family's standing in the community. There was no information about leads or possible suspects. In other words, there was no real interest in the case outside of Alpine. That, I decided, was just as well.

I'm fairly adept at premonitions, so I was chagrined, but only mildly surprised when Chris didn't show. I gave him until eight-fifteen to be late, but by eight-thirty, I was wor-

ried. I stalled the waitress for the fourth time and went out
to the desk.

A cheerful Vietnamese man told me there was no Chris
Ramirez registered. It hadn't occurred to me that Chris
would use a different name, but it made sense. Milo
Dodge could have been already looking for him. In fact, it
dawned on me that the sheriff might have sent out his
APB at the crack of dawn.

I described Chris, and the round-faced clerk nodded
in recognition. Mr. Jones had checked out early, around
six A.M. Was I, by any chance, Mrs. Lord?

I told him I was. The clerk handed me a Ramada Inn
dry-cleaning bag that contained Mark's leather jacket and
a note with my name on it.

The waitress pounced as soon as I got back to my table.
Although my appetite had dwindled in the past five minutes, I felt coerced into placing my order and asked for the
special. Appeased, she scurried off, leaving me to peruse
Chris's note.

He had surprisingly elegant handwriting, and his spelling was amazingly accurate for his generation. "Dear Mrs.
Lord," the note on motel stationery read,

> "I feel bad about taking off before you got here. The
> fact is, I should never have come back to Alpine. It was
> a mistake for a lot of reasons. I don't know how to ex-
> plain this to you, but seeing the town and the people
> stirred up a lot of memories I'd tried to forget. I'm still
> not sure what's real and what isn't. Maybe if I go away,
> I can sort it out. Or else forget it all again. Thanks for
> everything. Yours truly, Chris Ramirez. P.S. Here's the
> jacket. Maybe Heather would like to have it."

I reread the note. The distress I'd heard on the phone
last night was mirrored by the written words. I recalled
how tense Chris had been when he came back to the house
Wednesday night. I thought at the time it was because of
his meeting with his relatives. Now I wasn't certain. A six-

year-old isn't attuned to the nuances of adult behavior. As a child, Chris might have felt disturbed by the estrangement between his parents and the rest of the family, but he wouldn't have fought to keep the memory at bay. Indeed, it seemed that Margaret had done quite the opposite, and Chris had followed her lead. His hostility indicated that he wasn't suppressing his emotions.

So what was Chris trying to forget? Was it something ugly between his parents? That seemed the most likely, yet his mother must have been a constant reminder of any such incident. Chris spoke of the town and the people jarring his sleeping memories. Neeny? But Chris hadn't seen his grandfather. At least not as far as I knew. Now I wondered. There was that three-and-a-half-hour gap to account for. Milo Dodge knew something about that lost time, but he wasn't telling me. I'd have to find out for myself.

The waitress came with my order. I further frustrated her by immediately getting up and going back to the lobby. Sure enough, there was a Greyhound schedule in the tourist information rack. A bus left Seattle for L.A. at six twenty-five. Chris was already two and a half hours down the road. I couldn't possibly catch up with him, but the sheriff could. I went back into the restaurant and ate my breakfast. The waitress finally looked happy.

I did not.

Durwood Parker, a serious competitor with Eeeny Moroni for the Worst Driver in Alpine Sweepstakes, had run over a cow two miles east of Sultan. Debra Barton, of the Barton Bootery family, had announced her engagement to a Tacoma prelaw student. Averill Fairbanks reported a UFO hovering over his toolshed, his fifth sighting of the year. Francine Wells chalked up $350 worth of damages at Francine's Fine Apparel on Front Street when the wind blew over a bucket of blue paint being used to freshen the exterior, and spattered not only the display window, but the sidewalk and street. Bessie Griswold, up on Burl Creek Road, called the sheriff to report a prowler that turned out to be a cougar who mauled her Manx cat. Vida was pleased.

Those were the stories facing me when I got back to the office around eleven. I confided where I'd been only to Vida, who took the news of Chris's departure with a disapproving shake of her head. She was, however, glad to learn that I had not let Milo Dodge ravish me. So, of course, was I.

After giving Carla specific instructions on the handling of the morning's accumulation of news, I called to check on Fuzzy's condition. It was listed as stable. He would not, as far as they could tell, be shipped to a larger medical facility.

As for the homicide investigation, Milo Dodge reported no notable progress. The funeral was set for Monday in Seattle, since Alpine had no Greek Orthodox church. I designated Vida as the *Advocate*'s representative. The rest of us couldn't be spared, since Monday was always a hectic day in getting the paper ready for publication.

Just before noon, Milo called me back. Could I come down to the sheriff's office? Certainly. In fact, I could hardly wait, since I assumed he'd unearthed something newsworthy in the course of the investigation.

The sun was still peeking in and out from behind dirty white clouds, so I walked, taking a moment to admire the darkening red and gold of the trees that mingled with the evergreens on the hillside. Baldy was clear, looking comfortable above the town, its crest still free of snow.

Milo didn't seem much like the bemused man of the previous evening who'd relied on my sophistication to distinguish a turnip from a crocus bulb. He was sitting very straight in his leather swivel chair, his hazel eyes steely and his square jaw set. I felt like a criminal, which I supposed I was, having concealed the whereabouts of Chris Ramirez.

"Emma," he began, not bothering with small talk, "I have some questions to ask you."

"Go ahead," I responded, sitting down and trying to act unconcerned.

He consulted his notes. "You stated that Chris didn't say where he'd been during the time Simon dropped him off about eight-thirty and when he actually showed up at your house around midnight. Is that correct?"

"It is. I asked, but he didn't tell me." Why, I wondered fleetingly, if truth was such a great ally, did I feel so defenseless?

"Did you know Simon had dropped him off?" The hazel eyes were not only cool, but remote, as if he didn't want to make any personal contact.

"No. That is, I realized later that I'd heard a car pull up and then leave. But it might not have been them." I thought back to the night before last, which now seemed so long ago. "The wind was really blowing. It's a marvel I heard anything at all."

He flipped through some papers and pulled out a single sheet. "Did you leave your house at any time during the evening?"

My eyes widened. "No. I had dinner at the Venison Inn. In fact, I ran into Eeeny Moroni there. He can verify what time I left. It was about seven, I think. Anyway, I came straight home and stayed put. I was beat."

Deliberately, Milo shoved the paper toward me. "This is a lab report on the tire tracks in Neeny Doukas's driveway." He tapped at the page with his ballpoint pen. "One set belongs to your Jaguar."

I debated the merits of candor. But half the town had no doubt seen Chris driving my car Wednesday afternoon. In any event, Mark wasn't killed in Neeny's driveway. Still, Mineshaft Number Three was too close to the Doukas house for comfort.

"It wasn't me," I asserted. Annoyance had surfaced in my voice. Milo Dodge had picked up the check at the Café de Flore the previous night. Now he was grilling me like a felon on the FBI's Ten Most Wanted List. I felt like snatching up his roll of mints and sticking them in his nose. Carla had been right the first time: the sheriff was acting more like *Mildo* than Milo.

Milo seemed unmoved by my deteriorating temper. "I know it wasn't you. I saw the Jag coming from the opposite direction when I went up to meet Mark at Mineshaft Number Three." He fingered his chin while I absorbed that particular piece of information. "Could Chris have borrowed your car?"

There was no point in sheltering Chris over the issue. On the other hand, anybody could have figured out I kept that extra set of keys under the car. But somehow I didn't think they had. The simplest answers are usually the right ones. "He'd borrowed it earlier. I suppose he didn't think he had to ask again."

"But did he?" persisted Dodge.

"I don't know." The baldness of my reply seemed to sink in. "If he did, was it to go see his grandfather?"

Milo Dodge hesitated, then inclined his head. "Yes. He saw Neeny. It wasn't a successful reunion."

I'd hoped for better but expected worse. "Did they have a row?"

Milo was unbending a bit, extracting a mint and popping it in his mouth. He did not, however, go so far as to offer me one. "According to Neeny, it was pretty one-sided. Chris gave him some lip, and then the old man lit into him. The kid left with his tail between his legs."

"According to Neeny," I quoted. Chris might have a different version. "When was that?"

"Around nine." Milo had glanced at his notes again. "Neeny isn't too accurate about time. The world turns on his schedule, not the other way around. It was before Phoebe made his cocoa, which usually transpires around nine-thirty." Milo looked a bit wry. "We haven't pressed Neeny much. He's not feeling too well, you know. He refused to discuss Chris at all at first. I stopped by for a minute yesterday to offer my condolences, and he admitted Chris had been there. Maybe later we can get more details."

"Like when Neeny isn't rich?" I knew Milo Dodge wasn't as likely as some to kowtow to the Doukases, but neither would he go out of his way to raise any hackles.

"Now Emma, the man's grieving," Milo admonished. "He was genuinely fond of Mark."

I ignored the comment. "Have you checked on Phoebe and Neeny?"

Milo couldn't restrain a little snort. "You were right about that, Emma. They were married by a J.P. in Vegas on August eighteen. Did Vida come up with that tidbit?"

I gave him a smug smile. "I can't reveal my sources. How does Neeny's will read?"

"How the hell do I know? That doesn't have anything to do with Mark's murder. Ask Simon."

"I will," I snapped, aware that my short chin was giving an imitation of jutting. "What if Neeny had a prenuptial agreement with Phoebe? What if she could only inherit if Mark and Jennifer and Simon died first? What if he figured out a way to circumvent the state community property laws?"

"Couldn't do it." Milo sat back, hands entwined behind his head. "Come on, Emma, can you see Phoebe Pratt whacking Mark Doukas over the head with a crowbar?"

"No. But I can see Phoebe *Doukas* doing it. As Neeny's wife, she might have more to gain." Indeed, Phoebe wasn't exactly a lightweight. She and Vida were the same age, about the same height, and though Vida probably outweighed Phoebe by a good twenty pounds, both women were solid citizens in more ways than one. I didn't know Phoebe very well, but Vida did, and that was good enough for me.

If Milo's more relaxed pose was designed to disarm me, this time it wasn't going to work. I was ready for him when he asked about Chris. And I was honest. Up to a point.

"You drove all the way into Seattle this morning?" the sheriff queried after I'd given my brief recitation. "Where did he go?"

"California, I guess." In truth, I couldn't swear that Chris had headed for L.A. In his present state of agitation, he might have changed his mind and gone up to British Columbia or back East. He might even have gone home to Hawaii.

Milo mulled over the situation. "It's no wonder he sounded scared. He ought to be. He might not have murdered Mark, but he hasn't been square with us."

"Oh, come on, Milo. He's twenty years old. Are your kids rational human beings yet? What about your daughter who's living with Gumby?"

"What?"

"Never mind. So what if Chris took my car and went to see Neeny? If anything, that gives him an alibi for Mark's murder. It sounds as if he was with his grandfather around the time Mark must have been killed."

Milo looked dour. "He could have done both. Chris was within spitting distance of the mineshaft when he was up at Neeny's."

"So was Neeny, if it comes to that. And Phoebe. No wonder Neeny hadn't been served his cocoa. Phoebe was probably too busy smashing Mark's skull to hear the tea kettle go off." I felt a bit proud of myself. At least I was coming up with theories that weren't any crazier than Milo's.

"You're too damned irreverent," Milo muttered.

I gave a little laugh. "That's part of the job description. I, like you, would have gone crazy a long time ago if I'd taken every godawful thing that came along too seriously." I paused, watching Milo mutely accept my appraisal of the occupational hazards we both faced. "By the way, it wasn't Chris and Mark who had words Wednesday night. It was Mark and Kent."

This time, the sheriff registered genuine surprise. I explained my visit from Jennifer. "Kent lied so he wouldn't invite suspicion. It may have been stupid—or maybe he has something to hide."

"At least he's got a motive," Milo admitted. "With

Mark out of the way, all of the money will eventually come to Jennifer. Which," he noted with a twist of his long mouth, "gives her a reason to get rid of Mark, too."

"True," I conceded, though somehow the image of Jennifer slamming a crowbar over her brother's head seemed more farfetched than most of our other wild ideas. "The only trouble with the money motive is that Neeny is still alive, and Simon is only about fifty. My guess is that Neeny's will is made out so that Simon inherits everything. I suspect that's why he set up those trust funds for Mark and Jennifer."

Milo didn't know about the trust funds. It occurred to me that from his point of view, the sheriff's office dealt only in hard evidence, not supposition or even motives. He did allow that maybe a check into the disposition of the Doukas fortune might be helpful.

Having dropped his interrogator's mask, Milo finally offered me a mint. This time, I accepted. The rigors of the past fifteen minutes had left my mouth dry. I was also hungry, since it was now well after noon. Before I could make my exit, Milo reached under the desk and hauled out a bundle of newspapers. "These belong to you?"

I stared at the papers, some fifty or so, tied with twine. "It's this week's *Advocate*, all right. Where did you get them?"

Milo didn't look too happy. "About twenty feet from Mineshaft Number Three." He waited for my reaction, but I didn't have one, other than puzzlement. "We also found an odd set of footprints—right one deep, the left a bare impression."

So Billy Blatt hadn't told his aunt all.

Now I was forced to respond. "Gibb Frazier?" Obviously, this stack of papers made up the missing overage. The bundle must have fallen off Gibb's truck. "Have you talked to him?"

Milo shook his head. "He's on a moving job for somebody in Snohomish. He won't be back in Alpine until Saturday night."

Vaguely disturbed, I left the sheriff to ponder his growing collection of evidence. Gibb could have driven up to Icicle Creek any time after he'd delivered the rest of the newspapers. But why he'd gone there baffled me. For the moment, I had to put that problem aside. Lunch would have to wait. Next on my schedule was a visit to Neeny Doukas. On my way out of the sheriff's office, I used the pay phone outside to call Vida and confirm the marriage between Phoebe and Neeny.

"Ooooh," she wailed, "doesn't that beat all! He finally made an honest woman out of the old tramp! Neeny's a bigger fool than I thought!"

"I'm going up there now. Shall I take them a wedding present in your name?" I asked, shielding my ear from the rumble of a passing truckload of logs.

"By all means," Vida replied. "The only trouble is, I don't know where you can buy a pair of jackasses on short notice."

Neither did I, so I arrived at the Doukas residence empty-handed. As I stood on the wide veranda with its ancient window boxes and rusty lawn swing, I was aware that I wouldn't be the most welcome of guests. The door was opened by Frieda Wunderlich, squat, square and toadlike. She had thick lips and protruding eyes the color of ripe huckleberries. I always thought of her as covered with warts, but that was only a figment of my imagination.

"His Royal Highness is resting," she announced with her usual lack of respect. "The Queen Bee went to Monroe."

Now I wished I had brought something with me—a bouquet, a casserole, even a sympathy card. "I just wanted to let him know I was very sorry about his loss," I said, getting a whiff of basil and oregano from the kitchen. "I spoke with him about Mark only a few hours before the tragedy."

The words were my ticket over the threshold. Frieda stepped aside with a mock bow. "He's in the living room, watching television. Make him turn down the sound."

I'd been in the elder Doukas's house on two or three previous occasions. The furnishings were massive and dark, remnants of the Victorian era. Heavy brown draperies shut out the autumn light, and the air was thick with the scent of hothouse flowers and those spices from a sunnier climate. The rooms were cluttered with too much furniture, too many paintings, classical sculptures, potted plants, and now, floral arrangements of sympathy.

Neeny Doukas sat in a big armchair that would have swallowed a smaller man. He was rugged of build, hairy of chest, with dark eyes and an olive complexion. His hair, which had once been black and wavy, was now streaked with white and receding from a forehead that was accented by slanting black eyebrows that matched a bristling mustache and full beard. Ensconced in the big gray mohair chair complete with antimacassars and with an afghan over his knees, Neeny Doukas looked for all the world like the King of Thrace.

"Emma." His voice boomed out as he beckoned to me with one crooked finger. "You got that story?"

"What story?" I said stupidly.

"The one correcting your screw-up. You said you'd show it to me." He waved in the direction of an occasional chair covered in faded red and black cut velvet.

Up close, Neeny looked haggard, older than when I'd seen him a week or two earlier. The flesh on his cheekbones sagged, the big hands trembled ever so slightly, the black eyes were a trifle cloudy. I sat. Next to Neeny was a tray with a half-eaten meal grown cold. A soap opera blared on TV.

"I haven't done it yet," I admitted, raising my voice in the hope that he'd take the hint and shut off the set. "I wasn't sure you'd want me to run it now that Mark's . . . dead."

Neeny reared back in the armchair, the afghan twitching on his knees. "Hell's bells, I sure do! All the more reason." Those extraordinary eyebrows drew together like a pair of black caterpillars. "You see what happened? Some greedy swine thought Mark had made a big strike and killed him over it! Pah!" He all but spat in the rest of his lunch.

The TV perils of a beautiful blonde and her handsome dark-haired lover were giving me a headache. I tried a different approach, this time lowering my voice so that Neeny couldn't possibly hear me without a Miracle Ear. "You don't really think that," I murmured.

Neeny took the hint, using the remote control to turn the sound off but left the picture on. "What?" He didn't wait for my response. "Hell, Emma, who else would wanna kill my grandson? Unless it was that no-good kid of Margaret's."

"Neeny, do you really think Chris Ramirez is a no-account?"

He snorted in disgust. "He's Hector's son, isn't he? Hector ran out on my daughter and the kid. Blood tells, Emma."

"Chris has your blood as well as Hector's," I pointed out. "Besides, half the town seems to think you bribed Hector to go away."

Neeny Doukas all but leaped out of the chair. The afghan fell to the floor. "That's a goddamned lie! Who told you that, old big-mouthed Vida? I wouldn't have given Hector Ramirez a plugged nickel!"

His vehemence exploded Vida's myth. Still, it had been a logical explanation. In general, people do not just disappear. Or if they do, there's usually a reason. In the matter of Hector Ramirez, I hadn't yet heard anything to convince me that he had cause to drop off the face of the earth.

"I'd hoped," I said, still keeping calm, "that you and Chris might have hit it off."

"Hell!" Neeny kicked at the afghan with his foot. I wondered if Hazel had made it for him. Phoebe didn't strike me as the domestic type. "He came in here the other night all full of bullcrap about the rough time I gave Margaret. Damn! Margaret made her own bed. She wanted to wallow in it with Hector. See where it got her. Right outta the family, that's where! She could have married ten other guys—lawyers, doctors, even a forestry professor from the university. They all were hot for Margaret. But oh, no, she had to run off with that greasy Mexican! It's a wonder she didn't go over to Hawaii and wind up with some Chinaman! Or a Jap!"

It was all I could do to keep from declaring my hope that Margaret had slept with every Oriental in the fiftieth state and had had the time of her life. But I'd been around prejudiced people enough to know that there was no changing them, especially when they were part of the older generation.

"Did Chris stay long?" I inquired innocently.

"Too long." Neeny bent down to retrieve the afghan. He looked up, the black eyes sharper now. "I don't wanna talk about it. You feeling around for an alibi for the kid?" His mouth twisted in the thick beard. "It won't work, Emma. He was here about twenty minutes. He could have killed Mark before he came or right after. The damned mineshaft is right over there." Neeny jerked his thumb toward one of the windows. "Imagine! My poor grandson died within shouting distance, and I didn't even know it! Do you wonder I won't discuss this Chris when he's alive and Mark's dead?" Neeny shook his head, and I actually felt sorry for him.

I said as much. Wordlessly, Neeny accepted my condolences. He didn't look ill, so much as devastated. I asked how he felt.

"How would you expect? I'm getting to be an old man. What's to look forward to at my age?"

I shrugged. "Lots of things. You could travel more. Didn't you enjoy your trip to Vegas with Phoebe?"

The black eyes narrowed, but before Neeny could respond, Phoebe Pratt Doukas glided into the room. As always, she was dressed expensively, if tastelessly. Today she sported bright green slacks and a matching blazer with enough gold chains to enhance a harem.

"Emma," she said, her usually languorous voice tense.

"How kind of you to call." She moved across the room, full hips swaying, her upswept hair plastered to her head. Phoebe was what you might call handsome, if artificial. Her attention was fixed on Neeny. "Doukums, did you eat?"

Neeny waved at the tray. "Swill. That Kraut can't cook Greek food. Fix me some soup. Chicken noodle."

Phoebe planted a kiss on the top of Neeny's head. "Of course, Doukums. Lots of crackers, too." She swayed away, leaving a scent of jasmine in the air and a sense of unease in the room.

"Hey," he shouted, "get me some cocoa, too, Big Bottom. Lots of sugar."

Phoebe's return from Monroe had thwarted my question about the trip to Las Vegas. In any event, I knew the answer. I decided it was time to leave Doukums and Big Bottom to their own devices.

It was Phoebe, however, who showed me to the door. She had put on a frilly apron that said RED HOT MOMMA and rattled her chains as she came down the hall from the kitchen. "I've a mind to take Doukums to Palm Springs for the winter," she announced with less than her usual aplomb. "The change would do him *soooo* much good."

"Phoebe, what did you think of Chris?"

Phoebe's gray eyes with their layered blue lids widened. She fiddled with her chains and avoided my gaze. "Chris? I didn't see him. I was upstairs watching TV." An uncertain hand smoothed the lacquered hair as she lowered both her head and her voice. "He sounds like a saucy boy, I'm afraid."

I couldn't help but make a face. "Don't believe everything you hear. Especially in this town."

Phoebe had the grace to look a trifle sheepish. "Well, I did hear he was quite handsome. My niece, Chaz, met him at the Burger Barn. Of course, he can't be as good-looking as Mark was." There was a slight catch in her voice as she shook her elaborately coiffed head. "I'd like to meet Chris, though. It's a shame he and Doukums didn't get on." She let out a nervous trill. "After all, Chris *is* family. I think it's *soooo* important to keep everybody close."

"Yes," I conceded, trying to envision a rollicking clan of Doukases, "but it helps if they don't hate one another." I gave her a bright smile and went out the door.

My Jag was wedged between Neeny's twenty-five-year old black Bentley and Phoebe's Lincoln Town Car. She had pulled in too close behind me, and I cursed her thoughtlessness. But as I was trying to figure out how to maneuver the Jag out into the open, I noticed that the red exterior of Phoebe's new car was dappled with blue spots. Curious, I thought, but I wasn't sure why the blemishes tugged at my brain. The real question I had for Phoebe was why she had written to Chris in Hawaii, but I wasn't going to broach the subject until I had the letter in hand. There were already too many unanswered questions about Alpine's extended First Family.

Chapter Ten

LUNCH WAS FISH and chips picked up at the Burger Barn and eaten at my desk. Vida, who was also running late, joined me with a hard-boiled egg, cottage cheese, carrot and celery sticks, and a water pistol.

"Roger shot me this morning," she said, speaking of her eldest grandson and looking annoyed. "He's supposed to be home sick with the flu, but he's running around like a savage. Amy and Ted don't know how to handle him."

A staunch fan of Louisa May Alcott, Vida had named her three daughters Amy, Meg, and Beth. Jo had never materialized. Amy was the only one of the trio to remain in Alpine, the other two having moved to Seattle and Bellingham. Roger, who was almost ten, seemed to devote his life to plaguing his grandmother. Naturally, Vida doted on him.

"Gibb's got some explaining to do," declared Vida, taking aim with the water pistol at the portrait of Marius Vandeventer that hung over my bookcase. "Maybe he went up to Icicle Creek to make sure there wasn't any gold after all. He never did trust Mark."

"That part of town sure was popular Wednesday. Between the mineshaft and Neeny's house, half of Alpine seems to have passed by."

"It's a small town, after all," Vida remarked while snapping off carrot sticks in rapid succession. "Everybody has to be somewhere."

I dipped a piece of too-dry cod into a small container of tartar sauce. "At any rate, Neeny says Mark didn't stop by

119

Wednesday night. And Phoebe didn't see Chris. She was watching TV."

Vida dug into her cottage cheese. "Maybe she was trying to figure out how to break the news of the elopement to Simon and Cecelia."

"I wouldn't think Neeny would care what his family thought," I said as the phone rang. It was Richie Magruder, acting mayor in Fuzzy Baugh's absence. He wanted to know if Carla could take a picture of the raccoon family that was setting up housekeeping at the base of Carl Clemans's statue in Old Mill Park. I told Richie I'd ask Carla when she got back from interviewing Darla Puckett about her two weeks in Samoa.

"Even Neeny would care about repercussions if he's changed his will," Vida said, not missing a beat. "Simon would raise more of a ruckus than a bear with a crosscut saw." She reached over to the bookcase and pulled out my Seattle phone directory. "I just thought of something."

"What?" The french fries were better than the fish. I washed them down with a swig of Pepsi.

"Why would Phoebe go all the way to Seattle to see an eye doctor? She only wears reading glasses." Vida glanced up from the Yellow Pages to wave a celery stick at me. "What if she went to see someone else?"

"Like?"

"Like a lawyer. Here." She tapped at the page. "Old Doc Dewey's daughter, Sybil, married an attorney who is in a big firm in One Union Square. Douglas Diffenbach. He specializes in estate planning. I think I'll give Sybil a call." Vida was wearing her smug expression.

"That's a long shot."

"Of course," agreed Vida, writing down the number and replacing the directory. "But Phoebe couldn't use Simon's firm. She wouldn't want him to know what she was up to. And Sybil's husband is the only attorney I know of in Seattle. I mean, personally. Phoebe wouldn't go to a stranger."

Of course she wouldn't, I thought. Small-town mentality

wouldn't permit such a digression. Vida might be right. "But what about client confidentiality?" I countered.

Vida shrugged. "It's no breach for Doug to say he's seen Phoebe. And he would say so. It isn't every day that someone from his wife's old hometown comes waltzing into One Union Square." She grabbed the phone and started dialing. As it turned out, she had called the law office, not the Diffenbach residence. Undeterred, Vida asked for Doug. I sat back, watching her operate. Vida was a lesson in subterfuge.

"Doug? yes, this is Vida Runkel in Alpine.... No, not since little Ian was christened ... Four already? Oh, my! Again in January? How lovely! Phoebe didn't mention it.... Yes, she was too excited about being a bride, I suppose.... Oh, I know, but life's like that, marry and bury, laughter and tears.... No, but Milo Dodge is doing his best.... Phoebe was so impressed with your work.... True, she's easily impressed by a lot of things.... My daughter, Beth ... Oh, that's all she'd want, too, but these things are necessary when you have children.... Yes, I'll have her call.... Thanks so much, Doug ... My best to Sybil. 'Bye."

Vida took a deep breath. "Phoebe had her own will drawn up." She gave me a hawklike stare. "Who do you suppose she's left everything to?"

I knew Phoebe was childless; I also figured that even if Vida had drawn the bare facts out of Doug Diffenbach, she couldn't possibly have extracted the details. "I don't know. Who?"

Vida sat back, munching on her hard-boiled egg. "Really, Emma, I'm not an oracle. I just wish I knew."

So did I.

At three o'clock, I swung by Alpine High School and caught Kevin MacDuff climbing on his bicycle. He took one look at my car and turned away. I honked.

"You must be awful mad at me," he said as I got out of the car and hurried up to meet him. "Kent sure is."

"It's not your fault," I said with a smile. "All I want to know is what you actually told Carla."

Kevin hung his head. At fifteen, he was far more slender than his eldest brother, and his skin was comparatively pale except for a spot of color on each cheek. His hair was strawberry blond, very short, with a wispy pigtail in back. "I called Carla about the paper route and we got to talking, and I said I'd seen Mark and he acted like he'd found gold." Kevin's head bobbed up, his fingers clutching the handlebars of his mountain bike.

I nodded. "Mark *acted* like he found gold, right?"

Kevin nodded back. "Right."

"Exactly how did Mark act? Were you at the mineshaft?" I queried as an old beater without a muffler roared past.

Kevin screwed up his face. "Well, he was kind of excited. Out of breath, you know. I was going to see Eric Puckett up the road and Mark came down from the mineshaft just as I was going by. He said . . ." Kevin paused, clearly trying to recall Mark's precise words. "Mark said he'd made a big discovery. I asked him what, but he just shook his head and got into his Jeep, so I rode off to Eric's."

Briefly, I considered Kevin's account. "But he didn't *say* he'd found gold."

"No."

"So Carla misinterpreted your remark." And, I thought, but didn't say so, that Kevin had misinterpreted Mark's reaction.

The entire student body seemed to be whizzing by us afoot, in cars, on bikes. The single-story high school, which had replaced the two-story red-brick building that had become the newly refurbished public library and senior citizen center, sprawled over a full city block, its playfield reaching to the edge of the forest.

Kevin screwed up his face. "Misinterpreted?"

"She took what you said literally," I said, still smiling.

"I guess." Kevin sighed.

I suspected he'd been taking considerable abuse from Kent. "Don't worry about it. I seriously doubt if that bit about the gold had anything to do with Mark's death."

Kevin didn't look convinced. "Kent was really pissed off. I guess so were all the Doukases."

"I don't know about that." I patted his arm. "Just be careful what you tell Carla next time, okay? She tends to go overboard."

"Yeah. Sure." He gave me a half smile. "I'd better go home and feed my snake."

"Kevin, what do you think Mark did find up at the mine?"

Balancing himself in mid-stride, Kevin turned to look back at me. "I don't know. Whatever it was, it must have been a big deal. He acted . . . weird." He gave a shake of his head.

"Scared?" I suggested.

"Maybe." His fingers clenched and unclenched the handlebars. "Yeah, maybe that was it. Scared." He gave me a curious look and pedaled off down the street.

I stared after Kevin. Mark Doukas didn't strike me as an easy person to scare. For a long moment, I stood next to the Jag, lost in thought. Maybe Fuzzy Baugh was right: the sheriff should open the mineshaft. I'd ask Milo what he thought, though I already knew he felt it would invite danger.

But Milo was out when I stopped by his office. Bill Blatt said he was paying a call on Neeny Doukas. That news buoyed me a bit. I hoped that Milo wasn't going to let the Doukases lead him around by the nose.

The sun was still out and the air felt crisp when I got back to *The Advocate*. Ginny was mailing out bills; Ed was at the Grocery Basket; Vida had gone to the drugstore; and Carla was taking a picture of the raccoons.

"Only four phone calls," Ginny said, handing me the slips of paper and showing off perfect white teeth in one of her rare smiles. "Some man is waiting to see you. He got here about ten minutes ago."

"Not Chris Ramirez?" I asked on a sharp intake of breath.

Ginny shook her head. "I never saw Chris, but it's not him. This guy's older."

I relaxed. Swinging my handbag over my shoulder, I strode through the editorial office and into my inner sanctum. The door was already open, and there was somebody sitting behind my desk.

It was Tom Cavanaugh.

Over the clutter of my desk and a chasm of twenty years, we shook hands. On the surface, we acted like civilized people who were mildly pleased to see each other. Tom was prepared for the encounter, but I was flabbergasted. A bit too quickly, I sat down, not in my own chair, where Tom was seated as if he owned the blasted place, but one of the pair reserved for visitors.

"Well, Tom," I remember saying in a voice about an octave too high, "how are you?" After that, I don't recall much except pleasantries. I suppose we spoke in clichés, acknowledgment of the years that had passed, the physical changes we had undergone, the quirks of fate that had brought us together in that tiny office in a small town on the slope of the Cascade Mountains.

Somewhere between noting the gray in Tom's black hair and his observation that I no longer looked as if I were starving to death, my brain began to take charge of my emotions. I nailed Tom down for the reason he had come to Alpine. Dave Grogan had contacted him, he said in that easy, mellow voice that also could have made a living in radio and television.

"Dave told me you were paddling a leaky canoe. Either you bail out or patch up the holes." He pointed to a bound volume that contained the first six months of my tenure. "I've been studying these. You'd have to be publishing out of a mud hut in the Third World not to make money with a weekly or a small daily these days."

My eyes narrowed. It was bad enough that he'd invaded

my life unannounced, stolen my chair, and forced me into a subservient role. But now he was lecturing me on how to run my freaking paper. I was getting angry, but the sight of him diluted my temper: Tom Cavanaugh was still handsome, whatever softness hammered out by life, leaving him sharp of feature and even sharper of eye. He was a tall man and had apparently kept fit. Tom looked so much like Adam that I wanted to cry.

"Except for Christmas and Easter and your loggers' festival, I don't think you've run a single promotion," Tom was saying. "You could do one a month—back-to-school, Halloween, Thanksgiving, you name it. Inserts are what make money, Emma. Chain stores, independents, co-op advertising. Who's your ad manager, Dopey the Dwarf?"

"Yes."

Tom lowered his head, looking at me in that dubious manner I recalled from twenty years ago. "That's what I figured. Dump him. Or her."

"Can't."

He started to look stern, then broke into that wonderful, charming, delicious grin. "Of course you can't. Old softhearted Emma. But you *could* hire someone to supervise him, a business manager, let's say, and . . ." He saw me start to argue and held up a hand. "In the long run, it would pay off. Unless you've had a personality transplant, you make a lousy boss, Emma. You couldn't even get the gofers at *The Times* to remember to put sugar in your coffee."

I shook my head emphatically. "Hold it. Listen, Tom, this is wonderful of you to offer advice. Really." I tempered my growing irritation with a thin smile. "But I'm in the middle of covering a murder investigation. It's big stuff, involving a very prominent old line family. I can't get sidetracked. Frankly, Tom, as usual, your timing stinks."

His eyes, which were so blue they were almost black, took on a hint of surprise, even hurt. "Dave Grogan painted a desperate plight. Leaky canoe, headed for the falls." His own smile was now a trifle limp, too.

I sighed. "Dave's right. But he probably didn't know about the murder." It crossed my mind that even as I had talked with Dave on the phone, Mark Doukas might have been meeting his killer. "Look," I went on, trying to sound more kindly, "come for dinner tonight. I'll have Ed Bronsky, the ad manager, and his wife, and Vida Runkel and Carla Steinmetz join us." If necessary, I'd ask the city council and the U.S. Forest Service, too. There was no way I'd share an evening alone with Tom Cavanaugh.

I'd risen, tired of Tom's advantage in my chair. Now he stood, too, and for one sharp, painful moment, it struck me that he looked as if he belonged behind that desk. But he didn't. I did.

He was still looking down at the back issues of *The Advocate*. His attire was casual, a navy blue sweater over a light blue shirt with gray slacks. He didn't look rich, just comfortable. Then, as I knew he would do eventually, he gestured at the framed photograph on the filing cabinet. "Adam?"

"Yes."

He stared at the picture. I suspected Tom had looked very much like that when he was in college at Northwestern. "Good-looking kid," he remarked. "Smart?"

"Fairly. Not motivated, though."

"Right. Nice?"

"Oh, yes."

"No big problems?"

In the context of today's teenagers, I knew what Tom meant. "No. Thank God."

"Not exactly," he said dryly. "Thanks to you, Emma. You've done well."

The dark blue eyes held mine just a moment too long. "So have you," I said lightly.

But Tom shook his head. "No, not really. Sandra did well. She was born into money. I just use it."

"How is Sandra?" I was trying to keep the light note in my voice, but it wasn't working very well.

"Bats." He shrugged.

"Define *bats*."

His expression was guarded. "She's unstable. Delusions. Paranoid. She also shoplifts. Fortunately, we can afford topnotch keepers."

"Is she at home?"

"Sometimes." He fingered a sheaf of papers in my in-basket. "If she undergoes a violent episode, her doctors and care givers recommend that I have her . . ." He stopped, apparently aware that he was reciting like a parrot. With a sheepish grin, he reverted to the irreverent candor I remembered so fondly: "I cart her off to the loony bin."

"Sounds like the place for her," I retorted, equally flippant. Now I understood the comment I'd heard about *poor Tom* at the Sigma Delta Chi banquet. "All the same, I'm terribly sorry."

He had sobered and shrugged again. "That's one reason I travel a lot. If I didn't get away, I'd go nuts, too. It's my version of a paper route."

"Only you buy them instead of deliver them," I noted. Fleetingly, I thought of Sandra Cavanaugh. I'd only met her twice, once at an office holiday party, and another time in a restaurant where she was lunching with other suitably well-heeled young matrons. She was a pale, pretty ash blonde, fine of feature, slim, and inclined to keep one eye on her handbag and the other on her conversational vis-à-vis. It not only made her look a little walleyed, but caused me to wonder if she thought the rest of the world was after her Big Bucks. Or maybe, it occurred to me now, after *her*.

Tom had come around to the other side of the desk, a scant two feet away. "Are you serious about dinner?"

I reflected. "Sure. Seven-thirty?" For safety's sake, could I possibly assemble another fifty people by then? I berated myself. What was I afraid of? Twenty years over the dam, and what was there still between us? Only Adam.

"Look," I said, lowering my voice as I heard Vida talking to Ginny in the outer office, "I may be able to use some advice, but I'm not a damsel in distress. Believe it or not, I've already come up with some ideas of my own for increasing revenue."

Tom's expression didn't change. "I'm sure you have. Like what? A Color-the-Pumpkin Contest?"

I, too, kept my face impassive. "Not quite. It's more like an Ask-the-Jackass-to-Dinner Party."

"Sounds like fun."

"We'll see."

"Who's the jackass?" asked Vida after Tom had left.

I explained, briefly. Since I'd never told Vida who had fathered my son, I felt there was no need to go into anything but the barest professional details. I invited her to dinner.

"With Ed and that fat, sad-sack wife of his?" Vida looked appalled. "And Carla? Don't feed that girl Jell-O. She'll giggle and jiggle all night! Ask Ginny instead."

I was looking at the pictures of the raccoons. Carl Clemans's bronze statue appeared to be feeding them. "Is that a yes or a no?"

Vida rubbed her eyes. "Ooooh—I'll come," she said grudgingly. "So will Ed and Shirley. That woman is so lazy she wouldn't get off a keg of dynamite if somebody lit the fuse."

As it turned out, everybody came, including Carla and Ginny. I left the office just before five, racing to the Grocery Basket before the commuters arrived. Luckily, sockeye salmon was in, if not exactly a bargain at $10.99 a pound. Local corn was still available, a new crop of Idaho bakers had arrived, and the bakery that supplied Café de Flore had made its semiweekly delivery to the store that morning. Dessert would be my lifesaving, timesaving, but not necessarily money-saving cherry cream cheesecake. Dodging Durwood Parker, who was driving down the wrong side of Front Street, I stopped at the liquor store before heading home.

It was when I was unloading the groceries that I saw the Ramada Inn laundry bag on the floor of the backseat. Mark's jacket, I thought with a pang. I should have given it to Milo Dodge. But I hadn't. Should I call and tell him where it was?

A glance at my watch told me it was almost six. My guests were due in an hour and a half. There wasn't time to spare. Or so I rationalized, as I tucked the motel bag into one of the grocery sacks.

I didn't want to admit that I could be afraid of what the sheriff might find on the jacket that Chris Ramirez had borrowed from Mark Doukas.

Chapter Eleven

VIDA CAME EARLY. "You need help," she announced, and without further ado, she put on an apron that displayed two pigs hunched over a trough. "My daughter, Meg, gave me this. It reminded me of Ed and Shirley. Where's your biggest kettle?"

I showed her. She shucked corn, and I greased potatoes.

"I went to see Fuzzy after work," Vida said. "That must be his real hair. It looked like it had died instead of him."

"How was he?" I asked, using a cooking fork to poke holes in the potatoes.

"Critical, my foot! He should be out of there tomorrow. Or Sunday, anyway." She filled the big cast-iron kettle with water from the tap. "At least I found out why he had the heart attack. *Spasm*, I should say. Or so young Doc Dewey told me. No wonder, Neeny is enough to give anybody a stroke. Or a spasm."

I closed the oven and eyed Vida curiously. She was dumping salt with one hand and sugar with the other into the kettle. I refrained from asking her why. Vida had been cooking a lot longer than I had, though, I knew from experience, not necessarily better. "What did Neeny do now?"

Vida looked at me over the rim of her glasses. "Fuzzy went up to see Neeny last night. He asked Neeny about opening up Mineshaft Number Three to see if it was filled with opium." She made a face. "Imagine! Fuzzy's such a dolt! Anyway, he had to ask Neeny because the mineshaft is on that old fool's property. And Neeny had a fit—not a spasm—and threatened to have Fuzzy impeached if he did such a thing. So Fuzzy got all upset, and his ticker went kaflooey." She wiggled her eyebrows at me. "Well, what do you think?"

I wasn't sure. Obviously, Vida's suspicions didn't bode well for Neeny. "Neeny has hidden something in that mineshaft?" I asked. "How about Hazel?"

Vida sniffed. "I saw Hazel Doukas on view at Driggers Funeral Home in 1986. She looked almost pretty, considering that in real life, she reminded me of the back end of a Buick. No, it's one of two things: there really is gold in that mineshaft, or else Neeny is just being a stubborn old goat. I vote for Number Two."

I wasn't inclined to disagree. Hastily, I shoved the potatoes into the oven. "I forgot to check the mail," I said, running out of the kitchen, through the front room, and straight to the barn-red postal box that stood next to the road. Three bills, four circulars, and a cheese catalogue made up the sum of my correspondence. Nothing from Adam. I cursed him, imagining several scenarios, the most likely of which was that he hadn't gone to the post office until it was too late to make the overnight delivery. Maybe tomorrow I'd get the letter Phoebe had written to Chris. I said as much to Vida when I got back to the kitchen.

"You already know what it says," she pointed out. "What else? Invisible ink that will show up when you put the stationery over steam?"

Vida was right. It was the fact that the letter existed in the first place that bothered me. "Why?" I asked, as much of myself as of Vida. "Phoebe is not necessarily the tart with the heart of gold."

"Correct," said Vida crisply. With one sure, lethal motion, she slit the larger of the two salmon from head to tail. "Phoebe had a reason for writing to Chris. Especially since she sent that letter right after she eloped with Neeny." She pointed the knife at me. I was glad I didn't consider Vida a serious suspect. Otherwise, I might have been scared stiff. "Why indeed?" she demanded. "I don't see Phoebe as the kindly new wife, trying to make peace between the warring family factions."

"Me neither." I sighed in frustration and inadvertently managed to stop our speculations by turning on the hand mixer to whip up my cream cheesecake.

For the next three hours we put the murder of Mark Doukas aside. Tom arrived with a bottle of white wine from the Napa Valley; Ginny trotted out a bouquet from her parents' yard; Ed and Shirley brought their prodigious appetites; and Carla dragged in a dead squirrel she'd found next to the street.

"We ought to bury him in the yard," she said.

I hastily agreed, pointing her and Ginny toward my gardening shed out back. "Wash your hands after you're finished," I urged, turning on the porch light.

It was already dark, though the evening had turned mild. Maybe autumn had suffered a setback.

I served drinks, dispensing with appetizers, which I'd forgotten about, and, naturally, the talk immediately turned to newspapers. Carla and Ginny came back to the house with a couple of handfuls of trash they threw into the kitchen wastebasket. Ginny was violently antilitter, and I was mildly embarrassed that she had found any in my yard. I resolved to spend part of the weekend getting the garden ready for winter.

The evening was a pleasant interlude. In retrospect, it was an island of peace in a tempestuous week. Tom was the center of attention, always a master of anecdote, and delivered several witty stories about his career in journalism, both as editor and publisher. I began to feel like a rank amateur. It was partly Tom's fault, for making me feel like a semifailure. But I was damned if I'd let him rescue me. Not after twenty years, all of which I'd spent nurturing his son. To hell with him, I thought, after my third glass of pinot noir.

The topic of Mark Doukas's murder came up only at the door. It was Carla who mentioned it, asking who intended to go to the funeral. Vida had volunteered; so did Ed, whose gloomy manner would fit right in at anybody's wake.

Since I had already decided that only one staff member should attend, I was just as pleased when Shirley Bronsky demurred: "I've so much to do, and I hardly knew Mark," she said in the squeaky voice that always sounded at odds with her bulk. "Cece Doukas is a nice woman, but Simon is too stuck on himself. Of course if Cece had raised five kids instead of just two, and if she didn't have help with that big house, and if I could afford to wear nice clothes like she does . . . well, we'll just send a memorial to our favorite charity."

"It ought to be Weight Watchers," Vida muttered after the other guests had left. "But I'll bet it's the Bronsky family vacation fund."

I was too tired to quibble. And relieved. Vida had offered to stay on and help me clean up, which eliminated any prospect of being left alone with Tom. "Thanks, Vida," I said, emptying the first load of dishes while she scraped the dessert plates. "You're a good egg."

"Hard-boiled, some would say." She gave me an ironic glance. "Or gone bad." She shrugged. "We've got to ask the sheriff to open that mineshaft."

"Vida, you're the one who told me not to play detective."

"It's not the same thing. The mineshaft has become part of the story. It put our mayor in the hospital."

I didn't try to unravel her peculiar brand of logic. "Would Milo Dodge force the issue with Neeny?"

"He's the only one who can," Vida noted, rinsing silverware. "Unless Eeeny Moroni could talk Neeny into it." Before I could suggest that I talk to Milo and she should take on Eeeny, Vida eyed me over the butcher block counter in the middle of the kitchen. "He *seems* nice. Where's the wife?"

I feigned ignorance. "Whose? Milo's?"

Vida snorted and flapped the dishrag at me. "Don't act like an adolescent idiot, Emma. Tom Cavanaugh looks enough like Adam to be his father." She gave me her gimlet eye, then, to my surprise, turned away so abruptly that she almost knocked an empty wine bottle off the butcher block. "Never mind. It's none of my business."

I decided to leave it that way. For the moment. But something she had just said bothered me, and it had nothing to do with Tom Cavanaugh. Unfortunately, I was too tired to figure out exactly what it was. Maybe it was just as well, since a little knowledge can be a very dangerous thing.

Tom Cavanaugh was staying up at the ski lodge, which was still offering off-season rates. Not that the economy rate would matter much to Tom, but the lodge was a lot more plush than Alpine's two motels, neither of which rated more than two stars in the AAA travel guide. The old Alpine Hotel on Front Street wasn't recommended by anybody, except the retirees and occasional transients who lived there. But the lodge had four stars pending, due to the current remodeling. Rumors that a restaurant was to be added on to the mediocre coffee shop were yet to be confirmed.

I had thought about driving up to the lodge on Saturday to talk to Heather Bardeen but decided against it. With Tom in residence, it might look like a ploy to see him again. As it turned out, I didn't need to call on Heather. Vida was mining her extensive sources like a squirrel gathering nuts for winter.

"I talked to my niece, Marje Blatt, this morning," said Vida shortly before ten A.M. "She works for Doc Dewey, you know. Old Doc." She stopped and muttered something I couldn't hear. A noise that was a cross between a squeak and a squawk carried over the line. "That's Cupcake. She won't take her bath."

"I thought it was Shirley Bronsky." I tried to envision Vida's canary in a tiny tub full of bubbles. The idea struck me as funny. Then I thought of Shirley in a much larger tub, with many more bubbles. That was not so cute. "What did Marje say?"

Vida emitted a little gasp of incredulity. "I can't repeat it over the phone, Emma." There was reproof in her voice. "You don't know who's listening."

Since Alpine had been converted to a sophisticated automated electronic switching system the previous year, I doubted if anybody west of Denver could have overheard us. But I didn't say so to Vida. Instead, I invited her over for coffee.

"Fifteen minutes," she said. "I've got to fluff up Cupcake."

I made sure I had enough coffee for both of us before using the spare minutes to confirm the bridge date at Darlene Adcock's that night. Then I emptied the kitchen wastebasket into the fireplace where I burn most of my nonrecyclable junk. On the way into the living room, I stumbled over the vacuum cleaner cord. Several items in the wastebasket were jostled onto the carpet. With a mild curse, I retrieved them. A blurred scrap of paper caught my eye.

It was a note, addressed to Chris. Apparently, Ginny Burmeister had picked it up in the yard, along with a gum wrapper, a UPS delivery notice from the next door neighbor's, and a pop can some kid had tossed over the fence. Ginny must not have looked at the refuse or she would have commented on the note addressed to Chris.

Unfortunately, most of the words had been smeared by rain. All I could make out was "Urgent . . . —me r—— away . . . off CR 187 . . . -eeny."

I was still trying to decipher the note when Vida banged on the door. She flew into the living room, her velvet beret cocked over one eye. "What's that?" she asked, jabbing at the piece of paper. "You look like somebody sent you a death threat."

I showed her the note. "Ginny must have picked this up when she and Carla were burying that squirrel. I'll bet it

had been left on the porch or stuck to the front door. It
must have blown off in that storm Wednesday night."

Frowning, Vida shoved the beret so far back on her
head that I marveled it could stay put. "That must be:
come right away. Is it signed Neeny or Eeeny?"

I considered. "Neeny's house is on County Road 187,"
I said. "But would he send Chris a note? Especially one
that said *urgent*?"

"Not likely." Vida paced the room in her flatfooted
manner. "But Eeeny Moroni wouldn't send Chris a note
either. At least I can't think why." She stopped in front of
the sofa, and we locked gazes. "That note is printed. Anybody could have sent it and signed Neeny's name. Everyone knows he'd never call himself *Gramps* or *Pop-pop
Doukie*."

Vida's reasoning made sense. "I wonder if Chris saw
the note," I said, taking it from the end table and putting
it under a dictionary to flatten out the wrinkles. "He might
have and then just dropped it." When Vida didn't say anything, I went right on conjecturing: "That would explain
why he didn't come in. Simon dropped Chris off, Chris
got the note, took my car, and drove up to Neeny's."

"Or," put in Vida, shrugging off her tweed coat, "he
didn't see the note but headed straight out to visit Neeny
anyway, because that was his plan all along." She scowled
at me; I scowled back. "Yes, yes," she said testily, "*or*
Chris went to the mineshaft and socked Mark over the
head."

"You don't really believe Chris killed Mark, do you,
Vida?"

Almost angrily, Vida hurled her coat onto the back of
the sofa. "No, I don't, though I've only your word for his
lack of homicidal intentions." She stared at me over the
rims of her tortoise-shell glasses. "By faith alone, as Pastor Purebeck says in his oh-so-tedious Sunday sermons.
Really, that man means well, and I suppose it's unchristian
to say, but . . ."

I allowed Vida her customary diatribe about the First—

and only—Presbyterian Church's pastor. Meanwhile, I
tried to figure out who had tiptoed onto my porch after I
got home Wednesday night and left the note for Chris. Actually, tiptoes wouldn't have been required, not with the
storm that had been raging at the time. But whoever it was
probably hadn't bothered to knock. My car was parked
outside, and the lights were on. The person who had sum-
moned Chris to an unspecified spot on County Road 187
had not wanted to see me. Or more to the point, had not
wanted to be seen by me.

". . . Wearing spats and nothing else!" Vida stopped to
take a deep breath. "What do you think Pastor Purebeck
did then?"

I didn't have the foggiest idea what she was talking
about. "Um—offered to resign?"

Vida looked shocked. "Of course not! He came straight
down out of the pulpit, took Crazy Eights Neffel by the
arm, and led him outside. It was a genuine act of Christian
charity."

"Oh." I was as accustomed to wild stories about Crazy
Eights Neffel, Alpine's resident loony, as I was to ha-
rangues about Pastor Purebeck. Luckily, the phone rang,
sparing me further embarrassment at my lack of attention.
It was Tom Cavanaugh. I automatically turned my back on
Vida.

"I was thinking that if you had some free time this afternoon, I could help you plot ad strategy," Tom said.

I was aware of Vida's eyes boring between my shoulder
blades. Frantically, I sought an excuse. "I can't. I'm going
to start writing up the murder story."

"What about tonight?" Tom was both a patient and a
persistent man.

"I'm playing bridge."

I thought I heard him suppress a chuckle. No doubt he
found it amusing that the one-time great love of his life
was spending a Saturday night gobbling gumdrops and de-
bating whether to bid one spade or two clubs. "And tomorrow?"

"I go to ten o'clock mass at St. Mildred's," I said, wildly casting about for whatever I could possibly be doing on a Sunday afternoon. "Then I really ought to work in the yard."

Persistence won out over patience. "I'll see you in church. We'll drive some place for brunch." He hung up the phone.

Turning around, I waited for Vida's comment. But none was forthcoming. In fact, she was stalking off to the kitchen, presumably to fetch us coffee. I followed her, like a kitten trailing a mother cat.

"Marje informs me that Heather Bardeen is not p.g.," said Vida, handing me a coffee-filled mug, sugar in place. I felt like calling Tom back and telling him I'd trained my staff better than those dimwitted gofers at *The Times*. "She had some sort of nasty infection and thought Mark had probably given it to her. Nothing serious, and according to Marje, he probably hadn't anyway." Vida sniffed. "Girls these days have no morals and less sense."

I wondered if Vida secretly said the same about me. But the very fact that she had made such a remark suggested that she did not. I was glad. But I was appalled at Marje Blatt's lack of professional ethics. "Does your niece blab everybody's case history around town?"

Vida looked faintly horrified. "Of course not! But I'm *family*!"

Since half of Alpine appeared to be related to Vida, I didn't quite see the difference. Still, a female is either pregnant or not, and given enough time, easy to prove one way or the other. I let the matter of Marje's big mouth rest. "So there's no help from Heather," I said, wondering if I should give Mark's jacket to her as Chris had suggested. Probably not—she didn't strike me as sentimental, and I supposed that if I didn't hand it over to Milo Dodge, I ought to deliver it to Cece and Simon Doukas.

"I didn't say that," Vida replied, and in my mental meanderings, it took me a moment to figure out what she meant. "Marje says—and this has nothing to do with patient confidentiality—that she heard from Dr. Starr's dental assistant, Jeannie Clay, who had talked to Chaz Phipps who said that Heather told her Mark wasn't the only Doukas in town." Vida wiggled her eyebrows.

I gaped. *"Simon?"*

Tapping her fingernails against her mug, Vida nodded. "It wouldn't be Neeny." She shuddered, sending ripples along the bustline of her floral print blouse. "Oh, God, I hope not! What a gruesome thought!"

It was indeed. But not as gruesome as murder.

After Vida left, I felt honor-bound to start putting together the story on Mark's death. I did the obituary first, after making a call to Al Driggers. Usually, he would bring obits by the office, but in this case, I didn't want to wait until Monday. I thought that maybe there would be some snatch of information in Mark's all-too-brief life story that would help solve the murder case. As far as I could tell, there wasn't: Mark had been born in Alpine in 1963; he'd graduated from the high school in 1981, where he'd lettered in football and baseball; he'd attended Everett Junior College for one year; he'd worked as a property manager for his grandfather and done a stint selling real estate. His hobbies were listed as prospecting, hunting, fishing, and watching sports.

I'm always amazed at how little obituaries tell about the deceased. I remember the first one I ever wrote while I was an intern at *The Times*. It was a woman whose name I forget, but the bare bones stated that she was a Seattle native, an enthusiastic gardener, a member of the First Church of Christ, was survived by her husband, four children, and eight grandchildren, and had "been beloved by all who knew her." I later learned that for twenty years, she had been the reigning madame in Seattle, with five previous husbands, and that she had also operated the highest-stake illegal poker game in Washington State. No wonder she had been beloved by all.

As for Mark, he sounded so ordinary. Even dull. Yet he

had incited someone to kill him. I started to organize the news story, listing the facts by hand.

Mark Doukas had been killed outside of Mineshaft Number Three on Wednesday night, around nine o'clock, his head bashed in by a crowbar. Something—or someone—had drawn him back to the mineshaft where he had exhibited some kind of excitement or fear that morning. Whatever had set him off was apparently unknown to anyone but him.

I paused, rubbing at the neck muscles which had grown stiff while I worked at my desk. The first time Tom had ever touched me was when he'd found me all tied up in knots over a complicated mutual fund story. It was late, almost midnight, and he took pity on me. I still remember the firm, yet gentle hands that relaxed my muscles but created other, more serious tensions. Damn the man, I thought, trying to chuck him out of my mind. I needed to concentrate on Mark Doukas. And the mine.

Despite Neeny Doukas, it had to be opened. I picked up the phone and dialed Milo Dodge's home number. He wasn't there. I tried the sheriff's office. Milo answered on the first ring. He sounded annoyed.

"Neeny and Simon are putting on the pressure," he admitted. "I've put out that APB on Chris Ramirez."

I suppressed a favorite four-letter word. "Chris could be anywhere," I said, hoping that wherever it was, the law enforcement officials wouldn't pay too much attention to the request of a small-town sheriff. Chris, after all, hadn't been charged with anything. I hoped.

"That's what Eeeny Moroni said," Milo replied, still testy. "He tried to talk me out of it, too."

Mentally, I thanked Eeeny for his caution. "Why?"

"Not enough evidence to require an APB." Milo sounded even more irked. "I know that, but if Chris didn't kill Mark—I'm saying, *if*, mind you, Emma—he may know something. Like what Mark and Kent were fighting about. Or some comment Mark may have made about somebody else."

"Or about the mine?" I ventured.

"Could be." The faint sound of paper shuffling reached my ear. "You going to the funeral?"

"No. Vida is, though." I wished we hadn't gotten off the subject of the mineshaft so fast. "Are you?"

"Yes. I shouldn't take the time away from the investigation, but I owe it to the family, personally, as well as professionally." His voice had lost its edge. This wasn't the sheriff talking now, but Milo Dodge, native Alpiner. "I went to high school with Simon, you know."

I didn't. "You aren't that old."

"I was three years behind him." Milo sounded as if he might be smiling. I decided to take advantage of his improving disposition.

"Milo, I think you'd better open up that mineshaft."

Silence. Then a sigh. "Neeny's dead-set against it."

"Why?"

"I don't know." I heard a clicking noise and figured Milo was lighting up one of his rare cigars. He exhaled into my ear. "With Neeny, he doesn't need a reason. Maybe it's because he's afraid somebody will get hurt and sue him. Maybe it's because Mark was killed there and he thinks of it as sacred ground. Maybe he just doesn't want the commotion. Hell, Emma, I don't know. The bottom line is, would forcing the issue be worth it?"

It was my turn to grow silent. I sat there at my desk, staring at my handwritten notes. "Yes," I finally said. "Think about it, Milo. Mark died on the spot where he seemed to discover something that made Kevin MacDuff believe he'd found gold. Obviously, Mark found *something*. Maybe if we knew what it was, we'd know who killed him."

Milo chuckled. "You sound like Fuzzy Baugh."

I ignored the remark. "Tell me this: do you know if Mark entered that mineshaft?"

"Not really. Have you ever looked it over? Up close?"

I'd never seen the blasted place until Thursday. Oh, I'd driven by it lots of times, but I'd never stopped. There was no reason for me to make a pilgrimage to an abandoned mine, especially on private property. "No," I confessed. "Vida gave it the once-over, though."

"Okay, then she might've noticed that somebody tried to open it up. Maybe with a crowbar." He paused to let that information sink in on what he no doubt considered was my thick skull. "But Gibb Frazier told me a long time ago that there was a second entrance, further up the creek. I'm waiting for him to get back from Snohomish to tell me where the hell it is."

I was suddenly exasperated. "Can't you and your deputies find the damned thing?"

"Sure we could," Milo snapped, his benign mood blown away, no doubt in a cloud of noxious cigar smoke. "Crank up your cranium, Emma. I've got five men for the whole county. One's on permanent traffic duty, one works nights, one's sick with the flu, and that leaves Jack Mullins and Bill Blatt. Jack's taken what little evidence we have into the lab in Seattle, and Bill is helping me at the office. In our spare time, we try to stop whatever other crimes may be going on in a four hundred square mile radius that includes some of the most rugged mountain terrain in North America. Any more dumbassed questions?"

"No," I said, hoping he'd swallow his cigar.

Chapter Twelve

IT WAS A beautiful fall day. I finished up the draft of my lead story, listened to the University of Washington Huskies trounce their hapless opponent of the week, and spent over two hours working in the yard. The letter to Chris did not come. I cursed Adam anew and considered calling him to see if he'd sent the blasted thing fourth class. But Vida was right. I knew the contents, and I couldn't see what bearing they had on Mark's death. I kept on weeding.

By five o'clock, I was bushed, the kind of tiredness that begets virtuous self-satisfaction. Mental and physical labor had refreshed my soul and let me feel at ease about running off for an evening of bridge.

Having grown up in a family of games players, I enjoy almost any kind of cards. Time is the problem. What little leisure I have, I prefer hogging for myself. Which, I suppose, is one reason Adam calls me antisocial. But playing bridge in Alpine is akin to doing research for the newspaper. I can learn as much in four rubbers of bridge as I can in four days of interviews.

Darlene and Harvey Adcock lived in an old but carefully restored house three blocks off Front Street, around the corner from Trinity Episcopal Church. Darlene's drapes were tightly closed, lest passersby peer in and observe some of Alpine's leading ladies sipping a glass of wine.

I didn't realize until I arrived that I was filling in for the bereaved Cece Doukas. Charlene Vickers insisted there was a madman on the loose and had forced her husband, Cal, to deliver her in his Texaco tow truck. Linda Grant, the high school P.E. teacher, thought the murder must be drug-related, chalking up a point for Fuzzy Baugh. Betsy O'Toole, whose husband Jake owned the Grocery Basket, asserted that it was a suicide. She had once known a man in Gold Bar who had hit himself over the head with a hammer. Eight times.

"Poor Cece," said Darlene Adcock, a mite of a woman with enormous gray eyes and flawless skin. "Mark could be a pain in the neck, as our Josh always said, but he was the apple of his mother's eye."

Francine Wells, who felt a professional duty to be the best-dressed woman in Alpine, adjusted the big bow on the blouse that went with her Chanel suit. "Mark was a twit, dead or alive. Cece spoiled him rotten, and Simon has always been too busy to be a real father. It's Jennifer I feel sorry for. The poor girl has absolutely no fashion sense."

My glance took in the other women who made up the three tables for the monthly meeting of what had started out as the St. Mildred's Mission and Anti-Communist Guild back in 1949 but had evolved into an ecumenical group who sent their annual dues to an inner-city school in Newark. Some day I intended to do a feature story on the guild's history and find out how both their membership and goals had changed in the last forty-plus years. But this was not the time for it. Instead, I'd see if I could ferret out any information about Mark Doukas and his clan.

Alas, at the first table, I was faced with the Dithers sisters, Judy and Connie, who owned a horse farm up on Second Hill. Two of the silliest women I've ever met, they took only their horses seriously, and were said to allow some of the animals to join them at the dining room table on special occasions, such as Christmas, New Year's, and, I presumed, the Kentucky Derby. The Dithers sisters spoke in fragments, a strange sort of shorthand that was understood only by them—and maybe their horses. I didn't expect much help from that pair. My partner was Linda Grant, who is normally very outgoing but seemed subdued by the Dithers sisters' presence. An hour and a measly part score later, I was glad to move on, to Edna Mae Dalrymple, the exceedingly nervous but very accommodating head librarian; Janet Driggers, the funeral home director's vivacious, if blunt, wife; and Mary Lou Blatt, Vida's sister-in-law. Mary Lou is a CPA and the mother of Marje the Indiscreet Medical Receptionist. Mary Lou is at least ten years younger than Vida, and for one of those obscure internecine reasons, the in-laws have not spoken in five years. Vida has never offered an explanation. In fact, if it weren't for Marje Blatt, I wouldn't know that Vida and Mary Lou were connected.

Edna Mae opened with a spade, Janet passed, and I responded with two diamonds. Mary Lou Blatt doubled and, before Edna Mae could react, put her cards face down on the table. "What's going on with Phoebe Pratt and Neeny Doukas?" she whispered, darting a glance over her shoulder at Vivian Phipps, who was studying her partner's dummy. Vivian is Phoebe's sister, and the mother of Chaz, Heather Bardeen's chum. Both Vivian and Phoebe were Vickers before they married, the sisters of Cal who runs the Texaco station. There are times when I feel as if I should carry an Alpine genealogy tree around with me. This was one of them.

Edna Mae jumped, making the wineglasses jiggle. "What do you mean? They've been seeing each other for years." Alpine's head librarian nominally disapproved of gossip. She pursed her lips and gazed into her hand. "Pass."

Janet sighed eloquently. "Frig, now I'll have to bid. Oh, hell . . . let me think . . ." Her tongue clicked off points. "Two hearts." She leaned across the table. "Do you mean Neeny can't get it up anymore?"

Mary Lou rolled her eyes, reminding me of her sister-in-law. "Hardly. I heard a rumor that . . ." She took a deep breath and spoke from behind her fingers. "Phoebe and Neeny eloped!"

Janet's sea-green eyes goggled; Edna Mae's overbite clamped down on her lower lip; I looked up at the small Venetian chandelier.

"Well!" Edna Mae gasped, clutching the stem of her wineglass. "Well, well!" She frowned, then shook her frizzy salt-and-pepper head and fidgeted with her cards. "You all know what rumors are. At least that one would put some others to rest."

Janet Driggers looked down her pug nose at Edna Mae. "Such as? God, I love stories about screwing! It sure beats all those stiffs Al has to put up with."

Edna Mae squirmed and turned a shocked expression on Janet. "Really, Janet! I couldn't say what I heard, could I?" Edna Mae nodded jerkily at me. "What do you say to that, Emma?"

"I'd say if it's only a rumor, it's all *alleged*. That's newspaper talk." I tried to appear ingenuous.

"No, no, no," said Mary Lou. "Edna Mae means Janet's three hearts."

"Oh." I glanced back in my hand. I'd lost track of the bidding. "Pass." I turned to Mary Lou, awaiting her response.

"I didn't hear it from Vida," she declared, rather huffily. "Vida thinks she knows everything that goes on in this town, but she doesn't. My sister-in-law is just a big windbag." Mary Lou gave me an arch little smile. "Sorry, Emma, I know you have to work with her. But that's not your fault."

"Thanks, Mary Lou." I shoved a handful of bridge mix into my mouth and wondered what Tom Cavanaugh was doing on a Saturday night in Alpine.

"She must be a trial," said Mary Lou, apparently referring to Vida. "Four hearts."

Edna Mae practically passed out. "Oh! You jumped! That's *game*! But I opened! Oh!" Her frizzy hair seemed to fibrillate.

Janet took a big swig of wine and bounced in her chair. "Then double us, you goose. Or get some balls and bid four spades."

"Four spades!" Edna Mae twitched and rearranged her cards for about the fifth time. "Oh! *Pass*." She scooted around in her chair, eyeing Mary Lou Blatt suspiciously. "Where on earth did you hear that Phoebe and Neeny got married? That's the sort of story that ought to come from a reliable source."

Mary Lou lifted her chin and looked at Edna Mae over her half glasses. "It did. My nephew's in law enforcement, you know."

I had a vision of Billy Blatt, his arms and legs being pulled this way and that by his aunts, Mary Lou and Vida. The poor kid didn't have a chance. I wondered what his mother was like. As far as I knew, I hadn't yet met Vida's other sister-in-law.

Janet's green eyes widened. "Deputy Billy? Wow! He ought to know. Simon Doukas must be wilder than a three-peckered goat! Pass." She swiveled around to look at Edna Mae. "*What* rumors? Come on, Edna Mae, if you aren't going to double us, at least dish out the real dirt. Marrying and burying are damned dull. How about more screwing stuff?"

Edna Mae blanched. "Really, Janet . . . It was nothing, just a silly story about Phoebe driving around town the other night." Her little round face crumpled. "Oh, my, I'm so confused! Who has the bid? Is it no trump?"

I was overcome with one of my perverse notions. "We're still bidding," I said with a sweet smile for my partner. "Five diamonds."

"What?" Mary Lou all but rocketed across the table. "Emma! How can you make an overcall like that!"

I couldn't, of course. Not with only seven points and five puny diamonds. "Where was Phoebe going?" I asked Edna Mae innocently.

"I don't know," Edna Mae said primly. "I worked late at the library Wednesday night, and I just happened to see that big red car of hers parked by the Clemans Building. That old truck with the wooden side panels was double-parked next to her. Isn't that illegal?" Still twitching, she cast a guileless look around the table.

Mary Lou arched her eyebrows. "Gibb Frazier! That's the old truck he uses to haul stuff in. What." she de-

manded, whipping off her glasses and putting her face in
Edna Mae's, "are you implying, Ms. Dalrymple?" Mary
Lou didn't budge as a single word fell from her lips:
"Double."

Edna Mae jerked about in the chair, hair flying, hands
shaking. "I'm not implying anything, Mary Lou Hinshaw
Blatt! All I said was that I happened to see . . ." She
stopped and looked at her cards. "Oh! She doubled us! Oh,
no! I pass!"

Janet Driggers was chortling. "Me, too." She leered at
all of us. "Phoebe and Gibb? That's hot. Then again, it
might be a hoot to make love to a man with one leg." The
leer intensified. "Think about it, girls."

Edna Mae shuddered, obviously not wanting to think
about it at all. I considered redoubling, just to prove how
truly perverse I could be, but decided that such a move
might cause my partner to suffer an aneurism. I passed and
waited for Edna Mae to lay down her cards.

"Poor Gibb," mused Mary Lou. "I wish he would find
somebody. He's a nice guy, really. But of course Phoebe
wouldn't do. Even if she hadn't gone off and eloped with
Neeny."

"Yeah, Edna Mae," said Janet, "how about it? When
was the last time you got laid?"

Valiantly, Edna Mae fumbled with her cards, getting the
suits mixed up and blushing furiously. "Honestly, Janet,
you say the most horrid things! Have you no decency?"

I grimaced at Edna Mae's dummy. She had no more
right to open with one spade than I had to overcall with
five diamonds. Doubled. We were up a stump.

To divert attention from what was going to be a slaugh-
ter, I posed what I thought was an innocuous question to
Mary Lou. "I wasn't around when Gibb had his accident,"
I said, waiting for her to lead. "What actually happened?"

Mary Lou tossed out the ace of hearts. She turned suddenly sly, no doubt because she knew how badly they
could set us. But that wasn't the entire reason. "Vida
thinks she knows so much," Mary Lou breathed. "Let me

tell you, she doesn't know what happened to Gibb, not even after all these years."

"Oh?" I kept my tone mild. "What did happen, Mary Lou?" I watched Janet scoop in the first trick.

Mary Lou was still smirking. "I used to keep the books for Simon Doukas when I was still working at home while the kids were young. I know this because I had to go over the medical expenses Simon paid out that year. Gibb and Mark Doukas got into a fight over some gold or something up above Second Hill, by those old cabins." She paused to lead the king of hearts. There went another trick. "Mark wasn't just a pain as a teenager. He was mean." She led the ace of clubs and exchanged knowing glances with Janet and Edna Mae. "He not only beat up Gibb, but after the poor guy was on the ground, Mark got into his car or whatever he was driving and ran over him." She led the ace of spades. "That's how Gibb lost his leg."

Of course I went set eight tricks and our opponents racked up several hundred points, but at least we weren't vulnerable. Gibb Frazier was, though, and the idea didn't make me very happy. I thought about that bundle of newspapers Milo Dodge had found by Mineshaft Number Three. I reflected upon Edna Mae's seeing Gibb and Phoebe downtown the night of the murder. That explained why Phoebe's car was splattered with blue paint. It had come from Francine Wells's store, blown about by the windstorm. Phoebe had lied about staying in that night. But what had Gibb been doing up at the mineshaft?

Shortly before midnight, we adjourned, walking out into the mild autumn air. The old moon sat above Baldy's black ridge, and the stars seemed so close, as if they were peeking over the mountains. About the time I polished off my third glass of wine and made a small slam to elude the booby prize, some of my fears had begun to ebb. It had been quite awhile since I'd strung together three nights of wine drinking. If, I thought with a giggle, I kept it up, I could be in the running with at least two dozen other people for the title of town sot. Waving good night to Vivian Phipps and the Dithers sisters, I reached my car and remembered to avoid the pothole on Cascade Avenue that I'd stepped in when I arrived. More resurfacing was needed, not just County Road 187, but on several streets in town. I must do some research for another editorial. I kept my eyes focused, more or less, on the dark pavement. Alpine could also use some new streetlights.

There was no pothole. I paused, giving myself a bracing shake. The fact was I hadn't drunk that much. Three glasses of chablis in a four-hour period had only given me the illusion of giddiness, perhaps a state I wished for to make my Saturday night more exciting than it might have been with Tom Cavanaugh.

The others were pulling out, including Charlene Vickers in Cal's tow truck. In the glare of Cal's lights, I saw the pothole just beyond my left front wheel. I was puzzled. Could I have been mistaken? My sense of well-being faded as I got into the Jag and drove home carefully. Maybe the murder case was getting to me. Maybe I was more worried about Chris Ramirez than I cared to admit. Maybe Tom Cavanaugh's arrival in Alpine had thrown me for a loop.

I pulled into my carport and scanned the front of my snug log house. The lights were on inside and over the front door. As ever, my home looked inviting, even reassuring. Yet I was nervous about getting out of the car. The night was very quiet. Through the trees, the neighbors' houses were dark.

Steeling my nerves, I slid across the seat and got out on the passenger side, nearer to the house. Dew glistened on the grass; a few leaves drifted off the maple. I hurried up the path, keeping watch over my shoulder. That was how I saw the dent in the Jag's right fender. Whirling around, I raced back to the car and swore aloud. Six inches across, deep grooves, paint scratched, my beautiful car was ravished. I'd have to call the insurance company in the morning, Sunday or not. A kid, no doubt, cruising on a Saturday night. I

stomped into the house and threw my purse on the sofa.
Then it dawned on me: the dent was on the *right* fender. I'd
parked that side against the curb. Nobody could hit me at
that angle. I thought about the pothole. It hadn't moved. But
my Jag had. Someone had driven it off while I sat inside
Darlene Adcock's closely curtained house, gulping bridge
mix and glugging wine.

I called the insurance company first, then dialed Milo
Dodge at home. It was shortly after eight A.M. "Somebody
stole my car," I said, not caring that I'd probably awak-
ened him from his much-needed sleep.

Milo sounded fuzzy. "Again?"

"Not again," I said crossly. "I loaned it to Chris." I explained what I thought had happened.

"Well," Milo said, yawning in my ear, "what's the big
deal? You got it back."

"With a dent in the curbside fender." I was trying to be
patient. "I suppose you blabbed to everybody that I had an
extra set of keys under the car."

"Blabbed?" Now it was Milo who sounded testy. "Hell,
Emma, you want me telling people Chris hot wired your
damned car? Besides, I only told my men about it."

Visions of Billy Blatt getting a hot foot from Vida and
Mary Lou flew across my mind's eye. "Look, Milo," I
said, reining in my exasperation, "are you going to do
something about this or not?"

Another yawn. "File a complaint. We'll check the car
out this afternoon." Suddenly his tone became more brisk.
"Say—do you think Chris is back in Alpine?"

Somehow, that had not occurred to me. I set my coffee
mug down on the desk and winced. "No. Why should he do
that?" Innocent or guilty, I couldn't think of any reason why
Chris Ramirez would return to the town he insisted he despised. Unless, of course, he had unfinished business. . . .

I desperately wanted to ask Milo if Neeny Doukas was
alive and well this morning, but I didn't dare. It took me

a moment to realize that Milo, now sounding fully alert, was talking his head off:

". . . A baseball bat, or even a shovel. They were probably going for the headlights. We had a rash of that kind of vandalism a year or so ago."

"What?"

"I said . . . Emma, pay attention! Jeez, what's with you?" Milo was annoyed. "Kids. They go around banging up cars, especially snazzy ones. Your Jag probably never budged from where you left it. Or," he added slyly, "did you check the speedometer?"

Of course I hadn't. I started to tell him about the pothole, but knew he'd dismiss it as a flight of fancy.

"Go ahead," he was saying in a more amenable voice. "File the complaint. Then we'll see if any other folks got their cars smashed, okay?"

It was pointless to argue. I mumbled my thanks and hung up. My watch told me it was 8:15, 10:15 in Anguilla, Mississippi. Ben would be riding his Sunday circuit, saying masses at five mission churches on the delta. He had never left Mississippi, having come to love its black poor and its white poor, and even some of the middle class.

I missed my brother. Except for a few, too-rare visits, we'd been apart for over twenty years. Ben hadn't been out west since I'd moved to Alpine. I needed to hear his crackling voice, to feel his brotherly love, and, I admitted, to tell him that Tom Cavanaugh had shown up.

I dressed for church with more care than usual, in a red cowl-neck sweater and a black pleated skirt. It wasn't for Tom's benefit that I put on black heels and made a serious attempt at combing my hair, but because we were probably going somewhere nice for brunch. Everett, or maybe all the way to Seattle.

St. Mildred's is old, but not as old as its eighty-eight-year old pastor, Kiernan Fitzgerald, who is officially retired. Father Fitz retains his Irish brogue, is rail-thin, and is completely bald except for three wisps of white hair that tend to stand on end. His sermons have been recycled over the years, and as he is somewhat forgetful, we still occasionally suffer through a Sunday diatribe about the Red Menace. Younger parishioners are mystified.

But on this last day of September, Father Fitz chose his basic Christian charity homily, urging the congregation to put aside their cares in the mill (it closed in 1929), sacrifice their Sunday picnic to Burl Creek Park (now the mall), and take food baskets to the poor families on the wrong side of the railroad tracks (the golf course since 1961).

My mind began to wander somewhere between a cautionary note not to let your youngsters ride on the running board of your Model-A and the dangers of drinking unknown beverages from a certain still near Icicle Creek. It was too bad, I reflected, that Fuzzy Baugh wasn't a Catholic. He might change his mind and decide that Mark Doukas had found white lightning in Mineshaft Number Three.

Naturally, my eyes wandered along with my mind. I was sitting at the back of the white frame church, near a side altar dedicated to St. Anthony of Padua. At the end of the pew, I spotted Francine Wells, resplendent in an Escada ensemble. The O'Tooles were in front of me. Ed and Shirley Bronsky and their fat little brood squatted cross the aisle. Up ahead, in about the third row, I could see the back of Tom Cavanaugh's dark head. He was wearing a gray tweed sports jacket. I frowned. Those broad shoulders still had their power to make me twitter like a teenager. Damn.

On the way back from communion, Tom caught my eye and smiled. I remained solemn, seemingly wrapped up in fervent prayers of thanksgiving. The fervor that should have been reserved for my post-communion prayers rose up to smite me in a most unspiritual way.

After mass, Tom hailed me in the parking lot between the church and the school. He had a rental car, some kind of American compact I didn't recognize, though I envied its lack of dents.

"Would you like to show me how you can drive your Jag?" he asked with that big grin.

"You can drive it," I said in a petulant voice. "I'm mad at it. Look." I showed him the fender damage, and he commiserated. I'd explain my theory later. At the moment, I was anxious to be gone. Most of St. Mildred's parishioners were watching us, no doubt speculating on the stranger's identity. Since Ed had met Tom, the news would soon be out. By afternoon, most of Alpine would figure that *The Advocate* was going broke and was about to be sold to a newspaper magnate from San Francisco. Or worse yet, they'd note the resemblance between Tom and Adam. I didn't know which scenario upset me most.

I followed Tom up to the ski lodge where he left his rental. While he was parking the car, I spotted Heather Bardeen and waved. She didn't wave back. Maybe she really didn't see me. I gave a mental shrug. What could I say to her anyway? Is it true you're having an affair with your late boyfriend's father? Even for an aggressive journalist, that seemed too harsh. Besides, she might sock me.

Once Tom was behind the wheel of the Jag, I regretted my impulsive suggestion that he drive. First my chair, now my car. Maybe he'd like to move into my house. To my horror, the facetious thought didn't strike me as all that absurd.

I was surprised when we headed east, not west. "Where are we going?" I asked as he pointed the Jaguar up Stevens Pass. "Not Leavenworth, I hope. They're having the Oktoberfest this weekend. Too much bratwurst and too many tubas for my taste."

"I know," Tom said. It seemed as if he always knew everything. "Have you ever been to the Cougar Inn on Lake Wenatchee?"

I hadn't, though I'd heard about it and had even gone so far as to ask Ed Bronsky to see if they'd like to take out an ad. Ed told me the inn was too far away. As it turned out, it was less than an hour's drive, a short stretch beyond the summit, then twenty miles north of Leavenworth.

The Cougar Inn was built in 1890, a big farm house converted into a restaurant and hotel. The lavish buffet included ham, sausage, a baron of beef, eggs, pastries, vegetables, fruit, and just about every other imaginable food a brunch addict might desire. With plates piled high, we made our way to a table for two that looked out over the sparkling waters of Lake Wenatchee. The sun was out, but the wind ruffled the evergreens. It was a perfect autumn afternoon.

At first we spoke of trifles. Tom had gone fishing Saturday, somewhere around Gold Bar. No luck, though the salmon were due to come upriver to spawn soon. Living most of the time in the Bay Area, he missed fishing. There was a place he liked to go on the Sacramento River, but that was ruined because of the recent disastrous chemical spill at Dunsmuir.

I asked about his two children. Graham was at USC, studying cinema. Kelsey had just started her first year at Mills. It was just as well that they didn't spend much time at home. Sandra's condition had turned Kelsey into an introvert. Tom worried about his daughter. He wished she'd gone back East to school. "The farther the better, I think," he said, briefly letting his carefully cultivated mask of good cheer slip a notch. He gave me a wry grin. "Sometimes I wonder if mental instability isn't contagious."

We were on our second round of plates. I told Tom about my car, including the mobile pothole. Unlike Milo, he didn't scoff. "The sheriff may be right about one thing," he said, digging into a mound of crisp hash brown potatoes. "It was probably kids, going for a joy ride."

Tom could be right. The Jag was tempting, and if word had gotten out that I kept a spare set of keys under the car, some of Alpine's brasher punks might have succumbed. After all, several of the women at the bridge party had teenagers. The kids might know I'd be at the Adcocks' for several hours and figure they were safe to take off for a while. At least that's what I wanted to believe. I didn't much like the idea of Chris lurking around town in the shadows.

"Well?" Tom spoke, and I realized I'd missed a beat.

Before I could respond, he put a hand on my arm. "Hey, this murder really has you upset. Why? I gathered from what everybody said at dinner the other night that Mark was a jerk. Did you think otherwise?"

"No." I felt the light pressure on my arm and couldn't help but smile. "To be honest, I didn't know Mark Doukas very well. It's his cousin I'm stewing over."

As briefly as possible, I explained about Chris. Tom listened closely, devouring more hash browns, eggs benedict, croissants, and link sausages. I was finally full, surfeited with cinnamon rolls, ham, beef, scrambled eggs, blintzes, asparagus, and two kinds of juice. When I concluded my recital, Tom took a slice of cantaloupe off my plate. His appetite had always amazed me.

"I can't see why Chris would kill Mark," he said, obviously giving the matter his usual thorough consideration. "No fight, no motive. So who had a reason to get Mark out of the way?"

"Nobody. Not a *real* motive."

But Tom shook his head. Outside, the wind was growing stronger, whipping up the blue waters of the lake. "Unless you accept the theory of a nut on the loose, your killer has a motive. The question is: *what?* His sister would benefit from the standpoint of money. She'd get his share, and so would her husband—Kent?" He saw me nod. "But from what you say of Jennifer, she sounds meek as milk. Of course," he added on an almost wistful note, "you never know about people."

"And Kent did quarrel with Mark," I reminded Tom. "Although Jennifer insists it wasn't serious."

The waitress was removing our plates and bringing more coffee. Tom waited until she was done before he spoke again. "As for your driver, he had a grudge. But why wait all these years?"

"I know. It doesn't make sense. All the same, I'd like to find out when Gibb Frazier was up at the mineshaft. It had to be after he got back from Monroe, which would have been mid-afternoon."

"Have you asked him?"

"He's been in Snohomish the past couple of days. Milo was going to talk to him when he got back. Today, I suppose." Gibb had been due in Alpine last night. I wondered if Milo had already seen him. Maybe I'd call the sheriff again when I got home.

The bill appeared at our table. I made a feeble gesture, but Tom laughed. "I'm rich, remember? Besides, this is a write-off. We were talking newspaper revenue."

"We should do that, I guess." I sounded vague.

This time he put his hand on mine. "We should do a lot of things, Emma. But not right now. You're preoccupied."

I started to bridle, then made a funny little noise in my throat that wasn't exactly a squeak but came close. "Damn it, Tom. I can't believe you're here."

He still had his hand on mine; his smile washed over me like balm. "Well, I am."

"For how long?" I hated to ask the question.

He took his hand away and leaned back in the chair. "Oh—a few days. I have to be in San Diego at a publishers' meeting the second week of October. Look," he said, leaning forward again, "I've put some preliminary material together for you, but I left it at the lodge. I need some more background anyway—demographics, per capita income, property taxes. It'd bore you. But give me a day or so, and I'll impress the hell out of you, okay?"

"Wow." I laughed in spite of myself. "Do you do this for every poor publisher?"

"Yes," he replied, "I do. It's the only way I can make a decision about investing." He glanced over at the buffet, where the last of the brunchers were lining up. "There are lots of appealing weeklies and dailies out there, just like that smorgasbord. But you have to pick and choose, or you'll end up with the financial equivalent of a stomachache." He palmed his credit card and stood up. "What are you thinking, that I must miss the writing?"

"Yes," I said, though that wasn't what I'd been thinking

at all. I'd had an evil speculation about whether or not the inn had a room available for the night.

"I do miss it. In fact, it's not the writing so much as the editing." Ever the gentleman, Tom helped me with my chair. "My greatest love was making a good story even better."

It was a commendable emotion. I resisted the urge to ask Tom to name his second greatest love.

We walked along the lake for a while, but the wind was too brisk to linger. We reached Alpine about four. In the lodge's parking lot, I felt compelled to inquire after Tom's dinner plans.

"I've got a date," he said, opening the door of the car. Between the trees, I could see the steep roof and dormer windows of the ski lodge. A weather vane twirled in the breeze and smoke curled from one of the stone chimneys.

"Oh." I tried to sound casual. "Just as well. I don't think I could eat until tomorrow."

He stuck one long leg out of the car. "I'll manage. Anyway, my hostess swears she's not much of a cook."

"Oh."

"Well?"

"Well what?"

"Aren't you curious?"

I let out a hiss. "Sure I am. But I'll be damned if I'll ask."

He braced himself on the steering wheel and leaned across the well between the bucket seats to kiss my cheek. "It's Vida Runkel. Do you think she'll try to seduce me?"

"Vida!" I gasped. "I hope so!"

It would be better than having her bombard Tom with a litany of embarrassing questions.

Chapter Thirteen

AMONG THE MESSAGES waiting for me was the voice of Milo Dodge, inviting me to dinner at the Venison Inn. "Catch a bite," was the way he put it, "and have a look at your busted British car." I felt as if I were playing a role in a French farce, where all the wrong people run off with one another.

Although I still wasn't hungry after the monumental brunch, I called Milo back and told him I'd meet him at the restaurant at six-thirty. Even as we spoke, I snagged my panty hose on the leg of my chair. They were my last good pair, and I could have faked it by wearing slacks if the run hadn't gone all the way from toe to hip.

Parker's Drugs stayed open on Sunday until six. Originally owned by Durwood and Dot Parker, the store had been sold almost ten years ago to a young couple from Mount Vernon, Garth and Tara Wesley. They'd kept the name and remodeled the premises. Durwood had been a fine pharmacist but not much of a retailer. He retired about the same time he hit his first cow.

Tara was behind the counter when I breezed in at 5:55. No one else was around, and she was closing up the till, but she gave me a warm smile.

"Just ring up a three-pack of No Nonsense, petite to medium sheer reinforced nude toe," I called out, racing to the rack.

"Will do," Tara said, "but I've got to scan it first."

I zipped up to the checkout stand. Tara was a pretty brunette, mid-thirties, the mother of two small children, and,

159

like her husband, a registered pharmacist. "Sorry I cut it so close. It was a last-minute disaster."

"That happens," Tara said, still smiling. "You're just the person I wanted to see. What's happening with the murder? There hasn't been a word on TV or in the weekend papers."

I told her there wasn't any substantive news. Sheriff Dodge was following up some leads, but he didn't have any serious suspects.

"That's scary," Tara said, no longer smiling as she gave me my change and receipt. "What if it's one of *us*?" Her big brown eyes widened with dread. "I'm always afraid of a holdup. Even in a small town, a drugstore is a sitting duck. Not the money so much as the drugs, I mean. That's why we came here. Mount Vernon was getting too big. We wouldn't have dreamed of going to Seattle or Everett or even Bellingham." With one wary eye on the street and the other on the cash pouch, she started removing checks from the till. "I'm here a lot at night because Garth works days so I can take care of the kids. I don't like being here alone." She took out the cash and stuffed it into the pouch. "I heard Mark was killed around nine last Wednesday. I was working by myself, and you know, I had the funniest feeling."

"Really?" Perfect hindsight always fascinates me.

Tara nodded twice. "I really did. It was so stormy. Nobody had come by in the last half hour. I had a mind to close up early and go home. Then Kent MacDuff stopped to pick up a prescription he'd had phoned in. I was sure glad I'd already made it up so I could get out of here."

I tried not to act surprised. "Kent came in so late? He's as bad as I am."

Tara lifted one shoulder in an offhand manner. "He'd hurt his shoulder. For such a macho man, Kent's a big baby. Unlike you, he didn't apologize for coming in at closing time."

"Jennifer said he was miserable," I remarked, wondering why I was making excuses for Kent MacDuff. To emphasize my superior manners, I thanked Tara and asked if she wanted me to wait and go out the door with her.

She laughed, albeit nervously. "Oh, no. It's only six. And there's the sheriff. I feel reasonably safe with him around."

Sure enough, Milo Dodge was just getting out of his four-wheel drive. I waved; he waved back. A minute later, I joined him on the sidewalk. "You're early," I said.

He was frowning, his shoulders hunched against the wind. "I stopped to see Gibb. He's not home yet." Milo's hair blew back from his forehead, but that wasn't what made his long face seem even longer. He was worried.

I decided to forget about stopping in the rest room to change my panty hose. Milo was in no mood to notice. "Do you think he's still in Snohomish?" I asked as we headed for the Venison Inn.

"No." Milo opened the door. He didn't speak to me again until after the hostess had greeted us and provided a table with a view of Front Street. I felt like a window display. "I checked. He finished the moving job about five yesterday and told the people he was working for that he had to go meet a steelhead."

"Maybe he caught one," I remarked, hoping to strike a light note. Steelheaders are a rare breed, inclined to suffer any hardship to catch their elusive prey.

Milo wasn't amused. "Even if he had, he'd be back by now. I sent Bill Blatt and Jack Mullins looking for him. I don't like this, Emma."

I debated about telling Milo what Mary Lou Blatt had said about Gibb Frazier at bridge club. I decided to hold back. "You think something's happened to Gibb?"

Impatiently, Milo pushed the unruly hair off his forehead. "I don't know. Gibb hated Mark's guts, but I wouldn't figure him for a murderer. Unless he got really pissed off."

Which, I reflected grimly, Gibb had a right to do. Next to Chris, Gibb was my least favorite suspect. Despite his rough edges, I liked him well enough, and he was my employee. I owed him a certain amount of loyalty.

Milo ordered Scotch; I opted for root beer. This was my day of total abstinence. Across the restaurant, the hostess was seating Jennifer and Kent MacDuff. Their arrival gave me the opportunity to change the subject.

"Kent's alibi won't wash," I said, trying not to look smug.

Milo stared at me. "How come?"

I explained about Kent's nine o'clock visit to the drugstore.

Milo looked thoughtful. "Kent never mentioned that. I suppose he was afraid to." He glanced over at Kent, who was haranguing their waitress while Jennifer hid behind her long blond hair. "But if Kent doesn't have an alibi, neither does Jennifer. They were supposed to be home together."

"True." I liked the idea of an alibiless Kent MacDuff. I wasn't as keen on the same status for his wife. But I was reminded of Phoebe. "According to Edna Mae Dalrymple, Phoebe was driving around downtown Wednesday night."

Milo's ears pricked up, like a hound on the scent. "What time?"

"I'm not sure," I admitted. "During the windstorm, though. She got Francine Wells's paint on her car."

The notepad came out. Milo wrote swiftly. Out of the corner of my eye, I saw that Kent MacDuff was on his feet, heading our way. So were the drinks.

"Hey, Sheriff," called Kent, oblivious to the stares from the other diners, "what's new with your dragnet for cousin Chris?"

Milo looked annoyed. "Nothing yet. That takes time."

Kent was blocking the waitress's path. She tried to get around him; he refused to budge. "Hell!" Kent waved an arm, narrowly missing the waitress. "Chris could kill ten other people while you guys screw around. Neeny's about to blow up. You'd better get Chris back here before the funeral tomorrow."

The chilly stare Milo gave Kent would have turned a more sensitive man to stone. "You'd better get your butt down to my office first thing tomorrow morning. Your wife, too."

"What?" Kent bellowed as more heads turned. The waitress executed as neat a step as I've ever seen outside of a chorus line and deposited our drinks. "We've got to leave early for Seattle. Are you nuts?"

Milo was unmoved. "Then show up as soon as you get back. I've got some questions for both of you."

"Oh, bull!" exclaimed Kent. He started to bluster but apparently realized the sheriff wasn't going to relent. "It may be pretty damned late," said Kent. "I hope you like overtime."

Milo shrugged. "I'm used to it."

Still belligerent, Kent wheeled away. Jennifer had been watching from over the top of her menu. Her blue eyes looked terrified.

"Dink," muttered Milo, taking a big swig of Scotch. "Why didn't somebody whack *him*?"

Before I could make a suitable rejoinder, Milo's beeper went off. He excused himself and went to the pay phone outside the rest rooms. I drank root beer and tried to avoid watching Kent and Jennifer MacDuff argue. Why weren't they with Simon and Cece? This must be a terrible night for the bereaved parents, with their son's funeral only hours away. Maybe the other Doukases had gathered at Neeny's. I hoped so. Even the most aggravating of families should cling together in a crisis.

Milo returned, looking downright dismal.

"What's wrong?" I asked brightly. "Did Durwood Parker mow down a herd of sheep?"

The sheriff didn't sit, but drained his Scotch in a gulp. "No." He drew a five-dollar bill out of his wallet and put it on the table, avoiding my stare. "Gibb Frazier's dead. Somebody shot him. I've got to go, Emma. Sorry."

* * *

After arguing all the way back to Milo's car, he finally relented and let me come with him. Out on the highway, he explained what had happened.

"Billy and Jack didn't find him. They were staying in our jurisdiction, this side of the Snohomish–Skykomish County line. But down by Gold Bar, some gun freaks stumbled across Gibb this morning in a gravel pit where they practice shooting. He didn't have any I.D., but somebody at the morgue in Everett recognized him."

I was still suffering from a mild case of shock. "I don't get it. Why would anybody kill Gibb?" My teeth were chattering, and my feet beat a tattoo on the floor of Milo's Cherokee Chief. It was his own car, and he'd had to put his temporary flashing lights on top of it before we left town.

Milo didn't have any answers, either. We covered the next fifteen miles in silence, whisking past the Sunday drivers heading for home. Outside of Gold Bar, Milo slowed down. "Over there, across the river—that's Reiter Ponds, a big fishing hole. Back off the road is the gravel pit."

It was dark; I couldn't see a thing. I knew about Reiter, though. Half of Alpine always seemed to be asking if there was any action there.

Milo accelerated. "The Snohomish County Medical Examiner said Gibb had been dead for at least twelve hours when they found him this morning around eleven."

"Poor Gibb." I held my head and tried to regain my composure. "Did he have any relatives? He never mentioned them."

"His wife died of leukemia almost twenty years ago. There was a boy about my age. He got married and moved to California—or was it the other way around? I forget." Milo was sailing past Startup, Sultan, the turnoff to Monroe. "Gibb and his son were never close, not even after Ruth died. There was a sister, too, but she moved to Portland a long time ago. I think Gibb went to see her when the spirit moved him, but she never came back to Alpine."

A lot of people seemed to leave and never come back. Was nothing left for them in their old hometown? Or, having moved on and maybe up, did they want to keep their roots well buried? I didn't know. But one thing I was sure of: I wished Chris Ramirez hadn't come back. And that Gibb Frazier's return to Alpine didn't have to be in a body bag.

The Snohomish County Coroner's office is fairly new but suitably drab, with metal and vinyl chairs, steel gray filing cabinets, and a framed front page of the Everett *Daily Herald*'s account of the 1916 I.W.W. massacre. The deputy coroner was anything but drab, however. A squat, rosy-cheeked cherub of a man, Neal Doke looked like he should be wearing a monk's robe instead of a white lab coat. Even his brown hair was balding like a tonsure.

Introductions were made, condolences were given, chairs were offered. Doke asked if we'd like to see the body. Milo said yes; I said no. I waited alone with a cup of weak coffee and the grisly reminder of what had happened to the radical Wobblies who tried to land in the Everett harbor seventy-five years ago.

Milo returned looking grim. He laid a hand on my shoulder, maybe for support as much as comfort. "It's Gibb, all right. Damn. I'm sorry, Emma."

"Me, too." I hate tears, and though I mourned Gibb, the loss didn't devastate me. More to the point, I was stunned and angered. Two deaths in less than a week were grounds for outrage.

Neal Doke was at his desk, leafing through papers. Jack Mullins and Billy Blatt had joined us. "Okay," said Doke, sounding too perky for the occasion. "Healthy white male, age fifty-eight, left leg amputated above the knee, small scars on forehead, both arms, left thigh, abdomen, etc. Time of death, approximately between five and eight P.M., Saturday, September twenty-eighth. Shot in chest, bullet passing through body, missing ribs. Probably from a distance of twenty feet, but that's guesswork." He looked up from his paperwork. "I did an autopsy on a giraffe once. Hell of a thing."

None of us commented, though it was clear from Neal Doke's expectant face that he had hopes of being asked. "I take it you didn't find the bullet?" Milo inquired, stony-faced.

Doke waved a pudgy hand. "Hell, no. That gravel pit is full of bullets, from all the gun people practicing. Oh, our deputies will come up with it eventually, but it'll take time."

As a journalist, I felt obliged to say something. Anything. "How will you know it's the bullet that killed Gibb?"

Doke was unwrapping a package of Ding Dongs. "It'll have blood on it. My guess is that the gun was a thirty-eight." He bit into one of the Ding Dongs. "Just a guess, mind you," he said with his mouth full. "You folks ever get any poison victims? I had one last year, woman from Mukilteo did her husband in with bleach. He must have been a real idiot." Doke shook his head and kept chewing.

We left as soon as Milo had called Al Driggers and asked him to drive the funeral hearse over to Everett. Billy Blatt and Jack Mullins finished filling out some forms, then took off in their sheriff's car. Milo and I stood outside of the county building and noticed that Everett didn't smell as bad as usual. Over the years, the paper mills have given the city an unfortunate reputation.

"You hungry?" Milo asked, zipping his down vest over his plaid shirt.

"I never was," I said. "I'm sure not now."

He gazed up at the dark sky that had grown partially overcast. "I feel like a jerk."

I looked up at him, the graying blond hair falling over his forehead, the long face glum, the hazel eyes shadowy. "Why?"

He kicked at a candy bar wrapper on the sidewalk. "Hell, this is my first real homicide. *Two* of them, god-damn it, and I'm getting nowhere fast. I've got an election coming up next year. The citizens of Alpine will burn my butt if I don't find the killer."

Casually, I linked my arm through his. "Oh, come on, Milo, it's only been four days since Mark was murdered. The poor guy isn't even buried yet. Let's go have a cup of coffee."

Traffic was heavy on Wall Street for a Sunday night. Milo scowled at the cars, as if he disapproved of so much coming and going. He gave a tug and pulled me along the sidewalk. "Come on, Emma, let's go home."

We did, driving in virtual silence along the black ribbon of highway. He didn't use the flashing lights on the way back but managed to exceed the speed limit most of the time.

"What happened to Gibb's I.D.?" I finally asked, somewhere east of Index.

"Damned if I know." Milo passed a big truck with British Columbia plates. "Maybe whoever killed him didn't want his identity known right away."

"Where's his truck?" I braced myself as Milo passed an R.V. from California.

"We'll find it," said Milo. "That's hard to hide."

I kept quiet for a while, trying to figure out any connection between Mark Doukas and Gibb Frazier. It was possible that the two men weren't killed by the same person. The weapons had been different. Yet I didn't really believe we had two murderers on the loose. I was about to spring a theory on Milo when he spoke:

"Who's the guy, Emma?"

I blinked. "What guy?"

"The big city type staying up at the lodge." Milo kept his eyes on the road.

"Oh." I cleared my throat. "He's a newspaper investor. He also gives advice." I felt the color rising in my face and was glad Milo wasn't watching me.

"You need advice?" Milo's voice was a little too casual.

"Of course I do. This is a tricky business. Marius Vandeventer was sort of old-fashioned. And Ed Bronsky isn't exactly a ball of advertising fire. I can use some help in terms of increasing revenues, expanding circulation, new marketing approaches. . . ." And making an ass of myself by babbling like an idiot, I thought. "It's very complicated." After that I lapsed into silence.

So did Milo, at least for the next five minutes. When he spoke again, he glanced over at me. "He's a good-looking guy."

"He's been very successful." I'd had time to regain my poise. My voice sounded natural. "The newspaper broker I bought *The Advocate* through recommended calling in a consultant." It wasn't exactly the strict truth, but it was close. "Listen, Milo," I went on, changing the subject as he swung out from behind a timorous driver in an old Honda, "you've got to open up that mineshaft. Why not do it tomorrow during the funeral when Neeny's not there?"

He shot another look in my direction. "I won't be there either. I'm going to the funeral, remember?"

"Oh. I forgot." I had. The conversation about Tom Cavanaugh had rattled me. I cringed as Milo took the Alpine turnoff too sharply. "Couldn't your deputies do it?"

"Maybe." Milo finally slowed to forty miles per hour. The road into town was deserted, dark, and unfriendly on this moonless night. "Why are you so set on opening that mine?"

I tried to state my case logically. "Mark's death occurred shortly after he showed interest in the mine. Gibb went there, too. That's how your men found the extra copies of *The Advocate*. Maybe Gibb made the same discovery that Mark did. At the very least, there's something strange about Mineshaft Number Three."

Milo didn't respond until we turned onto Front Street. "I'll sleep on it. You could be right. I'm sure as hell not getting anywhere otherwise."

Just as he was pulling into an empty parking space two cars down from my Jag, I remembered to tell him about

Mark's deliberate maiming of Gibb. With Gibb dead, the revelation couldn't matter now. Milo was shocked.

"So Gibb had a motive," he mused, awestruck.

"Of sorts. But it's ten years old."

Milo drummed his fingers on the steering wheel. "I don't suppose Gibb killed Mark, then somebody—like Simon—took out Gibb for revenge." He sounded faintly hopeful.

"It's not impossible," I said, but secretly I felt that it was unlikely. Still, I was trying to bolster Milo's spirits.

He was silent for a few moments, then threw open the door. "Hey—let me check your car. For the dent." He looked a trifle condescending.

It was still windy, but there was no sign of rain. Milo had gotten out a flashlight and was examining the Jag's damaged fender. "Kind of odd. I wonder what they hit it with? It doesn't look like a baseball bat or a tool. The dent's too big."

I was about to ask if he wanted me to reiterate my car damage theory when a big white Cadillac careened down Front Street, braked with a screech, and almost ran into a mailbox. Eeeny Moroni stepped out, leaving his car parked halfway up the curb.

"What the hell's going on, Milo?" Eeeny moved toward us with his quick, fluid step. He nodded vaguely at me. "Emma, *cara mia*," he said without his usual fervor. "I just saw Billy and Jack at the Burger Barn. They said Gibb was dead."

"That's right." Milo was suitably grave. "Shot. He was found down by Reiter."

Eeeny had pulled out a big red and white handkerchief and used it to mop his face. "Holy Mother of God! What did Gibb ever do except shoot his mouth off now and then?" He gazed quizzically at me. "You heard from Chris again?"

"No." I shifted my shoulder bag to the other arm. "I thought you didn't think Chris was guilty."

Eeeny gestured with his hands. "I never said that. I only

warned Milo here that he didn't have much to use against Chris. Making wrongful arrests isn't a good habit for sheriffs to get into." He paced a bit, rubbing the back of his head. "Damn it, this is getting ugly. In all the years I was sheriff, I never had anything like this happen." He gazed at Milo, dark eyes sympathetic. "Look, if there's anything I can do, let me know. This thing with Gibb has got me down."

"And me." Milo sighed, leaning against a lamp post and looking as if he'd like to disappear inside his orange down vest. "Emma thinks we should open the mineshaft. Do you agree, Eeeny?"

The ex-sheriff made an expressive gesture with his hands. "I think Neeny would sue us. He's dead-set against it, you know."

"We can get a warrant," said Milo with a touch of truculence. "Neeny doesn't own this damned town."

Eeny wriggled his heavy eyebrows. "He used to. And he still has a pretty big chunk. What's the point, Milo? You don't really expect to find a six-inch vein of gold."

Milo sighed. "No." He glanced at me and looked away a bit too quickly. "I guess it was just a whim."

"It isn't a whim," I declared, getting a bit pugnacious. "As I explained to Milo, both Mark and Gibb were up at that mineshaft not long before they were killed. It's the one thing they have in common. So maybe there's something about it that . . ."

Eeny was giving me a withering look. "Emma, *mio cor*, *dolce* Emma, you sound as pigheaded as Vida. That mineshaft has been closed off for fifty years. What could it be that would cause murder?" He turned to Milo. "Look for rational answers, concrete evidence, real motives. You need facts, not fancies. Hey, Milo, do your homework. You've got an election coming up next year."

"Don't remind me," Milo muttered, once again the picture of gloom.

Eeny danced over to Milo and took him by the arm.

"Come on, *amico*, let's go to Mugs Ahoy and have a beer. Emma?"

I shook my head. "Thanks, Eeeny, but no, I quit drinking after a rowdy evening of bridge. Besides, I'm beat. You two go cry in your beer without me."

Eeeny shrugged and Milo uttered no protest. The past and present sheriffs moved off down the street while I got into my Jaguar to head for home. I wondered if Vida had heard the news about Gibb. I wanted very much to call her, but I was afraid Tom Cavanaugh would think I was checking up on him.

By the time I pulled into my carport, I realized I was being ridiculous. What Tom thought shouldn't make any difference. I was involved in a double homicide investigation. I strode into the house and dialed Vida's number. Nobody answered. I put the phone down with an uneasy feeling, triggered by various fears. It was after ten o'clock. I decided to wait and call Vida again in half an hour.

But it was six in the morning when I woke up on the sofa with the phone off the hook and a can of Pepsi spilled on the rug. I hadn't been lying when I told Eeeny Moroni that I was beat. Murder, it seemed, was an exhausting business.

Chapter Fourteen

By the time I put on the coffee, took a bath, got dressed, and ate some toast, it was almost seven. If Vida had to be in Seattle for the funeral at ten, she was probably up. To my relief, she answered on the first ring. I'd made up my mind not to ask any questions about her dinner guest. Not that I was jealous of Vida—she was older than Tom and not exactly my idea of a femme fatale. Besides, it was none of my business.

"Where the hell were you at ten o'clock last night?" I blurted.

There was a pause. Inwardly, I groaned at my lack of self-control. Then Vida's voice caromed off my ear. "At the Burger Barn, trying to get Billy to make sense about poor Gibb. Where were *you* at eleven?"

I laughed. I couldn't help it. Vida made a noise of exasperation. "Sorry, Vida," I apologized. "I'm kind of strung out. I fell asleep on the sofa and somehow knocked the receiver off."

I expected her to commiserate, but she was already off on another tangent. "I've already written up Gibb's obit. I'll drop it off on the way to Seattle. I called his sister last night, but she works and can't come up from Portland until the weekend. Al Driggers will have to wait till Saturday to hold the funeral."

It seemed that Vida had matters well in hand. I knew she was in a rush, so I told her I'd talk to her when she got back.

It was a busy morning at *The Advocate*, with the usual

Monday prepublication pressures and the added burden of at least thirty phone calls inquiring about Gibb Frazier. There could have been more, but it seemed that half the town had headed out for Mark Doukas's funeral in Seattle.

By two P.M., I had my share of the day's work in hand. I'd left some extra space for any late-breaking news on the homicides and reserved a small box on page three for an account of Mark's services. Vida could whip that out when she returned. I was just making some final corrections on a feature Carla had written about Linda Grant's personal fitness program when Tom Cavanaugh strolled in, looking resplendent in jogging togs.

Tom didn't sit down, saying he had to get back to the lodge because he'd asked for a lot of information to be faxed there. "I'll get back to you after I get a chance to go over it. I'd like to meet with Ed, too." He moved a step closer to my desk. "How are you doing? I couldn't believe the news when Vida got the call about Gibb last night."

"It's getting pretty grim around here," I admitted. "People are scared."

"It's not a random killer," Tom said. "Gibb Frazier must have been deliberately lured to that gravel pit. Vida's nephew said there was no I.D. on him."

"I agree." I tapped a half page of hard copy. "I wrote a short editorial to that effect this morning, urging Alpiners not to panic. At least four callers today insisted we've got a serial killer on the loose. That's nonsense, I think." Frankly, I wasn't sure which was worse—some sociopath indiscriminately knocking off the population, or a cold-blooded murderer with a motive. "How was dinner?" I couldn't resist the question.

Tom grinned. "Gruesome. Chicken and dumplings. The chicken was almost done and I could have used the dumplings in a softball game. Slow pitch. But Vida's a font of information. She ought to be your ad manager instead of Ed."

"Anybody ought to be instead of Ed," I moaned, glancing out into the news office to make sure he wasn't around. "Say, will you do me a favor?" Tom inclined his head, a mannerism I remembered as tacit assent. "I was just going to call Bill Blatt and ask him to get a warrant to open the mineshaft at Icicle Creek. If Vida isn't back by three, will you go up there with me?"

Tom glanced at his watch. "Okay. Shall I pick you up?"

Since the back road to Icicle Creek went past the ski lodge, and I also wanted to check the mail at my house, I told Tom I'd drive. As soon as he left, I called the sheriff's office. Bill Blatt hemmed and hawed, insisting that in Milo's absence, he didn't have the authority to issue a warrant. I figured he was hedging because he was scared of Neeny Doukas. But if we were going to have a look at that mineshaft, we'd better do it before Neeny got back to Alpine.

"To hell with Billy and the stupid warrant," I said, hurrying past Carla to the door.

Carla looked up from her portable makeup mirror where she was plucking her eyebrows. "What?"

"Never mind." I banged out of the office. Carla was almost as oblivious to the two murders as she was to everything else that qualified as news in Alpine. She'd also spelled the high school P.E. teacher's name as Linda *Grunt*. Some day I was going to ask to see Carla's diploma from the University of Washington.

There was nothing from Adam in my mailbox. I would have to call him after five, when the rates were down. In the present atmosphere of murder, I began to worry about him, too. He might be thousands of miles away, but I felt as if the danger in Alpine could somehow span the Pacific Ocean and menace my son. It was a silly notion, but it wouldn't go away.

The ski lodge was a classic structure, four stories of pine logs on the exterior, knotty pine interior, stone fireplaces, and snug little rooms with bright plaid curtains. The renovations that were being completed included plumbing and electrical updates, conversion of the basement pool room into a conference center, and expanded kitchen facilities. Perhaps there was still hope for a new restaurant after all.

I had purposely gotten to the lodge half an hour early because I wanted to talk to Heather Bardeen. As luck would have it, Monday was her day off. Disappointed, I went to the pay phone in the lobby to call Kip, the middle MacDuff, and ask if he would fill in for Gibb and use his pickup to take the paper into Monroe. Before I could find a quarter, Phoebe Pratt Doukas came through the main entrance with her niece, Chaz. I was startled. Did her return mean that Neeny was back, too? I greeted Phoebe with more warmth than I actually felt.

"I couldn't bear any more grief," said Phoebe in a broken voice. She was dressed in black crepe with lots of pearls and dangerously high heels. "I couldn't even go up to the casket. I'd rather remember Mark the way I last saw him, with those dark eyes looking out at me from under that baseball cap." Briefly, Phoebe turned away, lower lip quivering.

For all that my memories of Mark weren't so fond, I certainly mourned his untimely death and didn't have to feign sympathy. "He was too young," I said. "Violent death is always a waste." So were my words of comfort, I decided, but Phoebe seemed to drink them in like rare wine.

"Isn't that the truth?" She had turned back to me, tugging at her black kidskin gloves. "I was so glad to head back to Alpine. Seattle is too big. Neeny rode in Al Driggers's limo, but I took my own car." The statement seemed straightforward, but I wondered if there hadn't been a scene with Simon. Whether or not he now knew his father had married Phoebe, Simon Doukas would not have been keen on letting her join the family in what Vida termed Al's *Mourningmobile*.

"It was a wonderful service, but *soooo* long," Phoebe was saying as Chaz, apparently on break from her job at the desk, went back to work. "Greek, you know. Then there was a reception at the church, but the real wake will be at the house after they go to the cemetery."

I calculated. The funeral had probably been over between eleven and noon; the reception wouldn't go on for more than an hour unless the ouzo flowed like motor oil. If the mourners actually formed a cortege, they could hardly break the speed limit going up Stevens Pass. I figured I was safe at the mineshaft until almost four P.M.

"How is the family?" I inquired politely.

Phoebe's eyes got very round, and she tugged at her rope of pearls. "Poor dears! Doukums is such a strong old bear, but inside, his heart is breaking. I try to treat him like a china doll." The image she had conjured up was of a bearded Kewpie, watching daytime television. "Cece is ever so brave, and Simon is like a rock! Of course," she went on, lowering her voice and leaning down since her normal height and abnormal shoes gave her at least a six-inch advantage over me, "Cece must be gulping tranquilizers. And Simon never is one to show much emotion, is he?"

"That all depends," I replied, thinking of his tears upon seeing Chris and his anger upon meeting with me. No doubt he'd have apoplexy Wednesday when the paper came out. But my real concern wasn't centered on the grieving Doukases. I didn't have a lot of time to spare, and I wanted to steer the conversation to another topic. "You must make good time in that Town Car," I remarked, trying to sound casually congenial. "I had my Jag dented over the weekend. Have you gotten that blue paint off yet? Or will you have to have the whole car redone?"

Caught off guard, Phoebe teetered a bit on her high heels. "I really haven't had time to tend to it." She tucked a few stray curls under the wisp of black veiling atop her head. "There's been so many other things going on."

I gave a sympathetic nod. "How true. Edna Mae Dalrymple said it was so bizarre how that bucket of paint blew over just as you drove down Front Street Wednesday night." I gave her my blandest gaze and hoped Edna Mae would forgive me for misquoting her. She sure wasn't likely to forgive me for bidding five diamonds.

Phoebe doesn't have the quickest mind I've ever encountered, but the implication of my words eventually took hold. "Oh—well ... that's right, I made a quick trip downtown the other night." I noticed she didn't refer to Wednesday as the night of the murder. Phoebe was virtually whispering now: "I wanted to see Simon about a legal matter, and Cece said on the phone that after he dropped his nephew off, he was stopping by the Clemans Building to pick up some papers. But he wasn't there."

"Gibb was, though," I said with feigned innocence.

Phoebe's carefully etched eyebrows lifted. "Gibb? Oh! Yes, poor Gibb! Isn't this all so *awful*? My, yes, it was the last time I saw him alive. He honked at me and told me the *naughtiest* story! I was *soooo* embarrassed, I couldn't laugh. But I had to giggle a bit on my way home." She gave me a meaningful look. Was it a question or a confirmation? I couldn't be sure. If *home* meant Neeny's house, maybe Phoebe was ready to acknowledge that they were man and wife. Was she just fishing? Or verifying that she'd gone nowhere else that night?

Tom was coming down the wide stairway, dressed in sweater and slacks.

I had one more comment for Phoebe in my arsenal: "It's too bad Chris never got that letter you sent to him in Hawaii. When he gets settled, do you want it forwarded?"

Phoebe pulled at a pearl earring. "Oh!" She was clearly marshaling her thoughts. "No, no, it was only my belated condolences on Margaret's passing. Though," she went on, looking over my shoulder to give Tom an inquisitive stare, "when you get an address for the boy, let me know." For a brief instant, her face sagged, and she gripped my wrist. "Emma, does the sheriff really think Chris killed Mark?"

Startled by the sudden shift in her emotions, my reply tumbled out mindlessly. "The sheriff doesn't know anything." Immediately I felt a pang of remorse. Milo Dodge had enough problems without my picturing him as an imbecile.

Her composure restored, Phoebe gave Tom a coquettish smile and teetered off. I didn't waste any time but hurried Tom along to the parking lot. On the way to Icicle Creek, I told him about my conversation with Phoebe.

"Let me get this straight," said Tom as we drove past the high school football field. "Phoebe claimed earlier she hadn't left the Doukas house. Now she admits she did, but says she went to meet with Simon at his office. He wasn't there, right?"

"Which means Simon was out, Cece was alone, Phoebe was tooling around in the Town Car, joshing with Gibb, and since she was Neeny's alibi, that goes out the window, too." Why had Mark gone back to Mineshaft Number Three after dark? Why had he called both Milo Dodge and Eeeny Moroni? "Hey! Phoebe said something odd—about how she'd like to remember Mark the way she saw him last, wearing a baseball cap. But the only time I know of that he ever wore a baseball cap was when he borrowed Chris's—the night of the murder."

Tom gave me an indulgent look. "You may be reaching a bit on this one. Are you saying that Phoebe saw Mark just before he was killed?"

I braked for the blinker light at the three-way stop below First Hill. "That's right. Mark must have come to the house. There wouldn't have been time for him to go anywhere else after he left his parents' place. I doubt he would have come to see Phoebe, but why didn't Neeny see him? Or did she prevent Mark from talking to his grandfather? I honestly don't think Neeny saw Mark that night. Neeny has a passel of unpleasant traits, but he's not a liar."

I had sat through the passing of two cars, one van, and a logging truck. Tom gave me a gentle nudge. "If this were San Francisco, you'd have been arrested for erecting an illegal barricade by now. You'd better concentrate on your driving, Emma."

I did, or at least tried to, but I was convinced I was

right. Mark had gone to see Neeny; Phoebe had put him off; shortly afterward, she had left the house, supposedly to see Simon. Had Mark told her what he'd found at Mineshaft Number Three? It was possible.

It had taken us ten minutes to get to the turnaround by the mineshaft. The wind of the previous night had dwindled to a mere breeze, and the clouds had blown away. For the end of September, it was quite warm. Tom and I gazed at the entrance to the mineshaft in silence.

He was the first to speak. "Emma, nobody's been in this thing." He pointed to the moss-covered wooden doorway. "It looks as if somebody tried." He pointed to a half-dozen recent tears in the smooth green moss. "But that's as far as they got."

"Mark, maybe. With the crowbar." I made a face. "I could be wrong about this whole thing." My ears were pricked for the sound of any oncoming cars. We had skirted the cemetery but there had been no sign of Mark's funeral cortege. I glanced at my watch; it was bang-up three o'clock. The Doukases and the other half of Alpine could be arriving in town any minute.

My taupe flats pawed the ground like an anxious pony. "Somebody said—was it Gibb?—there was another entrance."

Tom walked up by the creek. I was pleased, if not exactly surprised, that he was being such a good sport about all this. Of course he was a journalist at heart and as curious as I was. Still, Alpine and its residents really had nothing to do with him.

He was about ten feet away, pushing at some vine maples. "Nothing here that I can see." He went around to the other side. I waited while he poked among some big boulders. "Say, Emma, these rocks have been moved recently."

I joined him. With a hefty heave, Tom displaced one of the boulders. We knelt down and peered into what must have been an offshoot of the main shaft. I let out a little shriek, and Tom swore under his breath.

Grinning back at us was a skull.

* * *

It took us at least a full minute to regain our mental equilibrium. Tom looked at me, and I looked at him. Leaves rustled above us. A chipmunk chattered somewhere close by. A blue jay called to its mate. The creek tumbled down the hill, rushing to the river. The amber and bronze vine maples bent low to form arches over our heads. It was all so peaceful, so natural, with the autumn sun filtering its golden light through the trees.

"Hell," breathed Tom, shaking his head. "When's the sheriff due back?"

I didn't feel like standing up just yet. "Any time," I murmured. I made a shaky gesture at the hole in the ground. "Is it just a skull, or . . ." I left the rest of the sentence unspoken.

Tom swiveled around and removed the other big boulder. He grimaced. "It's a whole skeleton." He put up his hand. "Don't look, Emma."

"A skeleton shouldn't scare me. After all, it's almost Halloween." My attempt at smiling failed.

"Seen one skeleton, seen 'em all, I suppose." Tom sat next to me and put an arm around my shoulders. "We'd better head back."

"Right." But I still wasn't ready to get on my feet. "How long has the . . . body been there, do you think?"

"I haven't any idea. It could even be some miner who got killed 'way back when." His dark blue eyes scanned my face. "Do you remember hearing anything about an accident?"

"No. But that doesn't mean there wasn't one. It's been—what? Seventy, eighty years ago." I tensed as a car approached and slowed down. "Damn. Somebody's coming."

We both stood up, Tom supporting me until I got my balance. A blue car had pulled in next to the Jag. I couldn't see the make of it from where we were. A moment later, Vida trudged across the little clearing, her black felt gaucho hat tipped over one ear.

"That knuckleheaded nephew of mine said you'd been calling about opening the mineshaft, so I figured you'd come up to—" She stopped as she took in the somber expressions on our faces. "Oh, Lord! What now?"

We told her. A mere skeleton held no terrors for Vida. She marched over to the open ground and bent down, exposing an inch of white slip under her black suit skirt. Clutching her hat to her head, she turned to face us. "I need a closer look. Tommy, can you get this out of here or will it crumble?"

Tommy, I thought. Had Vida adopted him? Tom didn't seem to notice; he was shaking his head. "I don't think I should try. What do you want to see?"

Vida jabbed a finger at the open ground. "There's a religious medal around the neck." She screwed up her face in the effort of recollection. "What do you Catholics call those things?"

I hazarded a guess. "Is it a St. Christopher Medal?"

"No, not that." Vida made more facial contortions. "Something marvelous." Her face lighted up, and she snapped her fingers. "That's it! A Miraculous Medal!"

"That's right," agreed Tom. He touched his chest. "I wear one myself."

Vida was brushing dirt off her black patent leather shoes. She gave us a sidelong look. "Yes. So did Hector Ramirez."

Vida and Tom stayed at the mineshaft while I went to get Milo. As I came to the intersection of CR 187 and Eighth Street, I saw the long funeral cortege wending its way into the cemetery. Vida had said Milo had left after the church service because he'd learned that Gibb Frazier's truck had been found at Reiter Ponds. Milo might have returned to Alpine by now.

He had, in fact, arriving about two minutes ahead of me. "Emma, we found—" Milo stopped, noting my wild-eyed appearance. "What's wrong? You seen a ghost?"

"Yes." I collapsed in the outer office's nearest chair.

Jack Mullins and Bill Blatt gaped at me from over the counter. In a garbled manner, I told them about the discovery Tom and I had made, along with the conclusions Vida had given.

"Jeez." Milo draped his big frame over a chair that was turned backward. He was wearing a rumpled gray suit, so outmoded that I suspected he had bought it for his wedding twenty-five years ago. "What makes Vida think it's Hector?" Milo's long face registered doubt.

Tom and I had been equally skeptical, but Vida had offered convincing arguments. "First," I recounted, "she remembered the medal Hector wore around his neck. Second, she swears she never discounted foul play. And third, she insists it couldn't be anybody else."

Milo hung his arms over the back of the chair. "I'll go along with reason number one, but I won't buy the rest of it." He paused as Jack Mullins passed out coffee in paper cups. "If Vida thought somebody killed Hector fourteen years ago, why didn't she speak up then?"

"She didn't want to believe it," I said, quoting her indirectly. "But the more she thought about it, the more likely it seemed. Vida kept quiet—" I raised a hand to fend off Milo's protest. "I know, I know, it doesn't sound like Vida, but she felt Neeny Doukas had Sheriff Moroni in his pocket and wouldn't press for an investigation."

Milo's head jerked up. "She thinks Neeny killed Hector?"

"She wouldn't put it past him," I allowed, trying to remember exactly how Vida had phrased it. "But mostly, she figured Neeny would say good riddance. He'd prefer that Hector not be found, dead or alive. If Hector had been killed, then he'd be some sort of martyr in Margaret's eyes, and Neeny couldn't go on saying what a rotter the guy was." There was still a glimmer of doubt in Milo's gaze. "Hey, you know these people better than I do. Vida's perception of Neeny hits home with me."

Milo was rubbing at his long chin. Bill Blatt looked

anxious, as if he didn't know whether to side with his aunt or his boss. Jack Mullins put on another pot of coffee.

"As for her third rationale," I went on when none of the men made a comment, "Vida will allow for a vagrant or an unknown prospector. But otherwise, she says nobody else has ever completely disappeared from Alpine."

Milo scoffed. "That's a crock of bull. I can think of three people in the last five years who—"

"So can Vida," I interrupted, my spirits restored and my need for action acute. I stood up. "But two of them were husbands escaping from impossible wives and one was a teenaged girl who ran off with her boyfriend from Index. Come on, Milo, let's get back there before the Doukases finish their graveside services."

Milo and his deputies led the way out to Icicle Creek. On the hillside in the cemetery, we could see at least a hundred people gathered under a green canopy. The line of parked cars reached almost back to the road.

At the mineshaft, Vida was sitting on a fallen log, a camera in her hand. Tom stood at the edge of the creek, probably watching for trout. I watched Milo as he shambled over to view the remains. His deputies followed him, somberly removing their regulation hats.

"I'll be damned," murmured Milo after an appropriate moment of silence. "It's *somebody*, all right."

"Of course it's somebody, you ninny," said Vida in annoyance. She had scrambled up from the log, damp earth clinging to her black skirt. "It's Hector Ramirez. Get Dr. Starr to dig out his dental charts."

Milo shot Vida a baleful look but didn't argue. "You three head out of here. There'll be all hell to pay when Neeny comes along and sees what's happening."

Vida glanced at me. "Do you have everything? I got some pictures. I had a couple of shots left over from the funeral."

I winced a bit at the gruesome tone *The Advocate* would be taking this week. "I'd like some positive I.D. before we send the paper into Monroe tomorrow," I told Milo.

He glared at me. "I can't promise that. What if Hector never went to the dentist?"

Vida pointed her camera at the sheriff. "Here, Milo, I want a picture of you so we can write a cutline saying 'Skykomish County sheriff Milo Dodge asserted today that Hector Ramirez never saw a dentist in his entire life.' Lift your chin, Milo. You look like you ate a bug."

Milo looked like he'd prefer eating Vida. A couple of cars passing by on CR 187 alerted me to the probability that the graveside services were concluded. "We're staying, Milo," I declared. "I wouldn't miss Neeny's reaction for the world." In my head, I was already rearranging the paper: Carla's feature on Linda Grant would have to be put on hold; maybe my piece on experimental logging practices would have to wait, too.

Milo gave me a fierce stare, then gestured impatiently at Jack Mullins. "Go get the van. We've got to move that skeleton out of here. See if you can bring Sam Heppner or Dwight Gould back with you. We could use some other deputies to help out." He turned back to me, fists on hips. "This isn't a tourist trap, Emma, it's law enforcement work. I want you people gone."

I set my jaw. "We're the press. We have a right to be here."

He jerked his hand at Tom. "He's not the press. He's a . . . *tourist*."

Tom strolled over to Milo, his engaging smile in place. "Actually, Sheriff, I'm the press, too. Would you like a list of my credentials?" He started to reach for his wallet.

Milo threw up his hands. "Never mind." Abruptly, he loped off to the open ground where the skeleton lay in blissful ignorance. At that moment, the Driggers Funeral Home car pulled up at the edge of the road. It was beginning to look like a parking lot out there.

Neeny Doukas, assisted by Simon, came tramping across the clearing. In contrast to his impeccably tailored son, Neeny was wearing a baggy black suit with a crooked knit tie. His olive complexion had a tinge of gray. "What the hell is going on here? This is private property!"

"It's a crime scene, Neeny," said Milo with commendable dignity. "We've found more remains."

"More?" Neeny's dark eyes bulged; a vein throbbed on his forehead. "Whaddaya mean, more? My grandson didn't come apart, did he? Whadda'd we bury? *Pieces?*"

Eeeny Moroni's white Cadillac and Phoebe's red Lincoln had also pulled in. The limo was now disgorging Cecelia Doukas, Jennifer, and Kent MacDuff. Al Driggers tried to maintain his stately decorum as he came from the front seat to assist the women.

"Here," said Milo, taking Neeny by the arm that Simon released with reluctance, "we found a skeleton. You don't have to look."

"Look, schmook," said Neeny, waving Milo away. "Lemme go, you dinks." He glanced back at Simon, making sure his son didn't miss the point. "No skeleton's gonna shake me up. I've had enough crap in the last few days." He tramped past Milo and Vida. I stood between Tom and Simon, watching Neeny bend slightly at the waist. For a fleeting moment, I thought I saw him flinch. But when he straightened up and turned back to face us, he appeared as formidable as ever.

"What were you doing digging around here without my permission?" he demanded of the sheriff.

With an air of deference, Milo Dodge indicated the strips of yellow and black crime scene tape that fluttered in the breeze. "We have a right to be here, Neeny. You want your grandson's killer caught, don't you?"

"You think the killer buried hisself? Are you nuts, kid?" He gave a sudden shake of his head, then waved back at the skeleton. "Naw, I guess not. At least you found that."

I held my breath, waiting for Milo to reveal the truth. But whether he wanted to shield Tom and me or take credit for the discovery himself was unclear. In any event, he just stood there stoically, as the others approached the mineshaft. Simon tried to steer them away, especially the women.

"A tramp, from the Depression," soothed Simon, putting a protective arm around Cece. She was ashen and fragile, in simple, expensive black.

Kent MacDuff marched straight to the open ground. He stopped abruptly, almost lost his balance, and took a deep breath. "Hey," he said, his florid face suddenly pale, "at least we know that guy didn't kill Mark. He was too skinny."

Kent's attempt at bravado fell flat. Phoebe was clinging to Neeny; Jennifer had collapsed on the log abandoned by Vida; Al Driggers was looking for someone to comfort; and Eeeny Moroni was dancing around the mineshaft like a rooster gone berserk.

"Goddamn it, Milo, this used to be a quiet little town! What the hell is happening now? I feel like moving to L-Freaking-A!" The ex-sheriff gave Milo an ugly look.

I felt sorry for Milo. "Can it, Eeeny," I said. "It's not Milo's fault that there's a killer loose."

Vida chimed in. "It sure isn't, you old noodle," she said to Moroni. "In fact, that bunch of bones over there probably got killed while *you* were sheriff."

Moroni sneered at Vida who tipped her gaucho hat over one eye and sneered right back.

I intervened again. "Listen, all this wrangling isn't getting us anywhere. We're hindering, not helping, Sheriff Dodge. Does anyone here have any idea who this might be?" I made a stabbing gesture in the direction of the skeleton.

Judging from the shocked looks of my audience, most of them hadn't considered the possibility that the skeleton had once been a real person who had walked and talked among them.

"Oh, no!" gasped Phoebe.

"Hell," breathed Kent.

"Indeed," murmured Simon.

"Screw off," muttered Neeny.

Jennifer began to cry softly. Al Driggers, finally discovering an object for his professional sympathy, went over to the log.

To my surprise, Cece Doukas asked the first intelligent question of the impromptu gathering: "Are there any clothes or other objects that might be identifiable?" So stunned was everyone that she apparently mistook their blank faces for confusion. "I mean keys or jewelry or possibly credit cards. Even a hobo might carry something other than a little bag on a stick."

Again, I waited for Milo to make a revelation, this time about the Miraculous Medal. But Milo was proving remarkably reticent. "We'll have any information available after we've removed the remains." He looked past the little group to the road. "Here come my deputies now. I'd appreciate it if you'd all move on out of here. I'd like to have the van come in as close as possible." His voice was unusually formal.

To my amazement, the Doukas clan began to disperse. Only Eeeny Moroni stayed put, looking sheepish. "Hey, Milo, *amico*, I apologize a thousand times." He put a hand on Milo's rumpled suit sleeve. "I'm what you call, you know, distraught. Mark's funeral today, Gibb getting killed, now this . . . I spent my life chasing shoplifters and catching people breaking the speed limit. Maybe," he confessed with an off-center grin, "I'm jealous. This is bad stuff—but it's big stuff. And it's *your* stuff, not mine."

Milo shrugged. "Forget it." He glanced at Tom and Vida and me. "You coming or going?"

"I'll be at the office for quite a while. Will you let us know if you find anything else?" I inquired. "Like what Cece suggested?"

Milo gave me a ghostly smile. "Sure. Thanks, Emma."

I stared at Milo. "Huh?" But he had already turned away, to where Jack Mullins and Bill Blatt were taking pictures of the skeleton. Then it dawned on me: Milo had appreciated my support in front of the others. Somehow, I was touched. And inexplicably pleased.

* * *

"Do all doctors get rich?"

I held the phone out an inch from my ear; I wasn't sure I'd heard my son correctly. "What did you say, Adam?"

"I was thinking," he said, sounding vaguely muffled, "that maybe I'd like to go into medicine. Save lives and like that. How long does it take?"

"Many years and many dollars," I replied, vexed. This was not the time for Adam to discuss his life's goals with me. "Are you certain you mailed that material?"

"Yeah, like I told you. I guess I had too much to do to get to the post office the other day before it closed. Plus I had to look for Chris's denim jacket. It was under the bathroom sink. Then I found all those other letters and junk that belonged to Chris's mom. So I put everything in a box and shipped it off to you. The guy at the post office said it should get to Alpine in five days." Adam sounded as if he were talking to an imbecile.

I sighed. That meant tomorrow. If I were lucky. "Okay. Did it cost much?"

"About four bucks. There wasn't a lot, just letters and stuff. I kept the rest, it looked pretty useless."

I hadn't any idea what Adam was talking about. "The rest of *what*?"

A door banged across the Pacific, and I heard distant voices. Adam had company. "Papers, you know, like old bills and insurance policies and car registrations—stuff like that. Chris got the insurance, so he doesn't need that, and I thought it would be kind of grim to send him his mom's death certificate and all the hospital stuff."

"Probably," I agreed. "But don't toss it out. He may want all that some day. Especially the death certificate. They cost money."

Apparently, Adam had turned away from the receiver to say something to his friends. When he gave his full attention back to me, it was as if I hadn't spoken. "Like I was thinking—maybe not saving lives. I mean, if you can't, then you must feel rotten when a patient dies, right? So being a baby doctor would be better. What's a *live* birth?"

I screwed up my face. "What do you think it is, dopey?" I was in my editorial office, wishing Milo would pass on any new information he might have gleaned from the remains at the mineshaft. It was after six o'clock, and Vida was out in the front office, typing like mad. Tom was there, too, answering the phones that were now bringing us renewed interest from the outside media.

"Yeah, I know what live birth *sounds* like," said Adam as masculine laughter erupted in the background. "But it can't be what I think it is. See, I'm looking at Mrs. Ramirez's records from when Chris took her to the hospital when she got so sick with the cancer. It says right here on this form: *Live Births: None*. So what does it mean?"

I almost dropped the phone. "Say that again?"

Adam's sigh vibrated over the ocean cable. Then he repeated the information. "So if it means what it sounds like, did Mrs. Ramirez find Chris under a rock? Hey, Mom, you used to think you were really cool with your open-minded sex education. I think you missed something!"

I stared at my computer screen, which seemed to look very fuzzy. "I think I did, too. Adam, what hospital was that?"

"Huh? Oh, not that big one up on the hill. It's the other one: Kuakini. Hey, the guys want to know if you think Chris is in L.A."

"I have no idea." I wished I did, but there wasn't time to speculate about Chris's whereabouts just now. "Is there a doctor's name on that form?"

"I think so. . . . Yeah, here it is, Steven Furokawa. He's Chris's doctor, too. Nice guy." Adam responded away from the receiver to a comment about girls and Malibu.

I saw Vida shoot an inquiring glance through the open door, then plod back to her desk. "Have you got a number for Dr. Furokawa?"

The noise inside Adam's room was building. "What?

Oh—a telephone number? No, but there's a phone book here some place. . . ." At last, he came up with Steven Furokawa's business and residential listings. "Hey, Mom, what's this all about? I haven't made up my mind yet. I just thought that being a doctor might be—you know, like fulfilling. You don't have to start checking around for—"

"Put a sock in it," I said, then added on a gentler note: "I love you. Hang up."

He did, and I immediately dialed Steven Furokawa, M.D., at his Honolulu clinic. To my relief, he was in; to my amazement, his receptionist put me through. In my best professional voice, I identified myself. "I understand you treated the late Margaret Ramirez for cancer. Her nephew was murdered five days ago, and her husband's body may have been dug up from an abandoned mineshaft this afternoon. Over the weekend, there was another homicide. Margaret's son, Chris, is also a patient of yours. He's wanted for questioning." If all that didn't impress Dr. Furokawa, I couldn't think what would—except telling him there was five hundred pounds of TNT under his office chair. "Doctor, I don't want you to breach patient confidentiality, but can you tell me this: did Margaret Ramirez ever bear a child?"

Silence. Then a quick breath. "You said yourself she had a son, Ms. Lord." His voice was dry, almost humorous.

Obviously, I couldn't cut corners. I explained about the admitting form from Kuakini, implying that I had it sitting right in front of me.

More silence. Then Dr. Furokawa spoke in a brisker tone. "I don't recall. I have a very busy practice. Mrs. Ramirez's records aren't available right now. Even if they were, I couldn't tell you."

"Doctor, this is extremely important. Three people have already died. The county sheriff can get an order to send Mrs. Ramirez's records to Alpine. But that could take a couple of days, maybe more." Doggedly, I kept speaking. This wasn't the first time I'd had to pry material out of an unwilling source. "You must have treated Margaret for some time. *Think*. Had she borne a child?"

Now the silence seemed to fill the thousands of miles between us, creeping along the ocean floor, washing over the coast, rising up into the mountains.

"No." Dr. Furokawa uttered the word with reluctance. "That's all I can tell you."

It was enough.

Chapter Fifteen

"WE'VE GOT TO go into Seattle tomorrow," declared Vida, ripping her account of Mark's funeral out of the typewriter. "That's where Margaret supposedly had Chris, you know. His birth would be registered at the King County Courthouse."

I was pacing the office. "It's a long shot," I said for the fourth time. "But Chris looks too much like a Doukas to be anybody else."

"I can go to Seattle," volunteered Tom.

He struck me as a bit subdued, and I wondered if he would like to have talked to Adam. But that would not be a good idea. My son didn't know that his father was in Alpine. Indeed, my son knew only the barest facts about Tom Cavanaugh. I'd always felt it was better that way.

"There are a couple of people I should see while I'm in the area anyway," Tom went on. "You two have a paper to get out."

Vida and I exchanged glances. "True," I said. Tom had gotten us a pizza and some salad. I sat down at Ed's desk. "Okay, let's nail this down."

Tom nodded. "Remember, though—even if you're right, it may have nothing to do with these deaths."

I didn't argue the point. Just because Margaret and Hector Ramirez were not Chris's natural parents didn't solve the murder investigation. But I still wanted to know who he really was. I doubted very much that Chris himself was aware of his parents' identity. In this age of candor about such matters, I found that suspicious.

Vida, who had been leafing through the 1971 volume of *Advocates*, clapped her hands. "Here! Chris's birth announcement—'August twenty-one, 1971, to Hector and Margaret Ramirez, formerly of Alpine, a boy, seven pounds, ten ounces, at Seattle.' "

Tom jotted the information down in a small leather-bound notebook. "Do you know where Hector and Margaret lived while they were in Seattle?" The question was for Vida.

She took off her hat and vigorously scratched her head. "Ooooh—not really, Tommy. A rental, out in the south end, I think. Neeny might know, or Simon and Cece. But even if they'd tell you, I doubt they'd have an address after all this time."

The phone rang. It was Milo, and his voice sounded strained. "Doc Dewey's here. He says the bones are at least five and maybe fifty years old. But because the clothing was so decomposed—all that damp up there by the creek—it's impossible for him to pinpoint without lab work."

"What about Dr. Starr?" I asked.

"He's got Jeannie Clay checking their records." The sheriff spoke away from the phone, apparently to Doc Dewey Senior. "No papers, of course, but there was that medal, a belt buckle, a key chain, and a wedding ring. Kind of fancy, gold with a sort of scroll design."

"Are the bones the right size for Hector?" I was making notes of my own on Ed's memo pad.

"Doc says yes, as far as he can tell." Milo's tone was grudging.

I gave Vida and Tom a thumbs-up sign. "Can we quote you as saying this raises the possibility of the remains being those of Hector Ramirez?"

A heavy sigh fell on my ear. "I guess. Hell, Emma, it could be Elvis."

"Or Elvis. Thank you, Sheriff Dodge." I imagined Milo's expression and tried not to laugh. "What about foul play?"

"Doc can't tell yet. No sign of a blow to the head. Poison, strangulation, stabbing would all be hard to figure at this point. A bullet might leave some mark on the bone, but there's a lot of discoloration." Milo paused again as Doc Dewey spoke to him. "We're going to dig some more in that hole. If the victim was shot, the bullet may be in the ground. As the body decomposed, Doc says the shell would eventually work itself into the earth."

I grimaced at my pizza. "Right." Hastily, I tried to think of any other questions I should put to Milo while I had him on the line. Then I remembered to ask about Gibb's truck. That part of the investigation had gotten shunted aside in the wake of the discovery at the mineshaft.

Milo couldn't add much, however. "It was just sitting there at Reiter, where all the fishermen park. Gibb's I.D. was on the floor. So were his keys. Lots of prints, mostly smudged, but we may find something yet."

After I'd hung up, Vida and Tom mulled over the information I'd relayed from Milo. "I wish," said Vida, rubbing at her eyes, "I could remember what Margaret's wedding ring looked like. It just might have been a gold band. I doubt that Hector could have afforded a diamond set."

Tom polished off his third slice of pizza. "How long were they away from Alpine?" Again, he addressed Vida as the font of all knowledge.

Vida briskly stirred dressing into her salad. "A year, maybe. I know they missed one Christmas, because Cece told me she was glad they were gone so that she wouldn't have to host what could be an awkward family gathering. But they were back by the next holidays, because Fuzzy Baugh wanted to borrow Chris to be Baby New Year for the Kiwanis festivities in Old Mill Park. Margaret wouldn't hear of it, since we had three feet of snow on the ground."

Tom made more notes. I ate more pizza.

Vida stared off into space, glasses in her lap. At last she spoke. "We're assuming the bones belong to Hector," she began, obviously having given her theory careful thought.

"Then we must assume Hector was murdered." She looked at both of us for confirmation. We nodded in unison. "Mark may have found the body when he was prospecting. That could be what set him off. But who did he tell? Not Kevin MacDuff. Could he have given his story to the murderer? Did he know he was talking to the murderer? And Gibb—did he find the body, too, or was he killed because he knew there was another way into the mine?"

Tom was drinking a large Coke. "Could Gibb have killed Hector?"

Vida shook her head and sprinkled a tiny packet of salt onto her salad. "I doubt it. No known motive. Unless he was in love with Margaret. He was a widower by then. That's possible, though I don't recall any rumors."

In my opinion, if Vida couldn't remember them, they didn't exist.

She was still speaking: "Margaret was a beautiful girl. Half the men in Alpine were crazy about her. That's why Neeny was so put out when she married an outsider like Hector. But even if Gibb had killed his so-called rival, why would he murder Mark? And who would kill Gibb?" She gave an emphatic shake of her head. "Let's put that aside for now. We can rule out some of the others as Hector's killer because of age." Setting down her plastic fork, Vida began to eliminate suspects on her fingers. "Hector disappeared fourteen years ago. Cross off Kent and Jennifer. They were too young. And Chris, of course. Anybody under, say, thirty."

"Okay," I agreed. "But I don't get it. Milo says it's virtually impossible to tell how Hector died. Why, after all this time, would the killer care if the body was found? If Mark and Gibb hadn't been murdered, would we all jump to this conclusion about Hector? And even if we did, nothing seems to point to any specific person as his murderer."

Tom stood up, brushing crumbs from his tailored slacks. "Emma's right. The trail is decidedly cold. Either the killer panicked or isn't very bright. Unless we're missing something."

The phone jarred us from our mutual absorption. I reached over my shoulder and fumbled at the receiver. *"Advocate,"* I croaked, still juggling.

Jennifer Doukas MacDuff's uncertain voice came on the line. "Ms. Lord, you said I could come see you if I had a problem. Did you mean it?"

"Sure." I finally had the receiver under control. "Yes," I said, not wanting her to think I was being too breezy. "When do you want to talk?"

Jennifer's words were jerky. "Now. Alone. At your house. Don't tell anyone. *Please.*"

Vida and Tom were watching me. "In fifteen minutes," I said.

My first reaction was to shield Jennifer. But fragments of movies and books passed through my mind in which the hapless heroine falls into a trap and only the intrepid hero can show up in time to rescue her from the arch fiend. I didn't want to set myself up for further damsel-in-distress scenarios. I broke faith with Jennifer and ratted, reasoning that I wasn't betraying a source because she hadn't really told me anything yet.

"If I'm not back in half an hour, send for Milo," I said, heading out the door over protests from Tom and Vida.

It never occurred to me that Milo might like to be a hero, too.

Jennifer was already waiting for me, hunched over the wheel of her compact car at the edge of my driveway. I kept my apprehension at bay as I let us into the dark house. It was after seven-thirty, and the sun had long ago disappeared behind the mountains.

After I turned on the lights and went into the kitchen to get us each a can of soda, the house seemed as snug and safe as ever. Jennifer had flopped down on the sofa where she'd sat on her previous visit. She had changed from the plain black dress of the funeral into faded jeans and a floppy shirt.

"This is a bother," she began, twisting her hands and

turning red-rimmed blue eyes in my direction. "But except for the sheriff, I don't know who else to talk to."

"It's okay," I said. "What's wrong?"

Jennifer sighed, untwisted her hands long enough to fling a strand of hair over her shoulder, and eyed the can of pop as if it were a bomb. "Phoebe is taking my grandfather away tomorrow. I don't think that's right."

"Where?" I asked, knowing I should have said *why*? But the picture of a docile Neeny Doukas, being carted off against his will by anyone, threw me off balance.

"Palm Springs. In California," Jennifer added, in case my sense of geography didn't extend past the Columbia River. "She says all this has been too hard on him. He needs to get away, to be in the sunshine. But it scares me." Her chin quivered.

Now I asked the proper question. "Why?"

Jennifer finally picked up the can of soda and took a sip. "I'm afraid he won't come back. My dad is really mad. Even my mom thinks Phoebe shouldn't take him away."

I leaned forward in my armchair, noting how the light from the table lamp emphasized the contours of Jennifer's face and added character. "Have you talked to your grandfather about this?"

The blonde hair swung to and fro. "No. There wasn't a chance, with everybody arguing and yelling. I came straight from the house," she explained, and I knew she meant Neeny's, not her parents' home. "After the guests were gone, Phoebe made her announcement to the rest of us. Then they all got to fighting. Kent and I left, and then I called you."

"How does Kent feel about this?"

"He thinks Phoebe's up to something. He doesn't trust her an inch." She ran her forefinger about that far on my coffee table to underscore her point. "I don't, either."

I hesitated. But what I was about to say was a matter of public record. "Phoebe *is* your grandfather's wife," I said quietly.

Jennifer stared at me blankly. Then her mouth opened and she started to speak, but no words came out. Her hands clutched at the pop can; her blue eyes grew enormous.

"They eloped to Las Vegas awhile back. Remember the trip?" I smiled kindly.

"The old tart!" Jennifer exploded, showing more animation than I'd ever seen her display. She thrashed about on the sofa, spilling soda and beating at the cushions. Dust flew; I winced. But Jennifer wasn't about to notice my poor housekeeping. "I hate my family! They're a mess! I wish I were somebody else!"

"This is hard on everybody," I pointed out. Maybe, I thought, it was time to change the subject. "How's Kent's shoulder?"

Jennifer stopped flouncing around long enough to consider the question. "Better. He didn't have to take one of those pills last night."

I tried to keep my manner casual. "I don't suppose he saw Phoebe Wednesday night when he was downtown picking up that prescription?"

"Phoebe?" She spoke the name with disdain. "He didn't mention it." Obviously, it hadn't occurred to her that she was admitting her husband had left the house after all.

"Or your father?"

"No." Jennifer ran her fingers through her hair in an agitated manner. "Oh!" Enlightenment seemed to dawn on her. "You know," she said uneasily, "I forgot Kent went to Parker's to pick up that medicine. So much else happened afterward."

It could have been true. "I heard your father was going to his office after he dropped Mark off at my house."

Jennifer dismissed the idea with a slight shake of her head. "I doubt it. Kent said he parked in Dad's place. It's reserved in front of the Clemans Building for him, you know." Behind the veil of hair, her face contorted with distress. "Are you trying to tell me my dad went someplace else that night?"

"I have no idea." I felt as if I were pillorying the poor girl. "Look, maybe it's advantageous for your grandfather to get away. Phoebe's right. He's been through a lot, losing Mark. You've all suffered this past week. And Palm Springs isn't exactly the Amazon Jungle."

From the expression on Jennifer's face, they were one and the same to her. "My father says the sheriff won't let Neeny go. Not until they've caught my brother's killer."

That sounded like a strange—and suggestive—remark, coming from Simon Doukas. "Did Milo say that?"

Jennifer shrugged. "I don't know. Why don't you ask him? There he is now."

Sure enough, Milo Dodge's Cherokee Chief had pulled up out front. I could see the vehicle's outline under the light I'd put on in the carport. I glanced at my watch. It was 8:20. Tom had taken me at my word.

Jennifer didn't want to stick around to talk to Milo. She went out as he came in, and I was left on the porch, feeling inadequate. Not only had I failed to console Jennifer, I'd ended up sowing doubts and doling out more bad news. Jennifer Doukas MacDuff had shown poor judgment in choosing a confidante.

"What was that all about?" inquired Milo, still wearing his rumpled suit and looking bone tired.

"Come in. I'll tell you." I offered him Jennifer's place on the sofa and a fresh can of pop. He accepted both, and from out in the kitchen, I heard him utter a long sigh as he sat down.

"Did you think I'd been killed?" I asked with a grin as I handed him his soda.

"Your adviser thought so," replied Milo. "Or is he dating Vida?"

I gave Milo a steady look. "He's not dating anybody. He's been married for years."

Milo's hazel eyes were ironic. "Oh? Funny, he doesn't act married."

"Knock it off, Milo." My voice had a rough edge to it. "You ought to be grateful he's helping with the case." I

stopped short of telling Milo everything, but I recounted
Jennifer's concerns for her grandfather. Milo wasn't
pleased about Phoebe's proposed trip.

"I can't stop them from going without causing a major
war, but it would be better if they stuck around." Milo put
his feet up on the coffee table. "They may be able to answer some questions. Like Chris."

"Are you hinting that Neeny may have killed Hector?"
I asked.

"I don't *hint* things, Emma." He gave me a disapproving look. "If you're talking motive, Neeny had one for
getting rid of Hector. But I still like the way Vida originally said he'd go about it—with money. Neeny could buy
anybody off."

I tried to picture Hector Ramirez, Hispanic laborer, who
had married into a wealthy small-town family. I didn't
know what Hector looked like, but I had an inkling of how
he felt. "Hector was proud, I think."

"But Neeny is stubborn." Milo made a slashing gesture
with his hand. "And no way do I believe Neeny killed his
grandson."

"Or Gibb?"

"Gibb's a different matter." Milo sank back against the
cushions and yawned.

"Go home," I said. "You're tired. So am I." I gave him
a feeble smile.

"Yeah." He took a swig of soda. "One thing, though."
His high forehead furrowed as he regarded me across the
space taken up by the coffee table. "We just got some tire
tracks back from the road into Reiter and the gravel pit.
Your Jag sure gets around, Emma." His expression was
vaguely abject. "I guess you were right about your car getting swiped."

Right or wrong, it was still a shock. It made me a bit
queasy to think that while I sat inside the Adcocks' living
room, Gibb Frazier's murderer was using my car. Suddenly my Jag lost some of its charm. I was staring open-
mouthed at Milo.

"Can I have the keys?" he asked.

With an effort, I recovered my voice. "Why ask? Nobody else does."

"The extra set is gone," said Milo. "Whoever stole them probably wanted to make damned sure no prints showed up. I'd guess they've floated out to Puget Sound by now."

I'd never looked to see if the spare keys were still in place. "You're going to check the car now?" I asked.

He'd gotten up and had gone to the window. "Sam and Dwight just pulled up. They've got the gear. It shouldn't take long."

"Great." I waved at my purse which was at the end of the sofa. "My keys are in there, right on top."

Milo bent over, then straightened up abruptly. "What's this?" He was holding the Ramada Inn laundry bag with Mark's leather jacket. I'd left it there throughout the entire weekend.

"Take that, too," I said with a sigh of resignation. "I forgot I had it." It was true. Sort of.

Milo opened the front door and called to Dwight Gould who took the keys and the bag.

I glanced through the window, watching Sam Heppner open my car. "I wonder where you'll find the green paint."

"What?" Milo was still at the door. The cool air felt good. "Oh, you mean from the dent."

"Right." The phone rang; it was Tom.

"Are you all right? What's happening? Did Dodge show up?" Tom's voice was full of concern, and I could hear Vida yapping at him in the background.

I took a deep breath. My watch said it was after nine. No wonder Tom was worried. "Milo's here. Everything's fine. Listen, Tom," I said, wishing Milo wasn't watching me so closely, "I'm going to head for bed. You and Vida had better go home. It's been a long day."

There was a moment of silence. "Fine," said Tom. He clicked off.

Milo was still gazing at me. "Will you be all right alone?"

I lifted my chin. "Of course."

Milo raised a hand in salute and loped out the front door. His deputies continued to subject my poor Jag to all sorts of scientific humiliations. I considered going outside to confer with them, but thought better of it. I'd had enough crime for one day. Besides, other matters had come home to roost for the night. I'd told Tom I was with Milo, and I was going to bed. Tom had become quite terse. Tomorrow, he would go into Seattle before I could explain. I could call him at the lodge, but it would be presumptuous of me to think an explanation was needed. Why should Tom—a married man—care what I did? Why should I care what he thought? Why should he think I was doing anything wrong? And why wasn't I?

There were times when I thought the opposite sex was not a good idea. This was definitely one of them.

Chapter Sixteen

THE FIRST CALL of the morning came from one of the last people I would have expected—Cecelia Doukas. At 7:35 A.M., just before I was about to leave for the office, she phoned to ask me over for a quick cup of coffee. While I was in a hurry to get to work, I could hardly refuse the invitation.

As I drove over to Stump Hill, I kept expecting the Jag to apologize to me for hauling a killer around. I squirmed a bit on the leather upholstery, trying to visualize who had sat in my place Saturday night. Maybe it was just as well I didn't know, or I might not have been able to drive the car at all.

The sheriff's deputies had left without telling me much. They'd have to wait for lab reports, Sam Heppner told me in his laconic manner. Obviously, they had not come up with the cliché cigarette butt or slip of paper bearing a mysterious phone number.

As I expected, Simon Doukas's car was gone from the driveway that led up to the Dutch Colonial in The Pines. I didn't think Cece would invite me over if Simon was around.

On this first morning after her son's burial, Cecelia Doukas appeared calm. I couldn't tell if her manner was induced by tranquilizers or an inner strength I'd never attributed to her. In any event, she was as well groomed as usual, in charcoal gray slacks and a light gray sweater. She led me into her big, airy kitchen, all white, with a few black accents. The only color in the room was a huge bouquet of autumn flowers, probably sent in memory of Mark.

"I know you're busy," Cecelia began, pouring us each a cup of coffee. "I'll be brief." She sat down across the dining counter from me on a matching stool. "Neeny and Phoebe are leaving tonight for Palm Springs. Jennifer says you told her they had gotten married. How on earth did you learn that?"

I reflected briefly on my need to protect sources. "We found out during the course of the investigation. Someone called the Clark County Court House in Las Vegas. They verified that there had been a marriage between the two parties back in August. You remember the trip?"

"Certainly." She offered sugar and cream. "I had no idea they'd gotten married. Neither did Simon." Cece's expression was melancholy. "I hope Neeny was sensible enough to have a prenuptial agreement drawn up. He didn't ask Simon to do it. That I know."

I could imagine Simon's fury when he learned of the elopement. And, if that is what it was, it occurred to me that Neeny probably hadn't bothered to consult a lawyer in Vegas. "Couldn't Neeny rectify any future unfairness by making a new will?"

"Perhaps." Cece gave me a wispy smile. "Isn't life peculiar? So often it blindsides us. I feel as if I'd been knocked down by a logging truck. Will I ever get up again?"

"You haven't any choice," I said frankly. "We have to get up if only so we can be knocked down the next time."

She saw the bitterness in my face and nodded. "Yes—I suppose you've had your share of trouble, too. It happens to everyone. But this all seems to have come at once." Her eyes brimmed with tears. "*All* of it."

I had the feeling she wasn't just talking about Mark's death and Neeny's marriage. "You mean Chris coming back?"

"Chris?" She seemed surprised. "Oh, well, I suppose, in

a way. It's funny, though—it seems as if he was here a long time ago. So much else has happened."

I studied her for a moment in silence. "I gather you don't think Chris killed Mark."

Cecelia picked up her mug and stared blindly at the glass-fronted cupboards behind me. "I don't want to think anybody killed him. If I knew who had, then I'd be forced to accept the fact that he's dead." Carefully putting the mug down, she gave me another tremulous smile, the tears still standing in her blue eyes. "That sounds silly, doesn't it?"

"Not at all." It had taken me weeks to grapple with the idea that I'd lost both parents. The call from the State Patrol, the visit to the funeral home, the memorial mass hadn't really sunk in. I was going through the motions. It wasn't really me. Those two dead people couldn't possibly be my mother and father. The realization hit me only when their birthdays, just four days apart, came along that September. "Did you know Phoebe was trying to see Simon last Wednesday night?"

"Yes. She called right after Simon left to take Chris back to your house. I told her my husband was going to stop by his office and she might catch him there." The blue eyes widened. "Oh! Do you think she intended to tell him she and Neeny had gotten married?"

I hadn't considered that possibility. "Wouldn't it have been better for Neeny to tell Simon? But Phoebe never found Simon." Again, I felt like the scourge of the Doukas women. "Your husband didn't show up at the Clemans Building."

Cece brushed at the tears with her fingertip. "No. He went somewhere else." She tilted her chin, looking both proud and vulnerable.

"I trust it was somewhere that gave him an alibi," I said, wanting to kick myself under the counter.

"It was." Her voice had turned cold. "But Simon would never use it."

I had to assume that Cecelia Doukas wasn't as naive as

she seemed. She must know about her husband's alleged affair with Heather Bardeen. It occurred to me that Heather might have tried to get revenge on Mark by sleeping with his father. No wonder Cece was so disillusioned with her life. "Do you think that skeleton could be Hector Ramirez?" I asked, going for a more neutral, if equally grim topic.

"It's possible. I'd hate to think so. I just want all this to end. It's not *nice*."

"Did you know Hector very well?"

She shook her head. "Margaret and Hector kept to themselves a lot. I saw him occasionally. He seemed well-mannered. But he didn't fit in, not with the family, not with the town. Neeny was quite unkind to him, and Simon felt the cultural differences were too great. It would have been better if he and Margaret had stayed in Seattle. People there are all rather different." She slid off the stool, going to get the coffeepot. I declined; I was already late. "By the way, I have no alibi for Wednesday night, if that's what you're trying to find out." She set the pot down and leaned on the counter, facing me. "Tell me, Emma—do you think I murdered my son?"

Impulsively, I put my hand on hers. It was ice cold. "No, Cecelia. I'm a mother, too, remember."

She gave her imitation of a smile. "Of course. Simon won't let me forget." She looked apologetic.

"You mean he won't let you forget I'm an *unmarried* mother."

Cecelia gave a sad shake of her head. I assumed it was not for me but for her husband.

Vida all but dragged me into the office. "Where've you been? I've got Chris on the phone!" She practically hurled me toward her desk. "Line two," she hissed.

"Chris? Where are you?" I was shouting into the earpiece. I turned the receiver around and repeated myself.

Chris's voice was calm. "I'm in Seattle. I never got to L.A."

Maybe that accounted for the fact that Milo's APB hadn't brought in any results. "Where have you been?"

"San Francisco. It's a cool place, but it costs too much to stay there. Everybody in San Francisco said L.A. had too much smog and too many nut cases. So I came back here." He sounded very matter-of-fact.

"Chris, let me ask you something." Even as I spoke, I scrawled a note to Vida, asking if Tom had left for Seattle. She didn't know. "Did you find a message at my house last Wednesday night?"

"What kind of a message?"

I explained to him about the piece of paper Ginny had found in my yard. "No," replied Chris. "I didn't see it. Neeny didn't send me a note. He wasn't that happy to have me come up to the house."

"Somebody signed his name and tried to lure you up there," I said. "Now listen, Chris, all hell has broken loose since you left. I want you to head back to Alpine." He started to argue, but I ran right over his words. "We think we know what happened to your father." I avoided telling him about the remains. That news shouldn't be delivered over the phone.

Chris let out a few obscene one-syllable words. "Won't the sheriff arrest me as soon as I come back?"

"No, of course not," I assured him, even though I wasn't certain. "Gibb Frazier, my driver, has been killed, too. You weren't around when that happened." At least Chris claimed he'd been in the Bay Area, but it suddenly dawned on me that he could be lying. After all, he was the one person who knew exactly where I kept that extra set of keys.

But I didn't want to think about that just now. The important thing was to get Chris back to Alpine. At Carla's desk, Vida was on line three, calling the ski lodge. She gave me a frantic nod and mouthed the single syllable, Tom.

"A friend of mine is coming to Seattle this morning," I told Chris, then went into details about the location of the county courthouse. Chris should plan on meeting Tom there at two o'clock. He would recognize him because I'd have him bring along a copy of last week's *Advocate*. "Where are you now?" I inquired, fearful that the rendezvous would never come off.

"The bus depot. I just got in." Chris was beginning to sound nervous.

With more admonitions to be sure to meet Tom, I finally hung up and pressed the button for line three. Tom was still distant, but he agreed to bring Chris back. "I assume I shouldn't tell him why I'm at the courthouse," Tom said in a formal voice.

Carla and Ed were coming through the door together. I tried to think of a way to ease the strain between Tom and me with most of my staff listening in. "By the way," I said to Tom, "Milo left right after you called, but his deputies stayed on to search my car. Gibb's killer drove it to Reiter."

Three faces registered surprise. But Tom's reaction was different. "Then I guess you really do like going it alone," he remarked. "I'll see you later."

Ed looked so downcast that I was sure the murders had hit him harder than I'd expected. But he had other matters on his mind. "I heard Safeway may be coming into town," he said morosely. "They want to build on the other side of the mall or maybe out by the golf course. God, what a mess that would be! Their media people like to use *color* inserts!" He made it sound as if their advertising department might ride into Alpine like the Four Horsemen of the Apocalypse.

Carla, of course, was much more upbeat. "Gee, I can't believe I missed more bodies! I knew I shouldn't have gone to Leavenworth for the weekend! But what a blast! I met this wonderful hunk who tried out for the Seahawks and he . . ." Ginny Burmeister came into the office and Carla rattled on, driving me into my inner sanctum.

Five minutes later, Milo called to say that Dr. Starr had

confirmed that the remains from the mineshaft were those of Hector Ramirez. He had made only two visits to the dentist, both in 1975, after he'd chipped a tooth while working on the Pine Street L.I.D. project. But that, coupled with the X-rays, was enough for identification. I relayed the news to my staff. Carla put on a tragic face, Ginny remarked that violence was often triggered by untidiness, and Ed complained that dentists overcharged. Vida, however, grew thoughtful.

"Did they find a bullet yet?"

"Not that I know of," I said. "Milo would have told us, wouldn't he?"

Vida gave me an enigmatic look. "Maybe."

Thanks to the time I'd put in over the weekend, we had the paper well in hand by noon. Since there still might be late-breaking developments, I wasn't ready to call it a day. At ten after one, Tom phoned from Seattle. Vida and I were alone in the news office, with Carla out to lunch in more ways than one, Ed supposedly getting an ad from Stuart's Stereo, and Ginny paying bills in the front office.

Tom's voice sounded considerably warmer. I gestured for Vida to pick up her phone, too. He might as well relay any information he had found to both of us. "I hit pay dirt," he announced. "It took awhile, because there was nothing for August twenty-one, 1971. But I went through the whole month, then back into July. Here, I'll read from the copy I made." I held my breath; Vida's tongue plied her upper lip. " 'Born July twenty-one, 1971, Baby Boy Pratt, to Phoebe Phipps Pratt and Constantine Nikinos Doukas.' "

Vida put her hand over the receiver. "Neeny!" she gasped.

I could hear, if not see, Tom's grin of triumph. "Well, Emma? Is that what you wanted?"

I laughed. "I don't know what I wanted. But it fits. Phoebe had Neeny's baby and gave it up to Margaret and Hector. No wonder she wrote Chris that letter! Wow!"

Tom was chuckling, too. "I don't know how this fits in

with the murders, but we can sort that out when I get back.
I'm going to get a sandwich and then wait for Chris." He
paused, then lowered his voice. "Emma, I'm sorry I got
upset about you and Milo. I never really believed you
were sleeping with him. It's just that I thought if you were
scared or didn't want to stay alone, you might have asked
me to . . . oh, hell, Emma, we'll talk about it later. And
Adam, too. See you."

I gripped the receiver tight and dared to dart a look at
Vida. She was putting her own phone down and gazing
straight ahead. "I wonder who handled the adoption," she
said in an ordinary voice. "A Seattle attorney, I suppose."

I knew I was blushing like mad. "Margaret and Hector
probably didn't get Chris until he was a month old. That's
why the announcement gave his birthday as August instead of July."

"Lucky for Phoebe that the Ramirezes wanted him."
She finally turned back in my direction. "No wonder he
looks like a Doukas." She rummaged in her tote bag. "My,
my, I seem to have forgotten my cottage cheese and carrot
sticks. Want to go get a burger?"

I stood up. "Why not?" What I wanted most was to hug
Vida.

Heather Bardeen and Chaz Phipps were just leaving
when we got to the Burger Barn. Vida jabbed me with an
elbow and then made her move, blocking the young wom-
en's exit.

"We need to have a word with you," she said in an im-
perious manner. "Where were you sitting?"

Despite their startled expressions, Heather and Chaz
didn't argue but led us to a booth at the rear of the restaurant. The waitress, who wasn't Kimberly this time, was already clearing off the table. She pocketed her tip and left
us in peace.

"This will be quick," said Vida, fixing her gaze on
Heather. "If the sheriff asks you—and he probably will—

can you tell him where Simon Doukas was last Wednesday night between eight-thirty and nine-thirty?"

Heather drew back against the booth's plastic maroon upholstery. "What a dumb question! Even if I could tell the sheriff, why would I tell *you*?"

Vida was unperturbed. "Because the sheriff will tell us anyway." She glanced at me from under the brim of her veiled green fedora. "We have a deadline, you see." Clearly, Vida was counting on Heather's lack of curiosity as to how our journalistic endeavor might be tied to Milo Dodge's interrogation.

But Heather was on her feet, pulling Chaz along with her. "I don't give a rat's ass about your deadline. If you want to find out where Simon Doukas and I were Wednesday night, you'll have to hear it from the sheriff." She gave Vida a nasty look, ignored me, and hauled Chaz out of the booth.

"Well," said Vida, picking up a menu, "that takes care of that. Heather certainly gets around. But it doesn't let Simon off the hook as far as the murder is concerned."

"Vida," I said, motioning to the waitress, "you don't think Simon would kill his own son, do you?" I couldn't believe it of Cecelia, whom I rather liked; neither could I believe it of the less likable Simon.

"Stranger things have happened," murmured Vida in her cryptic manner. She threw down the menu and looked up at the waitress. "Oh, why bother with all those decisions about calories and fat and cholesterol? I'll have the bacon burger, fries, a small salad, and one of those pineapple malts. I hope the pineapple chunks aren't so big they plug up the straw this time."

Privacy wasn't ensured by the booth in which we sat, so Vida and I spoke of the case in whispers, pooling our information and drawing certain conclusions. It was, we agreed, possible that Hector, Mark, and Gibb had been killed by the same person. With Hector, it would be almost impossible after fourteen years to establish alibis—or the lack of them. Even Vida, with her encyclopedic memory, wasn't precisely sure when Hector had disappeared.

"Only Margaret would have been likely to remember the date," she said, dumping large pools of catsup on her fries. "A pity she's dead. Chris would have been too young to recall much."

Briefly, I thought about the note Chris had left for me at the motel. He had mentioned memories. Was his father's—or adoptive father's—disappearance one of them? Could we assume that Neeny was Chris's real father? Vida felt we could, since she asserted that Phoebe had been carrying on with Neeny long before the boy's birth.

"Nobody has an alibi," I said once more for the record. "The real problem is that nobody has a motive, at least not for killing Mark."

Vida wagged a finger at me. "Not true," she said around a mouthful of bacon burger. "Hector's killer had a motive if Mark had found the remains."

I didn't agree. "Hector's killer had no reason to think that finding a bunch of bones could trigger a fourteen-year-old murder investigation."

Under the brim of her green hat, Vida's expression wavered, but she wasn't quite ready to throw in the towel. "There's *got* to be a connection. Oh, I know, I know," she insisted, waving her fork and sending lettuce in the direction of the two men across the aisle. "You said you thought Phoebe had seen Mark the night he was killed." She swirled more lettuce around in her little plastic bowl. "Would he have come to tell Neeny about finding those remains?" As usual, Vida could best answer her own questions. "I think he would, they were on Neeny's property. Maybe he told Phoebe. It would be just like Mark to try to get a rise out of her with a ghoulish story—and for some reason, she didn't want Neeny to know."

"His health?" I suggested.

Vida gave an absent nod. "That would be my guess. So she put him off. And then went haring off to see Simon.

Why?" This time she had no answer. "We're missing something. Tommy thinks so, too."

Tommy. I refrained from giving Vida a look of reproach. "I wish he'd get back with Chris. My biggest fear is that Chris won't show."

"It's possible." Vida assaulted her malted milk, a noisy business at best. "Don't start worrying until after four. It's going to take them awhile to get to Alpine, especially if Tommy has to meet with those people he mentioned."

It was now almost two o'clock. I suggested that we get my car and go see if the mail had come to my home. When we arrived, there was a notice saying that since nobody was home, there would be a parcel from Honolulu waiting at the post office after five P.M. Vida and I decided it would be easier to chase down the mail truck. We found it at Fifth & Cascade, across from the middle school. Naturally, the driver was a Runkel once or twice removed.

We opened the package inside the car, just as the first contingent of prepubescent students charged out of the school. There was Chris's denim jacket and several piles of correspondence, mostly addressed to Margaret Ramirez. Judging from a cursory look at their varying rates of postage, they went back several years. The letter from Phoebe to Mark was on top.

Vida all but ripped it out of my hand. "You've heard it already," she said, whisking Phoebe's eggshell stationery from its matching envelope. Swiftly, Vida scanned the two handwritten pages. "Hrmph. If I didn't know that Phoebe is probably the poor boy's mother, I'd have lost my lunch." Thoughtfully, she refolded the letter and handed it to me. "Why did she write that, I wonder?"

I was about to speculate when Vida slapped at the dashboard. "Let's go ask her. Now."

"But Vida," I protested, "we've still got some last-minute details with the paper."

"So we work late. Let's go. To Neeny's," she added, sitting back and bracing herself as if she expected me to take off at ninety miles an hour.

I didn't think this was the best idea Vida had entertained lately, but if Phoebe and Neeny were about to leave for Palm Springs, this might be our only chance to talk to either of them for a long time.

Frieda Wunderlich, looking as sour as a leftover lemon, greeted us at the door. "The Queen Bee isn't here and Himself went to get a tune-up from Doc Dewey. You want them to call you before they take off?" She didn't wait for an answer, however, but shook her gray head. "Going to the *desert*! Can you imagine anybody leaving beautiful country like this to go look at *nothing*?"

"With Phoebe around, Neeny's always looking at nothing as far as I'm concerned," retorted Vida. "Where is the old cow?"

Frieda screwed up her homely face, reminding me of a gargoyle. "She's over at her own place, packing. I heard— not that I'd ask—she's putting it up for sale." Her inverted eyebrows lifted like a pair of apostrophes.

"How much?" asked Vida, getting right to the point.

Frieda leaned forward; the two women huddled like a couple of drug dealers on a street corner. "Eighty-five," said Frieda.

"Ridiculous!" snorted Vida.

"Lucky to get sixty," agreed Frieda.

They were probably right. Phoebe's post–World War II rambler needed paint, and the garden showed neglect. A few scraggly dahlias leaned against a fence with several missing pickets. Under a sparse rhododendron, a little stone gnome was covered with moss. The house's location wasn't noteworthy, either, just one block off Front Street, facing the rear of the Lumberjack Motel.

A frazzled Phoebe Pratt Doukas met us at the door. "Oh—what a surprise!" Her face indicated it wasn't a pleasant one. "I'm just packing a few things. My niece, Chaz, is going to take care of the rest while I'm gone. Oh!" She fluttered about in the small entryway where several half-filled cartons, three suitcases, and an old gas barbecue reposed. "Come in, sit down—if you can find a spot." She sounded dubious.

The living room was also littered with cartons, mostly empty, and there were piles of clothes on virtually every piece of furniture. "I'll never get everything done in the next three hours," Phoebe declared, making a valiant effort at freeing up the Naugahyde sofa. Dust was thick on the few surfaces showing, the windows were smudged with dirt, and—as Vida had said—the curtains looked as if they hadn't been washed in years. The room had a musty smell, and the jade plant on the fireplace hearth looked dead as a dodo. It was obvious that Phoebe spent very little time in the home she had made with the late Clinton Pratt.

On the drive to Neeny's, Vida and I had discussed the best way to approach Phoebe about her illegitimate child. I had suggested that Vida's blunderbuss tactics could backfire. To my surprise, she had agreed. Vida and Phoebe had a history spanning almost sixty years, whereas I was only a casual acquaintance. And, as I readily volunteered, Phoebe and I had something in common: our bastard sons.

Consequently, as we tried to get comfortable on the sofa's sagging springs, I was horrified when Vida unleashed her barrage:

"See here, Phoebe, we know you're Chris's mother and Neeny is his father. The only thing we want to know is why, out of the blue, you wrote him a letter a couple of weeks ago."

Phoebe, who for once wasn't plastered with cosmetics, went white, then red. She began to shake, while tears welled up in her eyes. "Vida!" she gasped, staring at the other woman as if she'd been betrayed to the Gestapo. "Oh, Vida!"

"Oh, bother!" huffed Vida. "This is the 1990s, and Emma's an unmarried mother, too. All we're trying to do is figure out who killed Mark and Gibb and maybe Hector Ramirez." She turned to me. "Where's that letter?"

I extracted it from my handbag. "It's a very nice letter,"

I said, hoping to keep Phoebe from having a stroke. "Chris never got it, though. My son forwarded it to me."

The tears were coursing down Phoebe's crimson cheeks. She wiped at them with the sleeve of her green print blouse and gazed at the streaked front window. "He was all alone," she said at last in a thin voice. "Margaret had been a good mother, despite what Neeny said. For all I know, Hector may have been a good father, given his . . . limitations." Her head bobbed this way and that, presumably in search of a Kleenex or a handkerchief. I offered her a little packet of tissues from my purse.

"Thank you." Phoebe gave me a grateful look. I figured we were bonding, in some odd, pathetic way. "At the time he was born, Margaret and Hector were living in Seattle. Clinton had been dead for over a year, so there was no way I could convince people the baby was his. I went to Seattle, too, and got an apartment on Capitol Hill. Doukums didn't know. It was better that way since his old-fashioned sense of gallantry might have forced him to make an honest woman of me. And a divorce would have killed Hazel. So I let him think I was trying out my wings as a widow." Her lips quivered in a little smile. "I could have simply put the baby up for adoption, but I knew Margaret and Hector wanted a child so much. They went to Simon and had him make the arrangements. Neeny always assumed the baby was theirs. It was quite clever." Now Phoebe was really smiling, the tears finally staunched.

"Did they pay for him?" Vida asked on a somewhat sour note.

"Oh, no!" Phoebe's hands were at her breast. "They had nothing of their own, poor things. And there I was, not quite as young as I used to be, proud to be bearing Doukas fruit!"

I didn't dare look at Vida. To her credit, she didn't say anything but allowed Phoebe to continue: "It was so much better than giving little Chris up to strangers. And until Margaret moved away, I got to see him now and then." She sighed, her hands tearing at the tissue I'd given her. "I was heartbroken after they went to Hawaii. When Margaret died, I thought of writing immediately. But I kept putting it off—I didn't know what to say." She made a gesture at the letter I was still holding. "Does he know the truth?" She finally gazed directly at us, her eyes showing both hope and fear.

"No," I said. "But he's supposed to be back in Alpine today."

Phoebe clutched at the neckline of her blouse. "Oh! Dear Chris! Poor Doukums! Is ignorance really bliss? What to do, what to do?"

"What *did* you do?" inquired Vida. "About your will, I mean. After you and Neeny got married, did you leave everything to him, or to Chris?"

Phoebe had recovered a little of her natural color, but now it drained away as if Vida had pulled a plug. Instead of tears, however, Phoebe resorted to anger. "Vida Blatt, you are the biggest snoop in Skykomish County! No wonder they used to call you Goose Neck in high school!"

Vida smirked. "They used to call you other things, Phoebe Vickers. Like Freebie."

I thought it best to intervene. "Excuse me," I said, leaning between the two women like a referee, "but Vida's question may be valid." I hated to say what was coming next, but it couldn't be avoided. "If you intended to leave your estate to Chris, it might have a bearing on the murder case."

Phoebe was still glaring at Vida. "Of course I left everything to Chris," she said in a voice still choked with anger. "After Doukums, of course. And a little something for Chaz."

Again, my question came with reluctance. "Is it enough to kill for?"

The rage was beginning to ebb as Phoebe considered her financial state. "Doukums settled three million dollars on me when we got married. Simon doesn't know—we had Doc Dewey's son-in-law in Seattle handle it. Then there's some stock. Doukums always believed in buying into companies right around here. He's a great booster for people getting started. Besides," she noted guilelessly, "he gets some bargains that way." She gave us a big-eyed stare. "You know—local businesses. Like Microsoft. Nordstrom. Boeing. He's done quite well."

It sure beat my one stock investment—which involved making cat food out of bottom fish. The Japanese had violated about six fishing treaties and wiped out the fledgling company, along with my $200 stake. That was the last time I ever listened to a tip from *The Oregonian*'s business editor.

Having made an attempt at composing herself, Phoebe got to her feet. "Really, I must get busy. Our plane leaves at nine, so we're heading for the airport about six." Suddenly, she was picking up piles of clothing and dumping them into the empty cartons. "There's nothing more I can tell you. I wish I could, but—"

"You might let us know why you went to see Simon Wednesday night," Vida said, still sitting on the sofa.

Phoebe came to a dead halt, a stack of shoe boxes in her arms. "Oh! That!" She gazed around the cluttered room as if she expected to see an answer written on the faded striped wallpaper. "It wasn't anything important. Just something about selling the house."

Vida slowly but emphatically shook her head, the fedora listing from side to side. "Phoebe, Phoebe, that's a parcel of pigeon poop! You wouldn't go out at nine o'clock to track down Simon in his office when you could call him on the phone. Besides," she went on, yanking her skirt down over two inches of slip, "you didn't decide to sell this place until the last couple of days. I'd bet my last dime on it."

Phoebe dropped the shoe boxes, scattering several wedgies, high heels, and a pair of golf shoes. "Get out." Her voice was cold, with all nuances of the aging coquette vanished. I was already standing, halfway between the sofa and the entryway. To my amazement, Vida also rose. The two women faced each other, the same age, the same height, the same small-town background. Yet for one fleeting moment, they were titanic, a pair of Olympian goddesses facing each other not over a pile of shoe boxes but a chasm of memory.

Vida was the first to speak. "You're a fool, Phoebe Pratt." She dropped her voice a notch. "But maybe you mean well." In a flurry of tweed, she whirled around and stomped out of the living room.

I hesitated just long enough to give Phoebe a faint smile. Then I followed Vida out of the house, past the red Lincoln Town Car, and through the overgrown garden with its drooping dahlias and the moss-covered gnome that winked goodbye.

Chapter Seventeen

Kip MacDuff had agreed to take the paper into Monroe in the morning. We were running thirty-two tight pages, at roughly a sixty-forty ad-to-editorial ratio. It wasn't a bad proportion, but seventy-thirty would have been a lot better. Still, this was one week when we needed the news space. Unfortunately.

I'd finished calling the printer in Monroe to request an extra two hundred papers when I realized it was almost five o'clock. Carla and Ginny had just left. Ed was on the phone, and Vida was opening the box from Adam.

"Maybe we should go through these old letters," she suggested.

I didn't have much enthusiasm for the enterprise. "Go ahead. Just give me Chris's jacket." I looked at my watch again. "Damn it, Tom and Chris should be here by now."

Ed had hung up and was hauling himself into his plaid polyester sports coat. "Wouldn't you know it? Barton's Bootery is having a pre-Halloween sale. They want a half-page ad next week with pictures of *real* shoes. That means I can't use clip art!" He shot a forlorn look at the dog-eared volume of ready-to-print drawings that were his standby. Mentally, I thanked my lucky stars and lack of budget that I hadn't yet taken the plunge for the clip art computer program that would have made Ed's life easier while eliminating all advertising creativity.

The telephone spared me having to soothe Ed. To my relief, it was Tom, calling from the ski lodge. Yes, he had brought Chris back. They were going to get a quick bite in the coffee shop, then Chris would stop by the office or my house, whichever was more convenient. I said I intended to head for home in about fifteen minutes.

I did, leaving Vida to mull over Margaret's correspondence and Ed to wander away in a burdened state. As I drove up the hill that led to my home on Fir Street, the autumn sun was beginning to dip over Stevens Pass and a few clouds were scattered above the mountains. It was a perfect fall evening, cold enough to bronze the trees, but not to freeze the flowers. Yet I felt as if Alpine had been touched by a killing frost. I was glad that Chris was back in Alpine, but I realized that his presence might put him in danger. Surely he couldn't know about his real parents or that Phoebe had named him as her heir. But how would Milo Dodge react? I wanted to avoid the sheriff and to keep Chris away from him, too. It was impossible, of course. There was no place to hide in Alpine.

I had changed into slacks and a sweater when Chris came to the front door. Tom's rental car was parked in the drive. Now attired in a San Francisco Giants cap and an Oakland A's sweatshirt from the 1989 World Series, Chris somehow looked older, almost weary. On impulse, I hugged him.

"I was sure you were lost somewhere in Disneyland," I said, stepping aside to usher him in. "Where's your chauffeur?"

Chris strolled across the living room to stand by the fire I'd touched off as soon as I got home. "He had to make some long distance calls, so he let me borrow his car." He paused, giving me a wry smile. "I did ask."

I smiled back. My brain was whirling. Should I tell Chris about his real parents? But that wasn't up to me, it was Phoebe's responsibility. Yet I knew she and Neeny were probably already on the road to the airport.

The phone rang and I started to answer it, then stopped. It might be Milo, inquiring after Chris. No doubt he'd been sighted by the locals. I decided to let the machine take the call. Whoever it was would assume I was out to dinner. The thought triggered some nagging idea, but it fluttered away before I could grasp it.

"Mrs. Lord," Chris began, pacing the length of the hearth in long, uncertain strides, "is that really my father you and Mr. Cavanaugh found in the mineshaft?"

I hedged a bit as far as the definition of *father* was concerned. "Dr. Starr's dental records confirm that the remains belonged to Hector Ramirez." I sounded very formal.

Chris nodded once. "Okay." He stopped to finger the fireplace tools. "This is so crazy. . . ." His face crumpled, and for a moment, I thought he was going to cry. "You see," he said with a gulp, "I've been trying to remember things. I wrote that note, telling you how coming back to Alpine was such a bummer." He turned away, staring blindly at the mantel. "Could we drive up to the mineshaft?"

"Sure." I went to the front closet to get a jacket, then remembered to give Chris the one Adam had sent from Honolulu. I didn't know if we were making a pilgrimage to Icicle Creek or taking an exercise in memory. I thought it best not to ask.

The denim jacket brought a genuine smile to Chris's face. "Hey—that was nice of Adam to send this. He's a cool dude." Chris gave a little chuckle as we went out the door. "It's weird, but that Mr. Cavanaugh reminds me of Adam somehow. He's pretty cool, too."

"I like being around cool people," I remarked, unable to look Chris in the eye. Five minutes later we were turning off CR 187 at Icicle Creek. There was only one light burning in Neeny Doukas's house on First Hill as we drove by. The newlyweds were probably halfway to Monroe. It was getting dark, with only the sound of the creek breaking the evening silence.

Chris and I walked wordlessly up to Mineshaft Number Three. I'd brought along a flashlight. We could see the crime scene tape, now extended up the hill to the second entrance. Chris followed my lead, then stood staring down at the hole in the ground where Hector Ramirez's remains had been found. The excavation was much deeper than when I'd seen it the previous afternoon. I wondered if Milo and his deputies had uncovered any more evidence, such as a bullet.

"He was shot," Chris said, startling me with the baldness of his statement.

"How do you know?" I asked in a breathless voice.

Chris was staring at the deep hole that had been Hector Ramirez's grave. He was silent for so long that I wondered if he were praying. "I was there. *Here*," he added, making a sharp gesture.

"You saw Hector get shot?" I was so surprised that I almost stumbled over a root.

With his profile outlined by my flashlight, Chris stared straight ahead. "I remember it. For so long, I couldn't. But I do now." He sucked in his breath and bit his lip. "It was real grim. I never told my mom."

The flashlight wavered in my hand. "Did you tell anyone?" I asked, the horror of Chris's revelation sinking in.

Slowly, Chris shook his head. "I couldn't. And then . . ." He turned to face me, his features lost in the shadows. "I didn't remember anymore. Not until I came back to Alpine."

Frantically, I tried to think of words that might console Chris. It didn't matter that he really wasn't Hector's son—the slain man had been the only father Chris had known, just as Margaret had been his only mother. Feeling helpless, I watched Chris button up his denim jacket, then shove his hands in his pockets. He didn't weep. No doubt he'd shed all his tears a long time ago.

Except for the tumbling creek and the wind in the trees, it was too quiet. I wanted to get away from Mineshaft Number Three, to head into town with warm lights glowing from behind homely little windows. Tentatively, I put my hand on Chris's arm.

"Let's go back to the house," I said gently. "We can talk about it there. If you want to."

Chris looked down at me with sad dark eyes. "I have to, don't I?"

I wasn't sure what he meant. "You mean for your own sake? Or to tell the sheriff?"

"Both." He set his jaw, lifted his chin, and for the first time, I could see not just Mark, but Neeny, and Simon, too. We were still standing by the mineshaft, with the darkness enfolding us. My flashlight made a small circle of pale gold light on the forest floor. Chris was staring off into the trees again, shaking his head. "That's the part that mixed me up at the time. I thought my dad deserved to get shot. So I made myself not remember."

I tugged at his arm. "What are you talking about? What was he doing?"

Chris's gaze returned to rest on my anxious face. "He wasn't doing anything, except maybe talking or arguing. We lived on Eighth Avenue, before it turns off onto that road out there." He gestured with his free hand. "It was a little house by the golf course, but it's been torn down for a new development. That's why I couldn't find it the night I went driving around. We'd just finished dinner and somebody called my dad."

"Do you know who it was?" I asked, and that nagging little idea fretted at my brain. Dinner. Phone calls. Icicle Creek. But I couldn't get distracted.

"My dad didn't say who phoned. He went out, and I thought he was walking up to Neeny's, so I followed him. It was getting dark—I think it was spring, I know it was warm—but he came this way instead of going up my grandfather's driveway. I saw somebody else by the mineshaft, so I hid in the brush by the creek." At last, he freed his arm from my grasp and passed a hand over his dark hair. "The creek made a lot of noise, so I couldn't hear what they were saying. Then there was a shot, and my dad fell on the ground. I yelled and ran off." He paused, worrying his lower lip. "I don't know where I ran. I don't remember anything until my mother took me to Hawaii."

I was incredulous. "You don't remember the search for your father?"

"Not really. Maybe I thought he was still alive. Or maybe it was better if nobody knew he was dead." He gave me a pitiful look. "Like I said, I thought he deserved it. A kid's mind operates in black and white, I guess. There are good guys, and there are bad guys."

Somehow, in my shock at learning that Chris had seen Hector murdered, it didn't quite dawn on me that he would also know who had fired the fatal shot. Chris had been so young. The killer might have been a stranger, or someone who no longer lived in Alpine. Whoever it was would look far different to a young man of twenty than to a child of six.

"Who?" I asked, though I believed I knew. Unbidden, the nagging little fragment had clicked into place.

The car that had approached so quietly had not used lights. Its arrival was heralded by a soft thud, as if a bumper had made contact with a tree. As my Jag had done, I thought dully. Chris heard the noise, too, followed by the click of the car's door. Then a big flashlight switched on, momentarily blinding us.

I saw the white Cadillac's outline before I saw its owner's face. Steeling myself, I attempted a smile. "Hi, Eeeny, are we having a party?"

"Emma, *cara*," came the ex-sheriff's voice. His heartiness rang false. "Sure, why not? You, too, Chris? You like to party?"

I heard the catch in Chris's throat. Instinctively, I moved a couple of inches closer to him, as if I could shield him from his father's killer. From Mark's. And Gibb's. But Chris had been shielded too long, especially by himself. I saw the gun, a standard .38 service model, in Eeeny's hand.

"That's good," said Eeeny, his voice like olive oil. "You stand together. I can see you just fine, this close." He raised the gun, pointing it at me. "You tried to stop him from running away. He shot you. Then he saw there was nowhere to run because I come along. So he shoots himself." Eeeny shook his head. "Sad. Very sad."

Next to me, I felt Chris tense. Would he, could he spring at Eeeny? But the ex-sheriff was still quick on his feet. I tried to think of words that would buy us time. "Milo will figure it out, Eeeny. You made one very bad mistake."

"Like what, *cara*?" He didn't sound as if he believed me.

"You said Mark called you Wednesday night before eight o'clock. He couldn't have. You were at the Venison Inn, remember?" My mouth was dry; the words sounded unnatural.

He gave a little grunt of a laugh. "No. And neither will Milo, when you're not around to remind him." Eeeny peered through his glasses down the end of the barrel. "He's a nice kid, but not so smart. He'll get his speeders and his shoplifters, though. Some day his pension." In the artificial light, his smile was grotesque. "No pension for you two, though." His finger squeezed the trigger, and I let out a shrill cry.

The voice that boomed through the night startled the birds from the trees and the animals from their lairs: "Drop that gun—you're covered from all sides! Now!" A great rustling followed, with twigs snapping and branches crackling. Eeeny Moroni hesitated just long enough for me to throw my flashlight at him while Chris leaped at the hand that held the .38. I missed Eeeny but hit his glasses. They fell to the ground, even as he and Chris struggled. Chris had youth on his side, but Eeeny was strong as a bull. Frantically, I looked around for the source of all the commotion. Surely Milo and his deputies were just inches away from rescuing us. But the figure emerging through the trees was alone, carrying a megaphone—and a gun. It was Vida, and for once, she was hatless.

"I said drop it!" she yelled, jabbing her weapon into Eeeny's thick neck. Chris jumped back; Eeeny cursed but complied.

"You old bitch!" he screamed at Vida, trying to writhe away from her.

"Oh, shut up, Eeeny!" Vida jammed the gun even deeper against Moroni's flesh. "I suppose you don't think I'd shoot you. Well, you're wrong. I think you're the most horrid man I ever met."

Dimly, I heard sirens. Chris was flexing his fingers, apparently injured while wrestling with Eeeny. I turned to him and asked the inevitable question: "Was it Sheriff Moroni who shot your father?"

"Yeah." He was breathing hard, staring at Eeeny with loathing. "That's what mixed me up. I thought my dad must be a criminal. Sheriffs are supposed to be the good guys, right?"

I gave Eeeny a disgusted look. "Right. But not this one."

Milo Dodge, Bill Blatt, and all the other deputies poured out of two sheriff's cars, guns at the ready. Eeeny seemed to shrivel with every step taken by his former comrades. I half expected him to turn into Rigoletto and announce that he was accursed.

Vida finally withdrew her weapon and all but recoiled from Eeeny. She turned not to Milo, but to Billy. "What took you so long?" she asked her nephew crossly. "I've been here for ages, tramping about in the dark like a mole. I even lost my favorite mauve pillbox."

Billy Blatt automatically removed his hat. "Well, you see, Aunt Vida, we had to rendezvous and make sure our guns were ready to fire and that we had a warrant and—"

"Oh, hush!" With her flatfooted walk, Vida headed back toward the road. I followed her, with Chris at my side. As a journalist, I should have stayed glued to Milo and Eeeny, but the arrest of one sheriff by another was not a pretty sight. Besides, I had more than enough news to fill up the extra inches.

"What on earth made you come here and bring the sheriff?" I asked, catching up with Vida at the edge of the road.

Vida gave me an impatient look. "Those letters, to Margaret. Half of them were full of mush from Eeeny. He was in love with her, too. But then I always said most of the men in Alpine were." She sighed. "I just didn't figure Eeeny was one of them. The old fool." She palmed her gun and waved the megaphone. "My car's parked in Neeny's driveway. We'd better get back to the office and get this story out."

"Wait a minute." I grabbed her sleeve. "Where did you get a gun?"

"What?" Vida looked blankly from behind her glasses. "Oh!" She held out her hand.

In it was Roger's water pistol.

The paper was put to bed, but the rest of us were still wide awake. Vida, Milo, Tom, and I were in the news office, drinking brandy out of paper cups and going over the extraordinary events of the past few hours. It was almost midnight. Milo had arrived only a few minutes earlier, looking exhausted. He was already into his second brandy.

"Where's Chris?" he asked, peering around as if he expected the young man to leap out of Ed Bronsky's desk drawer.

"I dropped him off at Jennifer and Kent's," I said. "What happens next is up to the family. He *is* a Doukas, after all."

Milo leaned back in Ed's chair and put his feet up on the desk. "I'm glad we caught Neeny and Phoebe at the airport. They're spending the night at a hotel and driving back in the morning. Neeny can't believe his old pal is guilty, but Phoebe will convince him." He laughed into his paper cup. "Damn, she thought Neeny killed Hector. When Mark came up to the house, he told her about digging up a body. He saw that medal, too, and remembered that Hector wore one like it. Phoebe wouldn't let Mark see his grandfather and she sent him away—to get killed, as it turned out. But she was in a stew, figuring that Neeny would have been the most likely person to have murdered

Hector. She went to see Simon, but she couldn't find him because he was out screwing Heather Bardeen." Milo laughed some more.

"Poor Cece," said Vida. "She'd better settle his hash, quick." The look she transmitted through her glasses should have melted the frames.

Tom was tapping a pencil on Carla's desk. "Jealousy and fear." He shook his head. "Ugly motives, when you think about it. Did Eeeny really think Margaret would marry him with Hector out of the way?" The question, as usual, was for Vida.

"How would I know, Tommy?" she replied. "He was certainly crazy about her. He didn't stop writing those letters until the postage rate went up to twenty-two cents. The sad thing is that he thought he had to kill again. Twice."

It occurred to me that I hadn't eaten since lunch. Along with that startling insight came another, one I'd been harboring ever since Chris Ramirez had walked in my door seven nights earlier. "The first one was the wrong person." I saw three stunned faces and clarified my statement. "With Mark, I mean. Eeeny thought it was Chris."

"Hey, Emma . . ." Milo began.

"Now, Emma," said Tom.

"Of course, Emma!" cried Vida. "Eeeny was blind as a bat! Mark was wearing Chris's cap and jacket!"

I nodded. "And they looked so much alike." I gave a little shake of my head. "Chris was really Mark's uncle, not his cousin. No wonder Simon cried when he saw Chris. He knew he was looking at his brother. I wonder how the Doukases will sort all that out?"

"Oh, they will, they will, knowing Neeny," said Vida impatiently. "But why kill Chris? Because he'd seen Eeeny shoot Hector?"

"Sure," I replied. "The return of Chris Ramirez spelled terrible trouble for Eeeny Moroni. The six-year-old boy who ran and hid was far different—and much less dangerous—than the twenty-year-old young man. You see," I said, leaning on Carla's desk where I sat next to Tom, "Eeeny never got a phone call from Mark. But he left a note on my door for Chris. It blew away. Chris never saw it. I don't know if he signed it *Eeeny* or *Neeny*. That doesn't matter. It was a ploy to get Chris up to the mineshaft. But of course Chris never went. Mark did, because he'd found Hector's remains. Maybe he actually told Eeeny—or Eeeny guessed. That in itself was no serious problem, but coupled with Chris's arrival, it spelled trouble. But when Eeeny went to meet Chris, there was Mark, waiting for Milo—and wearing Chris's clothes. Eeeny may have used Mark's crowbar or one of his own, but he was light on his feet, and he probably sneaked up from behind. I suspect Eeeny swung first and discovered later he'd gotten the wrong Doukas. But it was easy to say he'd been called up there and found Mark already dead." I lifted my hands like a conjurer. Brandy on an empty stomach had magical effects.

Vida was nodding. "Yes, yes, then Gibb shot his face off—as usual—about the second mineshaft opening, so Eeeny had to lure him out of town, down to Reiter to watch the salmon come upstream or some such blarney, and then shoot him." She gazed at Milo. "Well?"

He gave her an off-center grin. "Same caliber bullet killed Gibb, killed Hector. We found the old casing in the dirt late yesterday afternoon. Fourteen years apart, but I'll bet they were both fired from Eeeny's .38."

"No wonder," said Vida, "that Eeeny didn't want Chris brought back to town, Milo. The farther away from Alpine, the better."

Milo turned solemn. "Damn. Eeeny was a good sheriff. He had a fine reputation around the state." Slowly, he swirled the brandy in his paper cup. "I might never have gone into law enforcement if it hadn't been for him. He set a hell of an example."

"Of what?" snapped Vida. "Homicidal mania? Honestly, Milo, if you ever grow up, you'll turn into an old fool, too!" She yanked off her glasses and rubbed her eyes with a vengeance.

Next to me, Tom was on his feet. "It's late, and I've got a plane to catch in the morning." He looked down at me. "Emma, I've got a lot of background for you at the lodge. Some suggestions, economic indicators, an overview and so on. I'll have Heather bring it by tomorrow."

I stood up, not too steadily. "You're leaving?"

He smiled. "You know what they say in news stories: personal reasons." Taking his navy blue blazer off the back of Carla's chair, he threw it over his shoulder. "Congratulations to all of you." The smile turned into a grin for me. "You not only caught a killer, but you got a terrific story. That should up circulation for a couple of weeks anyway." He paused to shake Milo's hand and give Vida a kiss on the cheek. I followed him out to his rental car, the brandy buffeting me against the cold night air.

"Tom . . ." I began, not certain of what I should say.

"Sandra took a jade penguin from Gump's this afternoon. It was worth eleven thousand dollars. She dropped it running up California Avenue." He looked less alarmed than bemused.

"Oh!" I felt terrible for him. I laughed. "Oh, Tom . . ."

He leaned down and kissed me, briefly, firmly. Then he turned away and looked over the top of his car, past the low-lying rooftops of Alpine, beyond the dense cluster of evergreens, up to the dark outline of Baldy with the moonlight bathing its contours. "You don't really need me, you know." He spoke so softly that I wasn't sure of his words.

My voice came out in a bit of a squeak. "I'm not the greatest publisher in the world."

He was still looking at Baldy. "I like this town." At last, he turned back to me. "Is it all right if I come back some day?"

I gave him a crooked smile. "Sure. Just don't wait twenty years."

"No," he said, opening the car door. "I don't want to

meet my son for the first time when he's middle-aged. Men get funny about that time."

"So," I said, "do women."

I watched the red taillights until they turned off on Alpine Way.

Kip MacDuff had driven the paper into Monroe. Vida was interviewing the mother of the bride about an upcoming wedding. Ed Bronsky was trying not to sell an ad to Stella's Styling Salon.

And Carla was chin-deep in reviewing the triple murder story. "I can't stand it!" she shrieked. "I didn't get to write a word about all these horrible things! Can I do the follow-up?"

"I tell you what," I said, stopping in the middle of the news office to take a handful of phone messages from Ginny Burmeister, "you can interview Chris Ramirez about his future plans. When he has some." For all I knew, Chris would be heading back to Hawaii in the next twenty-four hours. Unless, of course, Phoebe told Neeny Doukas the truth and he acknowledged the young man as his son.

Vida had put the phone down and was looking at me over the rims of her glasses. "She spelled it Al and Son."

"Who did what?" I tried to ignore Ed, who was telling Stella that he could solve all her problems with clip art.

"The mother of the bride," said Vida, shaking her head. "She submitted a description of her daughter's gown and spelled the lace on it as . . ."

"Oh," I said. "Alençon." That sort of thing happened a lot in Alpine.

"Exactly." Vida swiveled in her chair and began pounding her typewriter.

I paused in the doorway of my office to survey my domain: Ed was still on the phone, Carla and Ginny were arguing about the minutes of the county commissioners' meeting, and somewhere down the highway, the latest edition of *The Alpine Advocate* was going to press. Neeny

Doukas and Simon and Fuzzy Baugh and maybe a lot of other people might not like what they were going to read, but truth has a way of triumphing over human beings' petty emotions. Usually.

I smiled to myself. Another week, another paper. We were still in business. It was always a relief to make a deadline. And I'd done it on my own.

I strolled over to my desk. Something was not quite right. I looked around the crowded, cluttered office. Adam's picture was gone from the filing cabinet.

Maybe there are some things we can't do on our own.